Prolo⌣

Brent Matthews awoke with a start.

Where the fuck am I?

His head throbbed and his world seemed to be spinning.

He groaned and felt his stomach lurch. Somehow, he managed to keep from vomiting.

Brent leaned to his right and felt something warm and soft.

"Get the fuck off me, man."

"Wha—?"

Lips tacky, he licked them and tried to focus. He was in a car, a car that was moving. And he was wedged between two people in the backseat.

"Brent?"

Something sharp pressed between his ribs.

An elbow.

"You awake?"

The voice came from his left.

"Yeah—what the fuck happened?" Brent's voice was thick and syrupy. He instinctively tapped his pant pockets, looking for his phone.

They were empty.

Brent lifted his ass off the seat and felt around.

Still no phone.

"Fuck off."

It was Theo, Brent realized. Theo's on my right, Ethan on my left. I'm in a car and we're driving away from…

"Dude, you grabbin' my ass? Fuck off," Ethan chirped.

"Naw, my phone." Brent slid his fingers between the seats. "I think I lost my phone..."

There was some light in the car, mostly coming from the dash, and Brent, squinting hard, looked down at their feet.

Nothing.

"Fuck—where's my phone?"

"Bruh, tell me you didn't leave it back at the shack," Ethan warned in his nasal voice.

When Brent didn't answer and continued to search, both with his hands and his eyes, Ethan lodged his pointy elbow into his ribs again.

"I don't... I don't know." Brent grimaced. "My fucking head hurts and I don't remember shit. I feel like I'm going to puke."

"You puke in my Chevelle and I'll fucking kick your ass," the driver threatened.

Why can't I remember? The Shack...

Flashes. Brent saw flashes. Beer bottles, a joint being passed around.

A curtain.

A mattress.

"You really forgot it?" There was a hint of worry in Ethan's voice now.

"I... just lift your asses up."

Ethan did and, with considerably more effort given his size, Theo did the same. Brent cringed as he slid his hand across the warm leather where they'd been sitting.

No phone.

"We gotta... we gotta go back. I need it. I need my phone."

As an eighteen-year-old senior at Tenbury Academy, the entirety of Brent Matthew's life was contained within the six-by-three-inch technological marvel that was his cell phone.

FILTHY

SECRETS

A Chase Adams FBI Thriller

Book 11

Patrick Logan

FILTHY SECRETS

Patrick Logan

But despite the expected anxiety of a teenager not being able to locate their lifeblood, Brent felt extremely uncomfortable.

"I need my phone. I need it."

A cold sweat broke out on his forehead.

"Fuck," the driver cursed. "You sure it ain't in here?"

Brent nudged Theo again, who had since lowered his fat ass onto the seat. He searched more thoroughly this time, wedging his fingers between the backrest and seat cushion. Ethan turned on the flashlight of his own cell phone and after recovering from the light that felt like an icepick in his brain, Brent scanned the floor of the Chevelle.

"It's not here, man. Fuck. We gotta go back."

The driver released a string of curse words and Brent expected to be told to fuck off. Especially by him.

The car suddenly lurched and the tires squealed. Brent felt not just his stomach rise into his throat, but all of his internal organs.

He gagged as the car whipped around and was forced to bring his hand to his mouth, thinking that vomiting was imminent and believing that covering his lips with his hand would somehow keep the vomit down. It was nonsensical, but Brent knew if he puked in the Chevelle, he would get his ass kicked.

"Fucking dumbass forgets his phone," the driver grumbled. "Fucking absolute moron."

Ethan had been forced onto him by the aggressive U-turn and Brent shoved him off.

"I'm sorry, fuck! It must have slipped out… I don't… I don't remember shit."

"How much you fuckin' drink, man?" Theo asked.

"I don't remember. Fuck."

The driver hit the gas and everyone in the vehicle was thrust back against their seats.

"Easy," Ethan said. "You don't wanna get pulled over. The fucking cops—"

"Cops, yeah, like they'll do anything. Brent, get your goddamn phone and get your ass back in the car, all right? Is it upstairs? Tell me it's upstairs, at least."

Something in the driver's tone suggested that if this wasn't the case, another U-turn was imminent.

"Yeah," Brent lied. "I left it... I left it by the front door."

More curses, but the car kept moving forward, still picking up speed. As the trees whipped by on either side of them, the fear of being pulled over was quickly usurped by just getting back to the Shack alive.

"Slow down, man," Ethan whined.

"Shut the fuck up."

Brent had no idea how the driver saw the small dirt road in the dark, but he did, once again yanking the wheel to the right. There was a short drop from the hardened gravel of the larger road to the much smaller dirt one and for a moment, he felt himself go airborne.

When the Chevelle's fat tires gripped the dirt, a thin stream of vomit filled Brent's mouth.

He somehow managed to choke the acrid bile back down.

The Chevelle came to a rocking halt a few moments later in front of The Shack. The plaster building, barely deserving of its namesake elsewhere in Hawkesbury, looked imposing jutting out of the woods and illuminated by the Chevelle's harsh headlights.

"Find your fucking phone, Brent!"

Brent wanted to answer but kept his mouth shut for fear of his stomach revolting.

He reached over Ethan and opened the door then waited for his friend to get out. But Ethan just grabbed him by the arm and pulled.

"Go! Just go!"

Brent slid over him and fell out of the car. His balance was still off, and he had a hard time getting off all fours, looking like a runner who was going too fast, and his legs couldn't keep up, even though he was barely moving.

Brent clenched his jaw, and this seemed to ground him a little.

What the fuck did I drink?

He was standing when he reached The Shack's rotted wooden door. It was partly open—Brent didn't think that it was capable of fully closing—and he instinctively reached for his cell phone to illuminate the darkness within.

But, of course, he didn't have it.

"Hurry the fuck up, Brent!"

Despite hanging open, the door took some effort to widen enough to slip inside The Shack. Brent took one step and nearly tripped over a bottle, sending it careening into the darkness where it collided with maybe a dozen more.

"Jesus!"

Brent backed out of The Shack and hurried to the car.

"You find it?" Ethan asked, hanging halfway out of the window.

"No, it's too dark. Gimme your phone."

"I ain't givin' you my—"

"Give me your fucking phone! I can't see anything in there!"

"I'm not—"

"Ethan, give him your phone!" Theo snapped.

Ethan slid into the car.

"You give him *your* fucking phone, Theo. He already lost—
"

"Give it to him!" the driver ordered.

"Fuck."

Ethan reluctantly held his cell out the window and Brent snatched it up.

"Don't fucking lose it like you lost yours."

Brent ignored his friend and dipped back inside The Shack, this time with the bright beam from Theo's iPhone to guide him. But even with the light, Brent realized that finding his phone wasn't going to be as easy as he first thought.

The floor of the fifteen-by-fifteen-foot structure was littered with bottles. The Shack had never been clean, of course, but Brent didn't recall it being *this* filthy. The bottles, mostly beer, had typically been confined to the corners of the heavily graffitied space but they'd since spread inward, like bacteria growing toward a central source of nourishment. There might have been a path through the middle, there had to have been just to make moving through the space possible, but when he'd accidentally kicked the bottle, he'd knocked over others that obscured the path.

He was supposed to be searching for his cell phone, but Brent had to expend most of his effort just trying not to trip and fall.

Every few strides, Brent stopped moving and scanned the floor, sills, anywhere he might have rested his phone.

"C'mon, *c'mon*. Where the fuck are you?"

Being inside The Shack did nothing to spur his memory. Brent still didn't recognize anything. All he could conjure were small, incoherent flashes. He thought about using Ethan's phone to call his but couldn't because his friend hadn't unlocked it for him.

Something moved in his periphery, and Brent whipped the phone in that direction. A rat the size of a small beaver hissed at him.

"Fuck!"

Something was hanging from its mouth: the tail of a smaller rat.

"Sick—get out of here! Go!" He waved the phone. "*Go!*"

The rat didn't move.

Brent jumped when a horn sounded outside. He instinctively glanced toward the door, and when he turned back to the rat, it was gone.

"Hurry up!" someone hollered from outside. "Brent, hurry the fuck up!"

Spurred equally by the sight of the mutant rat and the horn, Brent began to move more quickly, no longer caring about the bottles underfoot.

After about a minute, he concluded that his cell phone wasn't on the main level. Which meant that it had to be in the basement.

Brent hated The Shack's basement. It didn't even make sense that this place, located in the middle of nowhere, with no access to electricity or water, had one.

But it did, and it was the only place left to check.

There was no door leading downstairs, just concrete steps behind the broken remnants of what might have once been a kitchen, descending into an earthy, dirt-floored open space.

Brent reluctantly took a step and then, forgetting the low ceiling height, cried out as the top of his head struck the plaster hard enough to send his neck jolting backward.

"Fuck."

Massaging the crown of his head, Brent more carefully descended into the basement that reminded him of something from The Blair Witch.

It didn't help that some asshole had had the same idea and had decided to draw child-sized hands all over the walls.

With his free hand, he reached into his pocket and pulled out his bottle of prescription Zoloft. He knew that the pills could exacerbate his nausea, but fuck it, he needed something to calm him down. His heart felt like it was going to explode from his chest.

He normally wasn't afraid of the dark, even in a place as creepy as this, but something about it made all the hairs on his body stand on end.

Brent dry-swallowed two pills and finally made his way to the bottom. It smelled bad down here, like damp gym socks and weed. Unlike upstairs, where everyone just stood when they hung out, the low ceiling made sitting more comfortable. There were six cigarette-scarred lawn chairs set up in a semicircle on the dirt ground.

Did I sit here?

Brent didn't think so.

He didn't remember coming down here at all. But he didn't remember much of anything that happened tonight.

And even that was an overstatement.

But his phone wasn't resting on one of the chairs or lying on the dirt beneath them.

Something crawled across Brent's foot and his entire body exploded into pins and needles.

It was another rat. And, unbelievably, this one looked even larger than the first.

Brent kicked reflexively, but rather than fling the beast across the basement as he'd intended, it just flopped onto its side and then, like an overturned slug, slowly righted itself.

Oh, fuck this!

The rat just stared at him, and Brent's trembling hand made the light he was holding bounce up and down. It reflected off something in the rodent's mouth. Something silver.

Something he recognized.

Despite the fear coursing through him, Brent leaned forward. It was a metal chain and dragging in the dirt attached to said chain was a sterling silver heart about the size of a nickel.

This inspired a memory. A burst of a scene, of this necklace pressed against a sweaty collarbone.

Breathing was difficult now as Brent's throat closed up like a gummy paper straw.

His phone was suddenly the last thing on his mind.

The basement was mostly just an open space, but there was one area that was segmented from the rest with three poorly erected, and now mostly rotted, walls. Perhaps the builder, whoever that might have been, had hopes of putting in an HVAC system or a hot water heater for a non-existent water supply.

Don't look, a voice of reason warned Brent. *Don't you fucking look in there.*

But he had to.

He *had* to.

Sweat, a moan, a thrust.

Instead of a door or wall to enclose the would-be utility area, someone had hung a thick curtain. Brent stared at this now, unable to remove his eyes from the soiled fabric. He shuffled toward it, kicking up tiny puffs of soil as he moved.

Don't look. *DON'T LOOK.*

With a shaking hand, he reached for the curtain. The fabric was thick with grime and years of collecting smoke debris from cigarettes and joints alike. The feel of this filth on the pads of fingers gave him pause.

He almost said, fuck it—fuck this place, fuck the shack, fuck the necklace, and fuck my cell phone—and ran back upstairs, likely braining himself in the same place he'd struck his head earlier.

But then he heard another honk, this time muted, from outside.

Don't be such a pussy.

Brent teased back the curtain and a scream immediately caught in his throat. His vocal cords weren't the only things that froze, either.

Two years ago, when he had been playing high-level lacrosse and on the verge of getting a full-ride scholarship to Penn, Brent had made a stupid, over-the-shoulder pass to a teammate in practice. Something in his arm didn't feel right afterward, but he didn't want to look weak and powered through.

The injury worsened and eventually escalated into a full-blown slap tear of his rotator cuff during a playoff game later that season, effectively ending his career. The morning after the injury, Brent had awoken to a strange sensation.

His shoulder had completely locked up and he was unable to move it.

This is what it felt like now, only the feeling wasn't confined to his shoulder; his whole body was frozen. If it hadn't been for a third honk of the Chevelle's horn, Brent was fairly convinced that he would never have moved again. But the sound shattered the ice encasing his nerves and Brent let the curtain slip from his fingers. At first, he backed away from the scene slowly, but then his heel struck something hard, and fearing that it was a rat again, he just turned and ran.

Brent sprinted upstairs toward the sound of the horn that was now incessantly blaring outside. Somehow, perhaps on account of him bending low to run, he managed to avoid concussing himself on the ceiling. He blasted through the bottles on the main level and then burst outside, falling to the ground.

Only now did he pause, his body heaving as if he were performing a dramatic version of the Yoga cat-cow pose.

"The fuck are you doing?" Ethan demanded. "Get yer ass—Brent, what happened?"

"She's dead." Hot tears soaked Brent's cheeks as he raised his face and looked his friend in the eyes. "She's fucking dead, Ethan! She's dead… she's dead… she's *dead…*"

PART I – CVU

Chapter 1

"I COULDN'T HELP BUT NOTICE you staring at me from across the bar," the man said as he sidled up next to Chase. "I was thinking that maybe you wanted to buy me a drink?"

It wasn't *just* a relationship of convenience.

It was a relationship that just happened to be convenient.

Rachel Abernathy and Georgina Adams… two young girls with past trauma but equally big hearts staying together for spring break? That was good. Getting Tate's nanny Marguerite to live with them in Virginia so Chase didn't have to worry about camp or any of that nonsense? All funded by Stu Barnes' generous donation?

Sign me the fuck up, Chase thought.

This arrangement also meant spending a lot more time with Tate, something that Chase was surprisingly still enjoying.

Apparently, not everything that happened in Vegas stayed in Vegas.

This came as somewhat of a shock as Chase had been worried that after reality sneaked back in, she would be less inclined to hang out with the man.

After all, for as much as she had a type, Tate wasn't it.

True, Chase was traditionally far from selective when it came to choosing a partner, but the man she'd married, Brad, was tall and lean, with what most would refer to as traditionally handsome features.

He had shaggy dark hair, and small, but manly features.

This was not Tate.

Tate was big and bold, everything about him grandiose from his mustache to the way he carried himself. He wasn't fat, *per se*, but was definitely on the heavier side.

Tate wasn't like Jeremy Stitts, either. And while Chase loved Stitts, she didn't love him romantically. But she had slept with him, and he was more like Brad than Tate.

Chase didn't know what to make of this strange dichotomy. Did it mean that what she felt for Tate was more or less real?

In the past, a question such as this one might have crippled her, but not now. For once, while Chase acknowledged these queries, she didn't find herself over-analyzing her actions or the underlying reasons for sleeping with the man.

And perhaps because of this, Chase had decided, explicitly, after a conversation with herself in the mirror, to just let things happen.

Let things happen.

A foreign concept but not one without evident merit. It had, after all, brought her back to Virginia, to Quantico, and had introduced Rachel to Georgina, who got along like two peas in a pod.

Chase had taken up running again, something that had fallen to the wayside during her travels across the country to confront Bryan Jalston, and she had even convinced Tate to come along with her on a few occasions, although all he did was grumble the entire time.

Floyd had made a full recovery and there were rumors that he was starting a cold case unit with Stitts.

By what could only be considered a miracle, Chase Adams' life had obtained an almost unheard-of level of normalcy.

Except for two things: her ex-husband Brad and her son Felix.

It was nice to see Brad. The animosity she'd once felt for the man for taking her son and fleeing the US had long since faded. He was only doing what was best for the boy and perhaps for him, for his sanity; Chase could see that now.

But Felix… just glimpsing the boy's round face was enough to conjure deep-rooted feelings of guilt and shame. These were so powerful that they threatened to shove Chase back down into the dark abyss that she was perpetually trying to claw her way out of.

It wasn't just that she hadn't thought about Felix, let alone spoken to her son, for so long that she had a hard time remembering his voice, but it was also about Georgina.

About how much time and effort and care Chase put into her niece while completely neglecting Felix.

Chase sighed and massaged her forehead.

Guilt.

That was what plagued her… plagued her since she was a little girl.

Ever since she and her sister had been taken, but only one of them had gotten away.

Stay with me, Chase. Please, Chase.

Even though Chase knew that Georgina had been an apparition, the creation of a madman in the metaverse, in Cerberus, the feelings invoked by seeing her deceased sister had been absolutely, one-hundred percent genuine.

"Chase, you gonna be okay? We don't have to do this now if you don't want to. There's no rush."

Chase forced her lips into a smile.

"You should know this by now, but I'm never okay," she said. It was meant as a joke, but it came off as self-pity.

"Don't do that," Tate said, shaking his head. "You don't need to do that with me."

Chase felt a defensive retort forming on her tongue, but she pushed it away. She wanted to say, *and you don't need to tell me what to do.* But she and Tate had agreed that if this, whatever *this* was, had any chance of working, they had to be brutally honest with each other.

Chase was.

For the most part.

Chase rubbed her temples again.

"I know," she said. "But this is what I want. This is what we both want, right?"

Tate nodded, apparently satisfied with the response.

"Okay, let's do it then." Tate gestured toward the door with the placard reading *Director Hampton* on it. "You want to do the honors?"

Chase grinned and this time the emotion was authentic.

"How chivalrous." She raised her hand and rapped her knuckles on the wood three times. The answer from inside was immediate.

"Come in."

Chase reached the door handle but at the last second, she paused.

"What if he doesn't go for it?"

Now it was Tate's turn to smirk.

"C'mon, does he really have a choice? Can he really turn down two of his best and most fucked-up Agents?"

Chapter 2

"GET YOUR SHIT TOGETHER, BRENT. Like, *now*."

Brent glanced over his shoulder as he finished taking a piss.

Theo was standing behind him, his hands on his thick hips, his even thicker lips turned downwards in a frown. He may have ordered Brent to get his shit together, but judging by the way his eyes darted back and forth, it was he who was on the verge of a breakdown.

"I'm not doing anything," Brent said. He shook and then stepped away from the urinal.

"That's the thing, Brent." Ethan stepped out from behind Theo and ran a hand through his long black hair. In almost every way, he was Theo's opposite. Ethan was thin and wiry, had a narrow nose, and his cheeks were almost sallow. This contradiction extended beyond physical appearance. Ethan didn't look worried, he looked angry. "You're *not* doing nothing. We've been in school for half an hour, and already three people, including Natalia, have asked me what's wrong with you."

Brent licked his lips.

"I'm not doing anything. I swear. I haven't said—"

Ethan stepped forward and placed a hand in the center of Brent's chest.

"Of course, you're not gonna say anything. Right? *Right?*"

Brent winced.

"I saw her, though. I know you don't believe me, but—"

Ethan twisted his hand into Brent's shirt and pulled him close.

"You were high and drunk, Brent."

There was no room for argument here. And while Ethan was right about Brent being drunk and probably high, he was wrong about Em.

Every time he closed his eyes, Brent saw her face, the blue veins standing out on her fair skin as if drawn in pen.

Her cloudy eyes.

The necklace clutched in the rat's mouth.

"She was *dead*," Brent nearly whimpered. "Fucking dead, man. I saw—"

"You were high and fucking wasted. You don't know what the *fuck* you saw," Ethan hissed through clenched teeth. Spit sprayed on Brent.

If only he could believe that.

If only he could chalk it up to a nightmare, maybe a bad trip although he didn't even remember taking a hit from a joint.

But she was looking at him. *Into* him.

Blaming him.

Blaming him for *everything*.

Brent shuddered and the reaction spooked both Ethan and Theo, the former finally letting go of his shirt.

Brent rubbed absently at the wrinkled fabric.

"You don't know what you saw," Ethan repeated, but his voice lacked the authority of moments ago.

"Is she at school? Is Em even here?" Brent countered. "Have either of you seen her? I tried calling, but she didn't answer."

Theo looked down and Ethan eventually shook his head.

"She's probably just sleeping it off. You know how her hangovers can be."

A two-day hangover wasn't unheard of, but one bad enough to keep Em out of school? Especially when they were only a few weeks from prom?

No. Ethan was full of shit.

Besides, Brent had seen her. And Emily wasn't hungover. She was fucking *dead*.

Ethan cleared his throat and then curled his upper lip.

"She'll turn up. But don't you fucking say anything. You say anything, and we're all fucked. Me, Theo, you, and… you know who else. Keep your mouth shut, Brent."

The glare in Ethan's eyes forced Brent to lower his own.

"Yeah, yeah, I won't say anything. I'm not an idiot, not a fucking retard." There had been a time before his injury when Ethan wouldn't have dared to speak to him this way. Then again, if it hadn't been for his torn rotator cuff, they might never have even become friends at all. "I'm fine, alright? I'm fucking fine."

Theo seemed happy with this response, but Ethan refused to move out of Brent's way.

"What?" Some of his lost bravado returned. "You want to do something, Ethan? Because—"

"Just keep it together."

"Whatever."

Brent brushed by both Ethan and Theo and went to the sink to watch his hands, deliberately avoiding his own reflection.

"Just don't ignore us. Answer your fucking text."

Theo left first and Ethan followed. Brent stayed behind, lathering his hands. Soap trickled down his wrists and it dawned on him that this was the first time he could remember washing his hands after taking a piss.

After rinsing, he finally looked up. But he didn't see his blond hair, square jaw, or pale blue eyes.

He saw her.

He saw Emily.

A shudder coursed through him, and the reflection slowly became his own.

Brent sighed and rubbed his eyes. *I can't answer your God damn texts,* he thought. *Because I still don't have my phone.* But he couldn't tell them that. He'd lied and said he'd found his phone in The Shack because he couldn't bear the idea of going back inside.

"Brent?"

Brent's eyes flicked to the door, and he was surprised to see Ethan still standing there, glaring at him.

"Yeah, I'll answer your texts. Now, can I please just finish washing my fucking hands in peace?"

Chapter 3

DIRECTOR HAMPTON DIDN'T SAY ANYTHING as Chase and Tate entered the room, he just stared down at a stack of papers on his desk. Having gone through this routine perhaps a dozen times prior, Chase knew better than to speak out of turn.

She often wondered what was printed on these ubiquitous pages. Clearly, the director wanted them to believe that they were important documents, requests from the President, or secret Pentagon transcripts, but Chase had a different idea: romance novels—the dirty kind, harems, perhaps, maybe one that takes place on a distant planet. Hell, why not one with dinosaurs, too? Tame dinosaurs *and* women.

Whatever his taste in literature, there was no doubting the man's experience. Before becoming Director of the FBI Academy, Hampton had been a top Agent, if not *the* top Agent in the Bureau. This was some time ago, however, although exactly how long had passed since the man had been in the field, was unknown. Director Hampton appeared to be in his late fifties, but being involved in the FBI had a way of ageing you prematurely.

He could be thirty-eight for all Chase knew.

And today, Hampton appeared particularly ornery, the lines around his mouth like deep chasms filled with disgruntled feelings. Without looking up, the man gestured for them to take their seats.

Tate replicated this motion, which annoyed Chase—precisely why he'd done it. Still, Chase sat first and then Tate followed suit.

Still nothing from the director. He shuffled the printouts of his Harem LitRPG, stacked them neatly to one side, then interlaced his fingers and leaned forward.

Finally, he gave them the privilege of looking up, his hazel eyes moving from Tate to Chase before coming to a complete stop.

"I knew I'd see you back here one day."

That was it.

No, *Hello, nice to see you.* No, *I'm so glad you're back, Chase.* There had been a time when Director Hampton might have led with something congenial, as the man had made it clear that he wasn't happy about Chase's decision to leave.

He'd even stated that she would be welcomed back from her indefinite sabbatical any time.

But that was before.

That was before the disaster in New York City with the suicide girls and Cerebrum. That was before the dual disasters in Virginia and Columbus when she'd had no business being involved at all. And then there was Stu Barnes and the fact that she'd dragged in Tate and Floyd, nearly getting the latter killed. The worst part was that the FBI couldn't claim Chase's "successes" given her non-affiliated status, but the media had no problem attributing her failures to the Bureau.

"That makes one of us," Chase replied, trying her best to reflect the Director's demeanor.

The two of them just stared at each other until Tate, like a kid being left out, decided to chime in.

"What about me? Did you expect to see me back here?"

Predictably, Hampton ignored Tate, which in and of itself was telling. If anyone else had made the inane comment, they'd likely be looking for another job by the time they left the room.

But not Tate.

Given all that she'd learned about her partner, Chase realized that the man's professional trajectory was something of a mystery. By reputation alone, she knew that he'd been with the Bureau for several years, more than both her, Floyd, and maybe even Stitts. She also knew that the man had worked with the once revered and now maligned Constantine Striker and that they'd both been instrumental in bringing down the notorious Sandman killer. Tate hadn't been shy about telling her that Con was the one who had taught him the ways of the Chameleon, so to speak, but other than that…

"Are you here to apologize for interfering in a federal case?"

Even if Chase felt motivated to reply, which she didn't, it was impossible to know which case Hampton was referring to.

"Or is it to apologize for getting one of my agents shot, an agent who has now left active duty to pursue cold cases?"

Chase did her best to suppress a smirk. This, too, was unclear. Was he referring to Floyd or Stitts?

Probably Floyd, she decided.

Yet, Chase was far from apologetic.

It was no surprise that being abducted at a young age, having your sister taken and indoctrinated, being addicted to heroin, and going through everything since had Chase leaning more toward Eeyore than Pollyanna.

But not Floyd. Somehow, he'd remained optimistic, unjaded, unconvinced that the world was filled with people who had but three simple desires: to fuck, to inflict pain, and to kill.

Deep down, she was glad that Floyd left before this inevitable attitude change.

"If you think I came here to apologize, then I might as well leave now," Chase said dryly.

"Expect *you* to apologize?" Hampton shook his head. "No. Not you." He finally looked at Tate. "*You*, on the other hand…"

Tate, for all of his ability to control his emotions, was taken aback and Chase saw the real Tate, which was rarely glimpsed in public.

Shocked, vulnerable, and more than a little sad.

She felt the urge to reach out and hold him then, which quickly made her feel silly and childish.

It was like witnessing a magician perform his signature trick, one that he'd successfully completed and awed the audience with hundreds, if not thousands, of times, only for it to fail miserably.

There was an innate desire to comfort them.

Maybe there was more to humans than fucking, hurting, and killing, after all.

"Me?" Tate hated filler words, but here he was, buying himself time to slip into a protective persona.

Director Hampton didn't bite. Perhaps he'd learned from Stitts that staying quiet often spoke volumes while running your mouth said nothing at all.

Tate's Adam's apple bobbed; the man was literally swallowing his pride.

Director Hampton was no fool. He knew that they'd come here because they wanted something, and the man wasn't above making them grovel for it.

"Yeah." Tate licked his lips. "I'm sorry. I fucked up."

Chase's relationship with Director Hampton had always been complicated and strained, which was no surprise given how she'd been brought into the FBI, duped, and nearly murdered by ex-Agent Chris Martinez.

But not until this very moment had she seriously considered physical violence against the man.

Chase felt a nearly uncontrollable urge to slap the smirk off Director Hampton's face.

Fuck, she hated that look.

"Let me guess, you guys want back into the fold? You want to partner up?"

This time, neither Chase nor Tate spoke—they just stared. Eventually, one of the director's untamed eyebrows rose up his forehead.

"There's more? There's an *and* to your request?"

Chase shrugged.

"Given that you're in the mood to open new FBI divisions, like cold cases, I was hoping that you'd considered one more."

The director's other eyebrow met his first.

"We only want to take on specific cases," Tate finished for Chase.

Hampton's eyebrows dropped, as did his eyelids as he squinted at the both of them.

"And let me guess, you only want cases that involve children?"

Chase wasn't surprised that the man had hit the nail directly on the head.

"That's right," she said, holding the man's glare. "Agent Abernathy and I are only interested in serious crimes against minors."

Chapter 4

ACCORDING TO BRENT'S SCHEDULE, HE had class for the rest of the afternoon. What those classes were and what was taught was a complete and utter mystery.

He couldn't stop thinking about Emily, about her milky eyes, pale flesh, and the strange bruising around her throat.

Her lips were swollen, reminding him of the time when she'd tried out a new lip gloss. It was supposed to plump your lips up and it worked... worked too well, in fact. Emily had had a reaction and her lips, especially the top one, had swollen to three times its normal size.

Brent had laughed uncontrollably, and Emily had been pissed.

No, she wasn't dead. Ethan was right. He was just drunk and high and all sorts of fucked up.

Emily, dead, lying naked on a filthy mattress.

No way. No *fucking* way.

Why can't I remember? Why can't I remember what happened Saturday night?

Brent ground his teeth violently.

What the fuck is wrong with me?

Brent, who barely registered the fact that he was aimlessly wandering the hallways even though he was supposed to be in class, was buried so deeply in his own thoughts that he nearly missed his name being called.

Maybe if it had been Ethan or Theo, he could have ignored them.

But it hadn't been his friends saying his name.

Instead, the voice had come from the school's PA system.

"Brent Matthews, can you please make your way to the principal's office."

Brent stumbled and nearly fell.

"Brent Matth—"

The voice was interrupted by the sound of Tenbury Academy's nearly one-hundred-year-old bell chiming, signifying the end of class.

The hallway suddenly flooded with students. They were so loud that the intercom was barely audible.

"—ews, please make your way to the principal's office."

Someone accidentally bumped into him, and Brent found himself bracing up against a locker.

What the fuck?

Brent put both palms on the cool metal and lowered his head between his arms.

This is not happening. This is not—

A hand gripped his shoulder and squeezed hm hard.

"What the fuck did you say, Brent?" Ethan hissed in his ear. "I told you to keep your mouth shut."

Brent shrugged free, but then bigger hands spun him around. He found himself face to face with Theo, with Ethan, the ever-scowling Ethan, standing behind his much bigger friend.

"I didn't say anything," Brent argued, but his voice was meek. He tried to step aside, but one of Theo's meaty hands shoved him up against the locker.

Hard.

"We warned you…"

"I know." Brent closed his eyes and he saw Emily. *Dead* Emily. "No," he moaned. "No, it's not real."

Theo shoved him again and again. The third time was strong enough to knock the wind from his lungs and forced him to open his eyes.

"I didn't say anything."

Even though he was the one holding Brent in place, there was some compassion on Theo's face. Not enough to let him go, but *some*.

"Get your fucking shit together, Brent," Ethan snarled. People were watching now—everyone in high school was on the lookout for a fight, and the esteemed Tenbury Academy was no different.

Ethan noticed this too and he nudged Theo in the ribs and whispered something in his ear. Theo's hands went from Brent's shoulders to the front of his once crisp white polo. To someone passing by, someone who didn't look too closely, it might appear as if Theo were helping smooth Brent's T-shirt. Strange, certainly, but not as interesting a fight. In reality, the man's knuckles were grinding into Brent's chest.

"She's dead," Brent said, grimacing against the pain. "Emily's dead and I—"

Ethan practically leaped over Theo's shoulder.

"She's fine! Shut the fuck up, Brent!"

Tears spilled down Brent's hot cheeks.

"No," he sniffed. "She's not okay. Em's dead and I don't know what happened to her but somehow, I'm responsible. *We're* responsible. I just can't remember—"

Theo suddenly wrapped an arm around his shoulder and practically carried Brent back into the bathroom, the site of their first altercation of the day.

Once inside, Ethan quickly checked the stalls, confirming that they were empty.

"Why don't you just tell me what happened?" Brent whined. "I need to know—"

"Block the door," Ethan ordered Theo.

Theo leaned his considerable bulk against the door and Ethan got right in Brent's face.

"Listen the fuck up, Brent. Nothing happened. *Nothing*. We all just drank and smoked a joint. That's it. They probably want you in the office because you forgot your lunch or maybe you flunked your fucking algebra test. I don't fucking know. Emily wasn't even there... why would she be? So, Brent, you're going to keep your mouth shut about Saturday night, alright?"

Brent whimpered like a wounded cat.

Ethan's face contorted.

"You mention Saturday night and I'll tell Jackson. I swear I will. And you think I'm mean? Huh? He'll fuck you up, Brent. Like he fucked up that Mexican kid. 'member that—yeah? *Worse.* Jackson will fuck you up worse, Brent. You know he will."

Brent wiped his face, and he took a deep shuddering breath. He still felt off. Ethan had mentioned a two-day hangover for Emily, but that's how he felt. Just... *off.*

Wait—Ethan had said that, hadn't he? That Em had a two-day hangover. Only now he was saying that she wasn't even there.

"I won't—I won't say anything."

"That's right, you won't. You'll keep your fucking mouth *shut.*"

Why is he lying?

Brent looked at Theo, but he refused to meet his gaze.

"Sorry."

"Fuck your sorrys. Just don't say anything." Ethan looked at Theo, who pushed off the door. "Let's go. And remember what I said, Brent. Think about what Jackson will do to you."

Brent made sure that they both left this time before splashing cold water on his face and pulling the skin beneath his eyes down.

They might have been able to convince him that what he'd seen was just a hallucination. Especially given how jittery and uncomfortable he felt. But then they'd lied. Or, Ethan had, at least. And now he knew. Emily *had* been there, and something *had* happened.

Did that also mean that she was really dead, too?

Brent, unwilling to even contemplate the possibility now, forced himself to leave the bathroom.

Class was about to begin, which meant that the halls were empty as Brent walked directly to the principal's office.

Mrs. Story, the cute secretary only a few years older than Brent himself, was known for her effervescent personality. Bubbly, overflowing with good humor. Brent's heart sank when he saw her thin red lips pressed into a frown.

"Mr. Matthews, please head right in."

Brent almost turned and ran. This didn't feel right. And when he looked through the frosted glass of the principal's door and saw the outline of not one, but two people, he nearly shit his pants.

"Brent? Please go in. They're waiting."

Someone was controlling him now; someone was making him reach for the door handle. But he couldn't open it.

Mrs. Story did that for him.

"Come in," the man with the salt and pepper hair seated behind the desk instructed.

Brent stood in the doorway; his eyes locked on the woman standing beside the principal.

"Brent? I said come in."

Mrs. Story gently nudged him inside the room just enough so that she could close the door behind him. When the latch engaged, Brent snapped back to reality.

"Brent, I believe you know Mrs. Iris Dawson? She's looking for her daughter. She hasn't seen Emily since Saturday night. Have you seen her?"

Chapter 5

"THAT WENT... WELL?" TATE ASKED as they walked briskly away from the FBI Academy headquarters. Chase wasn't sure if their pace was deliberate or if they were worried that if they didn't get the hell out of there as quickly as possible, Director Hampton might change his mind.

"I... guess?" Chase was still shocked. They'd gotten pretty much everything they'd asked for. "Not a huge fan of the name... Children's Victim's Unit? Sounds like a hospital ward."

Tate chuckled.

"Yeah, and CVU sounds like an STD. But I know why he did it."

Chase gave him a quizzical look.

"I've known Director Hampton for a long time; he's no idiot. We basically asked to be part of the Bureau's VCAC—Violent Crimes Against Children. But if he does that, we're no longer under Hampton, we're reporting to the big man in D.C."

"And that means he can't keep an eye on us."

"Or get credit for our massive successes," Tate countered jokingly.

Chase laughed.

"Yeah, sure."

Aside from the cheesy name, Chase could have done without the probationary period, which meant that both, either, mainly her, could be subjected to random drug testing at any time. The lack of a raise might have bothered some people, but not her. Stu Barnes had made sure that both hers and Tate's bank accounts were flush. He also took care of Rachel's outstanding medical bills and paid for Marguerite. The cash wouldn't last forever, but it would last a while.

There was one issue that Chase had argued with the Director for a good five minutes before Tate had signaled for her to let it go.

"It doesn't bother you that Hampton is going to pick our cases for us?" she asked as they reached her car. Chase grabbed the handle and opened the door but didn't get in.

"Does it bother me?" Tate cocked his head. "Yeah, it bothers me, sure. But like I said, I know Hampton. He wants *some* control. He'll give us one or two easy cases and then lengthen the rope. Give it three months and we'll be completely autonomous."

Chase was skeptical. She'd had the ability to select her own cases previously and that hadn't ended well. Hampton would be foolish to make the same mistake again. But Chase was nothing if not persistent.

And stubborn.

Tate's phone began to ring, and they both got into the car.

"Hello?" he said loudly, then he lowered his voice.

Chase tuned him out as she drove, not sure where they were going.

It felt strange to be back, to officially be an FBI Agent again. It felt strange to have a different partner, too, her third.

First Stitts, then Floyd. Both shot while on duty, both relegated to cold cases.

Would Tate be next?

She looked over at her new partner who now had a finger pushed into the ear opposite the cell phone.

No. Tate was different.

Chase shook her head.

Was he, though?

"Take a left here," Tate said, hanging up his cell.

Chase did as she was asked.

"Where we going?"

"Just make another left up here, two blocks."

"Tate, you know how—"

"Yeah, yeah, I know, you hate surprises. But you'll like this one. Just take a left."

Chase grumbled but again did as her new partner instructed.

"Can you just tell me where we're going?"

"I'm sorry, but you heard the Director: we may be partners, but I am technically your superior. I am under no obligation to answer your questions."

Chase rolled her eyes.

"I could have done without that, too."

Two more directions and Tate instructed her to pull into the parking lot of a pub called *The Taverne*.

"Really?"

The left side of Tate's mustache rose in a half-grin.

"What? I'm hungry. Where did you think I was taking you?"

Chase shook her head, but she was actually a little hungry, too. Five miles this morning, no record pace but she'd gotten a good sweat on. The only running that Tate had done was to the bathroom.

Her new partner held the door to the bar open and waved his hand in a dramatic circle.

"After you," he said in a terrible British accent.

"Are you ill?" Chase was greeted by the sound of Irish music, but thankfully it was turned down low. It was, after all, not even eleven in the morning.

Tate shut his eyes and continued to hold his hand out.

"*M'lady.*"

What the hell have I gotten myself into? Chase wondered. *What do all the experts say? Don't mix business and pleasure? And I've gone ahead and partnered up with the man I'm sleeping with? The man I'm practically living with? Chase, are you—*

"Hey!" someone shouted, drawing Chase out of her own head. "Look who it is!"

Chase glanced at Tate who had since entered *The Taverne* and was now smiling broadly.

"What?" he said with a shrug. "I told you, you were going to like this surprise."

Chase shook her head again, but now she was smiling, too.

"You asshole."

"Guilty as charged."

Chase turned back to the two smiling men who greeted her, pints in hand.

"Welcome back," Floyd said, tipping his glass. The kid's smile was so big it threatened to split his face in half.

"Yeah," Stitts added. "Welcome back to the shitshow that is the FBI!"

He leaned in close and kissed her on the cheek.

"I missed you, Chase."

"I missed you, too." She raised her voice. "I missed both of you so *fucking* much."

Chapter 6

"BRENT?" THE PRINCIPAL ASKED. "YOU alright?"

Like in the hallway when he'd heard his name over the intercom, Brent Matthews felt all the blood in his body begin to gel.

He was trying everything in his power to appear normal, but the sight of Mrs. Iris Dawson, with her chestnut brown hair bouncing to her shoulders, her face youthful but also a little too smooth in places, a telltale sign of Botox use, nearly broke him.

Brent's heart thudded in his chest, the muscle desperately trying to send his thickened blood to his brain, to his limbs.

"Brent?" the principal repeated. The man started to rise, a look of genuine concern on his face, but Brent somehow managed to raise his hand.

"I think," he rasped, "I think I'm coming down with something."

The principal's sharp blue eyes narrowed.

"Right, but did you hear what I said?"

Brent resisted the urge to look at the distraught woman for fear of his mind superimposing Emily's pale—*dead*—face on top of hers.

"Yes, sir."

"And have you? Have you seen Emily Dawson today?"

Today? No, not today. But on Saturday night, technically Sunday morning, I guess, I did. I saw her lying on her back, nude, her milky eyes open, bruising around her neck.

That's what Brent wanted to say. That's what he *should* have said.

But he was too chicken shit. Saying it made it real. And it wasn't real. It couldn't be real.

Em's just wasted. A two-day hangover.

"No." Brent shook his head. "I don't see her that often now that we broke up."

The principal grunted, and Brent wondered why he'd added the last part. Nobody had inquired about his relationship status, and they didn't need to: both the principal and Mrs. Dawson knew that they had broken up. Everyone in Tenbury knew that.

"Brent, are you sure you haven't seen Em?" Iris Dawson probed, a tremor in her voice. On the many occasions that Brent had been invited over to the Dawsons' for dinner, he'd never seen the woman even close to losing control. Not even when she'd burst in on Brent and Emily, their faces locked together, Brent's right hand high under Emily's white sweater, groping her breasts. But now... now, the woman appeared on the verge of a breakdown. "I'm pretty worried."

For some reason, this break of character served to anger Brent.

Why don't you ask her new boyfriend, then? Huh? Why are you harassing me?

"Em said she was going out with friends on Saturday but didn't tell me where. I haven't heard from her since. Do you know where she might have gone? Or with who?"

"No, sorry."

"What about her phone?" the principal asked. "Can you track it?"

Mrs. Dawson's curly hair swung in front of her face as she shook her head.

"No, it's dead."

Dead.

The word wreaked havoc on Brent's still foggy brain. He went from angry to guilty in one sluggish heartbeat.

What the fuck is wrong with me?

"So, you don't know?" Mrs. Dawson pleaded.

Brent felt his stomach clench, and he was about to answer when a vision flashed before his eyes.

He was back in the basement, not alone this time, but with others. Five, maybe six people in total. And they were shouting, jeering, cheering someone on. But who? And why?

"I already spoke to Ava, Natalia, and Laura—they haven't seen her either," Mrs. Dawson continued.

Yeah, because they're not friends anymore. They're not friends because I forced everyone to turn their back on her when Emily broke up with me.

But the vision… Brent saw Ava and Em talking, saw them clinking their glasses full of only god knows what.

They weren't friends, but they sure as hell looked like friends on Saturday night.

What the fuck happened?

Brent blinked and once again he saw Emily on the mattress. This was accompanied by a sudden visceral revulsion, a shuddering wave of disgust.

"I think..." Brent began with a series of hard swallows. He slumped against the closed door behind him and said the first true thing since entering the principal's office. "… I think I'm going to be sick."

His stomach, which had been clenched so tightly it felt as if an iron vise was squeezing his intestines, suddenly let loose, and hot vomit spilled from Brent's mouth and soaked the front of his wrinkled polo.

Chapter 7

IT HAD BEEN A SETUP, of course. The only question was whether the faux impromptu meeting was Tate's, Stitts', or Floyd's doing.

It didn't matter—it was just good to see them all again.

"Your hair," Stitts remarked, taking a sip of his beer. "Trying to look more distinguished, are we?"

Well, that didn't last long, Chase thought, taking a long haul of her own pint. *Actually, my hair is gray because I was force-fed Cerebrum, a pill that drives non-believers to suicide. Why I didn't feel compelled to take my own life, you ask? C'mon, my brain just doesn't work the same as others... you know that.*

"Yeah, distinguished." She reached out and flicked Stitts' chestnut brown hair, which, of course, fell back the way it had been before.

"And your hair is exactly the same," she remarked with a smirk. "Literally."

Stitts shrugged.

"What can I say? The more things change, the more things stay the same."

Chase was two pints in now, two and a half, and she was feeling happy. Even thinking about Cerebrum and the poor high school girls who fell victim to the pill hadn't permanently soured her mood. She just felt *good*. Good and comfortable, two foreign concepts in absentia and even rarer together.

After congratulating her and Tate for forming the CVU, a name that they hated even more than she did—*sounds like the pilot for a failed network TV show about crime scenes and family cars*—Stitts and Floyd opened up about their own work.

They had indeed formed a cold case unit working out of Quantico. Their focus was on violent crimes that took place twenty or more years ago, cases that other divisions, including other cold cases departments, had failed to solve. They seemed excited, reinvigorated. Especially Stitts who, toward the end of their tumultuous partnership, had started to become a little jaded. The case they were working on now involved a jogger who had been running through Central Park in broad daylight thirty-six years ago. Someone had accosted her and had, with near-surgical precision, removed her hands and feet. People found her while she was still alive, but there was nothing they could do to prevent her from bleeding out.

The topic of conversation changed when Stitts returned from the bathroom. All eyes were on the man as he leaned heavily on his cane.

Chase expected that this topic would arise; Tate and Stitts in the same room meant that it was inevitable that they would tease her. She was just surprised that it was Tate who brought it up.

"Okay, come on, let's see it—let me see what my future holds. Floyd, you first."

It took the young man a few seconds to figure out what Tate wanted. And then, quiet and unassuming as he was, Floyd glanced around first to make sure that no one was standing near them. Despite the early hour, *The Taverne* wasn't completely empty—some grinders were slurping down Guinness, but they were deliberately seated in the darkened corners of the bar.

Satisfied, Floyd lifted the hem of his shirt, revealing a nasty scar, pink and thick on his dark skin, just below his right nipple.

"Oh, *sick*," Tate joked. "Can I touch it?" He reached out with two fingers in a decidedly sexual manner, but Floyd slapped his hand away. "Kidding, kidding. But chicks are going to love that."

Floyd dropped his shirt and Tate turned to face Stitts. "Your turn."

Jeremy Stitts, who had been living with his wound for much longer than Floyd and was thus more comfortable, made a show of his reveal. He leaned heavily on his cane, wincing for effect as he teased up one leg of his track pants. The fact that the man was wearing track pants, which Chase had never seen him wear before, made her think that perhaps this, like the get-together, had also been planned.

Stitts' scar, albeit nowhere near as fresh as Floyd's, was equally, if not more, off-putting. There was the bullet wound, of course, but there was also a vertical cicatrix from an incision that ran nearly the entire length of his thigh. Chase could even make out the small dots on either side of the line that had once held thick sutures.

"Nasty," Tate hissed, and Stitts let his pant leg fall to the floor. All of them took a sip of their drinks. "I wonder where I'm gonna be shot while working with you," Tate teased. "If Stitts took a bullet here," he indicated his thigh, "and Floyd here," now he pointed at his chest, "I'm guessing I'm going to be the lucky one and get a piece of lead *riiiight*..." Tate took a finger and planted it right between his own eyes. "...*here*."

Chase smirked.

"Yeah, that sounds about right. But the main difference is," Chase paused to drink, smacking her lips obnoxiously before continuing, "Floyd and Stitts were shot by bad guys. If you don't shut the fuck up, the bullet in your forehead is going to be from my gun."

Tate laughed heartily and Chase realized that she loved his laugh. It was loud, boisterous, and real.

"Touché, Chase," Tate said wrapping his arm around her and squeezing her tightly. "Well, in honor of our wounds, past and future, I say let's do some shots. Tequila, anyone?"

Chapter 8

THE ONE GOOD THING ABOUT vomiting all over yourself is that it was a one-way ticket out of school, which meant that Brent didn't have to answer any more questions about Emily or the weekend. At least, not now.

The nurse took his temperature, which was surprisingly normal—Brent felt as if his head was on fire—then gave him a spare shirt to throw on which was a little bit too tight despite his small frame.

Away from Iris Dawson and the principal and in his car, Brent started to feel a little better. Not good, he severely doubted that if Emily really was dead, he would ever feel good again, but good enough that he wasn't about to collapse. He felt even better after hopping in the shower and rinsing the residual vomit off him.

He didn't like his body, not anymore. Before tearing his shoulder, he'd been solid, not ripped, but he'd held a considerable amount of muscle. He had a soft four-pack, too. Emily had loved his body. She said she loved it even after he'd been forced out of lacrosse and hadn't been able to work out for three months. But Brent thought she was lying. How could anybody like this? Weak, skinny fat.

Pale.

Fuck, I'm pale.

Brent brushed his teeth, which was difficult given that it felt like he had lockjaw. That, and he was trying his best not to look at his reflection again.

Pieces of Saturday night were coming back to him now. They'd planned a party—was it Theo's idea? Or Ethan's?—a get-together of the old gang. All seven of them.

No, *eight*—Emily was there, and that made eight of them. But why? Why was she there?

They hadn't hung out in months. They didn't even say hi if they passed each other in the hallway. And why would Emily? After what he'd done, she had every right to ignore him.

And she's with that prick. Don't forget that.

Brent began drying himself off.

Was he there? Brent wondered. *No, he definitely wasn't. I'd remember if he was.*

His memory might be coming back but it was cloudy and disjointed.

Why the fuck were we doing at The Shack, anyway?

It was Tenbury Academy tradition for seniors to party at the abandoned building three times: once, before spring break, which had passed nearly three months ago. The second time was after prom, and that was the big one: not everyone came during spring break, some had holidays with family, but everybody showed up after prom. Finally, most seniors came back for one final jam the week before leaving for college.

But last Saturday had been none of these occasions.

Why the fuck were we there?

Brent set his jaw and tapped his forehead aggressively.

Why can't I remember?

He'd had some epic hangovers before, some of the two-day variety that Ethan had mentioned. But never like this. Never with such utter voids in his memory.

Brent reached into his pile of clothes on the floor and found his prescription bottle. He popped two pills and dry swallowed them, which was particularly painful on account of puking up sour bile less than an hour ago.

He changed into a pair of track pants and a loose-fitting tee and sat on the edge of his bed. This comfortable position caused another memory to surface, but not one from Saturday night.

From the last time Emily had been in his room.

Brent lay down and closed his eyes.

"I just... I just don't love you anymore, Brent." Sweet, even when she was breaking his heart, Emily Dawson was sweet.

Brent felt his cheeks flush. There had been rumors about someone else, but he'd been too proud to believe them.

"What do you mean?"

Emily tucked her red hair behind her ears. Her lower lip was trembling as if she were the one being broken up with and not the other way around.

"I don't want to hurt you, Brent—I don't. But I need to be honest. I just... I don't have the same feelings for you I once did. I'm sorry."

By nature, Brent wasn't a violent person. But it was midterm finals, and his stress levels were through the roof. He hadn't slept all night and he was operating on near-lethal levels of caffeine and Adderall.

Still, this was no excuse for what happened next. There would never be an excuse for that. After it happened, Emily started to cry. Not tears of pain, but of anger as Emily went from sweet to acerbic.

"You wanna know why I don't love you anymore?" Emily wiped her cheeks. "Because I met someone else, that's why. I don't love you, Brent Matthews—I love someone else."

And just like that, Emily was out of his life. Gone.

Maybe if he hadn't slapped her there might have been a chance at reconciliation. So, she loved someone else? So what? In time, they could've been friends. In more time, they might have been able to harness their hormones and tumultuous 18-

year-old feelings and figured out that they were actually good for each other.

But not after hitting her. That was the end.

Brent had never struck a woman—*never*—and it didn't even feel real.

Things didn't have to be this way.

Things didn't have to end with Emily dead on a mattress.

Brent was terrified of falling asleep, his fear of nightmares, of giant rats eating more than just sterling silver, was almost palpable. But he could no longer keep his eyes open. And when he drifted off, it was anything but an ordinary afternoon nap.

Brent Matthews slept like he was dead.

Chapter 9

"THAT WAS YOUR DOING, WASN'T it?" Chase asked as they approached the front door of Tate's house. It still felt strange to think that she'd moved in with a man that she'd known for barely six months and had been dating for less than three. But it made sense on so many levels.

"Well," Tate shrugged, "it was a collective decision. I'll tell you one thing, though, Floyd was more than game. He made sure that Stitts was available. And that Stitts... only met him a handful of times but he seems like a good man."

"That he is," Chase said absently as he reached for the door handle. "That he is."

She was surprised to find the door locked and instinctively rang the bell while Tate reached into his pocket for his keys. Chase had a few hours to kill before she and Georgina were scheduled to meet up with Felix and Brad for dinner.

Tate unlocked the door and she pushed by him into the foyer.

"Georgina?" she hollered. "Rachel?"

Marguerite rarely locked the door when they were home and it was the middle of the day, meaning that Rachel should be napping.

Her words were met by silence.

A bad feeling began to form in her gut, one that intensified when she spotted what appeared to be Georgina's clothing—a pair of leggings and an off-white T-shirt—lying on the stairs.

"Georgina?"

Behind her, Tate called out for his daughter.

Chase rushed upstairs, taking them two at a time, using the rail to propel herself at an even greater speed. The first room was Rachel's, and she barged into it. There were clothes tossed on the bed and one of the dresser drawers hung open.

"Shit."

Chase dashed to the next room, her and Tate's.

No clothes here, no indication of someone rummaging through their things. The relief she felt at not having been robbed was short-lived; the alternative was that whoever had broken in here wasn't looking for material goods.

They were looking for people.

"They're not here!" she yelled down the stairs. "Tate, they're not here!"

Chase moved to the last room, hoping to find the three of them, Rachel, Marguerite, and her niece, sitting on the bed, perhaps all wearing headphones and listening to a podcast. But she wasn't surprised to find Georgina's room empty, either. Unlike Rachel's room, not one, but two dresser drawers hung open, tights hanging out of each like soiled tongues.

"Chase?"

She barely heard Tate calling her name.

It was Brian Jalston. She *knew* it was him, the sick fuck. One of the crimes that he'd been charged with, probation violation or whatever the fuck Stu Barnes had orchestrated, had fallen through and he'd been released. And true to the man's word, Brian had come for his daughter, for Georgina.

A hand came down on her shoulder and Chase, still picturing Brian's face, spun and delivered a hard kick to the groin area. She missed the man's testicles and instead collided with his inner thigh. He cried out, hobbled, and almost went down.

"Jesus, Chase!" Tate cursed as he bounced on one leg.

Chase leaped backward, her posture still primed for action.

Tate held one hand up, the other massaging his sore leg.

"The fuck, Chase! Don't hit me again." Chase noticed a piece of paper on the ground, which Tate had probably been holding prior to her attacking him. He followed her gaze. "It's a note from Marguerite. She said sorry about the mess, that they were late heading out to go watch a movie. She said they'll be back around 4:30."

Chase snatched the paper off the ground and read it. It said almost exactly what Tate had just told her.

"Call her," she said flatly. "Call Marguerite."

"It's her handwriting, Chase. It's—" He must have seen something on her face because he didn't finish the sentence. Instead, Tate reached into his pocket and pulled out his cell phone. He put it on speaker.

"Hello? Mr. Abernathy?" There was no concern in the woman's voice.

"Hi, Marguerite. Sorry to bother you, but I was just checking to make sure that you'd still be home around 4:30. You know that Georgina has dinner plans with her mom."

"Oh, yes, of course. Very sorry about leaving a mess, but like I said—"

"Don't worry about it," Tate reassured her. "Not a big—"

This explanation may be acceptable for Tate, but not Chase. Someone could be holding them hostage, someone could be putting a gun to Marguerite's head, telling her what to say. As quickly as her leg had shot out to strike, her hand moved to grab the cell.

"Let me talk to Georgina," she ordered.

"Mrs. Adams?"

"Let me speak to Georgina."

"She's in a movie. I think—"

"Don't care. Get her, now."

Tate gave her a disapproving look.

"Oh, okay, one moment."

Chase listened closely, trying to pick up any and all information she could. There was nothing, just random noise, then what was clearly the sound of a movie soundtrack. Marguerite whispered something incomprehensible, and a moment later there was more movement, then the sound became muted.

"Georgina?"

"Chase?"

Relief washed over her when she heard her niece's voice.

"Yeah, it's me," Chase replied. This was good—Georgina sounded calm. Still… "Honey, I'm just planning our summer vacation. Where would you prefer to go? Cancun or Montreal?"

There was a beat and then Georgina said, "Montreal, of course. Cancun's too hot in the summer."

And that was it, Chase could finally breathe normally, and she felt her chest loosening.

"Chase? Is everything okay?" Georgina asked in a small voice.

"Yeah, of course, just wanted to check in. Also, don't forget that we have dinner tonight."

"I know."

"Good. See you soon. Love you, Georgie."

"Love you, too."

Chase hung up and felt Tate's eyes on her. Her cheeks flushed as she handed his cell phone back.

"Sorry," she said, unable to meet his eyes.

Tate massaged his thigh once more then stepped forward and grabbed her around the waist.

"Don't be sorry."

"Yeah, but—" He kissed her then, awkwardly because her mouth was half open.

Chase kissed him back.

Maybe it was the three beers and one shot of tequila that she'd had, or maybe it was just the relief of finding out that her niece was okay. Or it could have had something to do with the fact that Director Hampton had agreed to them forming a new unit, which she'd been stressing about for the past few days. It could also be related to her upcoming dinner with her ex-husband. Whatever the reason, Chase needed an outlet.

And this was it.

Before she knew it, they were dropping clothes, first her top, then her bra, then his shirt, as they stumbled into their bedroom. Despite his sore leg, Tate had no problem picking her small frame up and gently lowering her onto the bed. Tate's lips moved from hers to her jawline, then the hollow of her throat.

"Maybe I'm the lucky partner," he said, continuing to move lower, his lips now grazing her sternum, then her belly button. "Maybe I won't get shot while being your partner, maybe I'll just get kicked."

"Shut up," Chase said, closing her eyes and wrapping her fingers in Tate's hair. Then she guided his soft lips and bristly mustache lower still. "Just shut up."

Chapter 10

Brent wasn't sure if the pounding was coming from inside or outside his head. All he knew was that it was all-encompassing. Even though he hadn't made a conscious decision to fall asleep, he had been hopeful that some of his brain fog would clear because of it.

But as he tried to sit up, which took three awkward, dizzying attempts, Brent quickly realized that this was not the case. He managed to make it to a seated position and then rested his forearms on his knees as he waited for the spins to stop. His lips were tacky, and a sour taste coated the inside of his mouth.

Holy fuck. What did I drink on Saturday night?

He closed his eyes but that only made the spinning worse.

The pounding returned and if there was any saving grace to this terrible afternoon it was the realization that the sound was indeed coming from the front door and didn't originate inside Brent's head. With great effort, he stood... and then immediately sat down again.

The temptation to sleep again was almost irresistible. But that thumping at the door... it was as if someone was using both hands and trying to burst through the wood.

The cops? Could it be the cops?

The only thing for certain was that, whoever it was, they weren't going away. Brent's second attempt to stand was more fruitful and he made it to the hall before having to stop and brace himself.

He felt like a child after riding the teacups at the county fair. The ride was over, but the spinning continued.

Bang, bang, bang.

Each thump reverberated inside his skull.

"Fuck," he groaned. Leaning heavily on the banister, Brent's wobbly legs guided him to the front door.

Had he had his wits about him, Brent would have looked through the peep hole and likely never opened the door. But he would have done anything in that moment just to get the banging to stop. And the second he unlocked the deadbolt and opened the door an inch, the person on the other side shoved hard.

His first thought as he was sent flying onto his ass was that it was the cops. They knew about Em, and they were coming to arrest him. Soon, they would be filling the air with shouts of "Sheriff's Department," "Search Warrant!", and firing off Miranda rights.

But that didn't make sense. Why wait for him to open the door? Why not just kick it in? They did that, right? They did it in movies, anyway. And if there was ever a time for such violence, it was now, it was after finding one of Tenbury Academy's sweethearts, Emily Dawson, naked and murdered.

Pain shot up through his elbows preventing Brent from rising even if he had the strength. Which, of course, he did not.

And then the figure at the door, decidedly not a police officer, pounced on him. Brent offered no resistance as the man gripped his shirt and pulled his torso off the ground.

"What did you do?" he hissed. The man's breath reeked of stale beer. "What the fuck did you do, Brent?"

Brent didn't understand what was going on.

Who is this man and why is he screaming in my face?

The man shook him violently and Brent's head whipped back and forth as if all the muscles in his neck had suddenly dissolved.

"What did you do to Emily? Where is she? Where the fuck is she?"

"Wha—what?" The mention of Emily's name brought with it a modicum of lucidity.

"Where is she!"

The shaking intensified and Brent felt nausea building. He was going to puke again.

"What did you do?" The man was screaming now, repeating the query over and over again, strangely in time with his shakes.

"Hey! Get the fuck off him!"

Someone else was here now, and this new person rushed into Brent's house like the first. He grabbed the man accosting Brent and heaved him backward. It was almost comical the way that the man fell on his ass as Brent had done seconds ago, but instead of just lying there, a drunken marionette to be accosted at will, he scrambled to his feet.

Both men looked familiar to Brent but for the life of him, he couldn't recall their names.

"He did something! Brent did something to her!" The first intruder yelled, and Brent detected a slight Spanish accent in his voice. His hands were balled into fists, but the second man was broader, thicker through the chest.

"You better get the fuck out of here, Carlos, or I swear to god this time I'm going to beat your ass bad enough to put you in the fucking hospital."

"I know he did something." There was fury in Carlos' eyes, fury that threatened to usurp common sense. Brent knew the other man—*what is his name? What the* fuck *is his name?*—would mop the floor with Carlos. "I know he did something. And when I find out—"

"Keep running your mouth and I'm going to bash your fucking teeth in worse than last time. The fact is, Emily's your cunt girlfriend, Carlos… if something happened to her, you're the motherfucker to blame. So, you better watch your fucking mouth."

Emily... sweet Emily...

Carlos didn't acknowledge the other man—his attention was fixated on Brent.

"If you hurt her—if you hurt her *again*—I'm going to kill you, Brent."

"Now you're threatening him? *You?*"

No, not sweet Emily. Bad Emily, mean Emily. Cheating whore *Emily.*

Carlos' eyes never left Brent as he said, "Yeah, Jackson, I'm threatening him. Brent, if you did anything to Emily, I'll kill you."

Jackson, that's it! The other man is Jackson Grimes.

Brent saw a flash of Saturday night: Jackson, beer in hand, a sly grin on his face as he brought an unlit cigarette to his lips.

He was there. He knows what happened.

"I've had enough of your mouth. Get the fuck over here."

But Carlos had other ideas. Before Jackson could grab him, he was gone, giving the door a hefty slam on the way out.

Jackson waited a moment then came over to Brent and hauled him to his feet.

"You need to sober the fuck up, Brent. And then we need to have a little chat."

Chapter 11

"HERE, LET ME FIX YOUR hair," Chase said, leaning down to adjust Georgina's ponytail. Her niece brushed her hand away.

"It's fine, Chase. Geez."

"Don't be rude, Georgina."

But the girl was right—her hair was fine, a French braid down her back that she'd mostly done herself.

Chase was just nervous, which was somewhat of a new emotion for her. She wasn't immune to butterflies in her stomach, but usually, these insects only fluttered during life-and-death situations. But this? Being nervous about a… what was tonight, exactly? Not a date, surely. A rendezvous? Perhaps. A get-together? In any event, she was incredibly nervous about meeting Brad and Felix, particularly the latter.

Was it the guilt? Sure. Guilt and nervousness were kissing cousins. But she'd agreed to this dinner, Brad's suggestion, and as much as she wanted just to run, that wasn't a viable option.

Chase was tired of running. Besides, that was the old her.

Stay in the moment, Doctor Matteo reminded her. *Don't think about the past, don't think about the future, just remain rooted in the present.*

"We're gonna be late," Georgina warned, waving a hand toward the double doors of the Italian restaurant.

"I know, sweetie. I know."

Chase straightened, ran a hand through her own hair and then flattened the front of her white blouse.

A white blouse? Is this a work event?

Chase was second guessing everything now.

Stay in the moment.

"You're going to be great, Chase," Georgina said.

Chase looked down at her niece and smiled.

At least I've done one thing right in my life, she thought.

Georgina smiled back.

"Come on, let's go," the girl said, grabbing her hand and pulling her toward the door.

The Italian restaurant was an odd choice for Brad. The man had always favored old-fashioned places, white tablecloths, and such. It wasn't that he was particularly keen on this style, but these restaurants were generally quieter and more amenable to talking. And back when they'd been together, Brad did a lot of talking. Chase, not so much. But this place, a small, Lilliputian-sized step up from the Olive Garden, was pretty much the antithesis of a high-end restaurant. It was loud, boisterous, and borderline obnoxious.

Does that mean that he doesn't want to talk? Did Brad pick this place so that we don't have to do the whole awkward how have you been, I missed you repartee?

Georgina yanked on her hand and then the girl very obviously rolled her eyes to the left. Chase looked up and saw a pretty, young maître-d' staring blankly at her.

"Sorry?"

"I asked if you had a reservation because we're booked solid tonight," the woman said, sounding annoyed.

"Yes, a reservation."

The maître-d' made no move toward the computer in front of her—she didn't do anything, and Chase had a curious thought: is this woman an NPC? Am I back in the metaverse?

The uncomfortable sensation gnawing at her guts reminded her a little of how she'd felt in *Cerberus*, in Tony Metcalfe's version of Hell.

The woman sighed.

"Under what name?" She didn't quite roll her eyes, but her hazel irises drifted upward ever so slightly.

"Cha—" She was going to say Chase, but that didn't make sense. Would it be under Brad? Adams, maybe?

Did he tell me? Did Brad mention what name the reservation was under? He must have. But—

"I think they're over there," Georgina said, pointing towards a table near the back right corner of the restaurant.

Chase's breath caught when she spotted them. There was Brad, handsome as ever in the most classical sense, with his sandy brown hair brushed to one side. He looked a little thinner and was sporting a five o'clock shadow that she didn't love. But it was still him, the man she'd loved and married.

Seated beside her ex-husband was Felix. The last time Chase had seen her son, he'd had shaggy blond, nearly white hair that hung over his ears and covered his forehead. Now, it was shorter, faded on the sides, and was more a dirty blond color that wasn't quite as dark as Brad's but getting there. His eyes were the same striking blue, however.

Despite their differences, these were the same people that Chase knew and loved. The only problem was, she was different. She had changed.

Brad looked up from the menu and spotted her.

He raised his hand in a wave.

Was it too late to run?

"Oh, yes, reservation under Felix. Please, follow me."

Georgina's hand found hers again and she squeezed it tightly. It was odd, the young girl comforting her when it should have been the other way around. Georgina was meeting her cousin and uncle for the very first time. But Chase was grateful for the support—she needed it.

As they approached the table, both Brad and Felix removed the napkins from their laps and rose to greet them. Brad closest but Chase had no idea how to interact with him. She started to raise her hand, but Brad leaned in and hugged her. Chase reciprocated awkwardly. Next up was Felix and she instinctively went to embrace him. Only he leaned away from her and stuck out his hand.

A fissure formed in Chase's heart, but she didn't force Felix to do something he wasn't comfortable with. She shook her son's proffered hand. The boy's grip was strong and professional. It felt rehearsed.

Chase wasn't sure what to say but Brad saved them all from an awkward silence.

"And this pretty young girl must be Georgina."

"Guilty," Georgina said cheerily. "It's nice to meet you, Uncle Brad."

She surprised everyone by giving Brad a huge hug.

"Not too hard, you're gonna break my ribs," Brad joked. Georgina responded by hugging him even harder. Then she let go and looked at Felix.

"Not much for hugs, are you? That's OK," she held out her hand and Felix shook it. "It's nice to finally meet you. I don't have any other cousins."

"Me... me neither," Felix said hesitantly.

They all stared at each other for a few seconds longer, before Brad said, "Come on, let's take a seat. We have a lot to talk about."

Chapter 12

HOT WATER CASCADED OVER BRENT'S body. He was pretty sure he'd already showered today but couldn't quite remember. The entire day was unclear as if everything was covered in a waxy film.

"I heard you were called into the office today," Jackson said. "I hope you didn't do nothin' stupid."

Brent filled his mouth with water from the shower head and then spat.

"I didn't say anything."

He heard rattling and assumed Jackson had found his Zoloft. Jackson hadn't met a drug, prescription or not, that he didn't like.

"Ethan told me you were acting all sus at school. Still goin' on about that shit, about Emily being dead."

She is *dead*, Brent thought.

"I saw her," he whispered.

He didn't think that Jackson heard him, but a second later, the man yanked the shower curtain back. Brent, suddenly exposed, tried to cover himself.

"You don't know what the fuck you're talking about," Jackson hissed. The man was only twenty-two but when he got angry like this and his face turned red, he looked much older, he looked like a drunk uncle who had a heart attack in his mid-forties. "And you're gonna keep your fucking mouth shut."

Brent grimaced.

"What happened, Jackson? I don't remember anything. What the fuck happened? I know we went to The Shack to party. If there was an accident and something happened to Emily—"

Jackson's hand shot out and he planted his palm in the center of Brent's bare chest, forcing him up against the tiled wall.

"We weren't there," Jackson said. "Nobody was fucking there, you got it?"

"But—"

Jackson pushed him again, this time hard enough to knock the air out of Brent's lungs.

"We didn't go to The Shack, got it?"

"Okay."

"What?"

"Okay, I got it."

Jackson kept his hand firmly in his chest and squinted at Brent, making sure he got the message.

"We weren't there."

Brent felt tears start to well and willed himself not to cry.

Jackson finally let him go and then turned the water dial all the way to cold. Brent sucked in a sharp breath.

"I think you might have missed a dose," Jackson said, scooping Brent's pills off the counter and throwing them at him. The container struck him in the shoulder and fell to the tub. "Take your fucking meds, Brent. And keep your mouth shut."

And then he left, leaving Brent shivering and crying beneath an icy rain.

***

Brent's leg tapped furiously in the front seat of his car as he waited for Ava to return home from school.

Despite both Jackson's and Carlos' threats, Brent couldn't just 'forget it'. That was ridiculous. They were lying to him, all of them were. They'd been at The Shack Saturday night.

Himself, Theo, Ethan, Jackson, Ava, Natalia, and Laura. The gang.

And Emily, of course.

What the fuck happened?

Another possibility unexpectedly entered Brent's mind. Maybe this was all just a setup. Maybe Em had finally told everyone that he'd slapped her, and all of his friends had turned against him. This whole thing might just be an elaborate scheme designed to make him lose his mind as payback. Unlikely, but not outside the realm of possibility. Jackson couldn't come up with something like this on his own, but with Ethan and Laura helping? Maybe even Ava, seeing as she used to be best friends with Emily before the breakup?

Possible.

But the makeup? It looked *so* real. And Em was *naked*. Naked, *naked*. She wasn't a prude, but she was far from an exhibitionist. Would she go to this length to get him back? And if so, why now? Why three months after the breakup?

Brent spotted Ava and Laura turning the corner and his heart sank. He didn't want to talk to them together. He wanted to speak to Ava. If anyone would tell him the truth, if anyone still cared about Emily, it was her. But then Ava and Laura hugged, the former turned, and the latter continued straight.

Brent waited until Ava was two doors down from her home, a house that was considerably larger than his own, before jumping out of his car. He tried to make the encounter look casual, waving his hand as he approached, but when Ava noticed him, the smile slid off her face.

"Ava? Can we chat?" Brent asked as he approached.

Ava had narrow features and was too skinny for Brent's taste. Bony shoulders, tight, perky breasts, and virtually no ass. When she tucked her blonde hair behind her ears as it was styled now, she looked cute, but that was the best she was going to get. Ava wasn't nearly as pretty as Emily.

"Brent? You look like shit," Ava remarked, her painted lips pursing.

"I know, I know. I haven't... I haven't been sleeping well. Bad dreams after what happened on Saturday."

A cloud passed over Ava's features and she licked her lower lip nervously.

"What do you mean?"

Shit.

He had hoped to trip her up.

"I mean, after The Shack. My memory is all fucked up." Brent tapped his forehead. "I think I drank too much or something."

"You don't remember?" Ava sounded almost accusatory.

"No!" Brent threw his hands up. "I don't remember shit. I just woke up in the car—Jackson's car, yeah, it was his Chevelle—missing my phone. I went back to get it and... fuck, that's when I saw Em's body. If you know anything, please..."

"Her... *body*?" Ava's words came out as mere gasps. "What are you talking about? What do you mean her *body?*"

Ava's shock appeared genuine, which went against the idea of a setup, not that Brent had really put much stock in this in the first place.

Before they'd broken up, Em, Ava, Laura, and Natalia had been inseparable. Sort of like him, Ethan, and Theo, only tighter. But then the shit hit the fan. Brent knew that he was at fault, that no matter what Em had said, he never should have hit her. That was a no-no and admitting to it would mark the end of his social life. It might even ruin his chances of getting into university, which, truthfully, had become bleaker after his injury and his bombed midterms. So, Brent had gone on the offensive, claiming that Em had cheated on him with Carlos. He'd expected her to counter with the fact that he'd slapped her, and Brent was prepared to call bullshit, but so far as he knew, Em never said anything about what he'd done.

And when Em showed up holding hands with Carlos just three days after they'd parted ways, her fate had been sealed. The girls had to pick a side, and nobody wanted to be on the side of the slut who was sleeping with the scholarship kid. It was high school, after all, and status meant everything. Especially at Tenbury Academy, where most parents had net worths in the mid-eight figures.

But that didn't change the fact that Ava still cared about Em.

"Brent? What do you mean, her *body*?"

Brent swallowed, trying to moisten his throat. He'd popped three Zoloft this time and he felt the familiar onset of cottonmouth. At least this time the pills seemed to help, to calm him, not like earlier in the day when they'd conked him out and he'd woken up feeling worse.

And while the meds hadn't done anything for his memory, they were making him think a little more clearly. Perhaps telling Ava, Em's one-time best friend, that he, a scorned ex-boyfriend, had discovered her naked corpse when he didn't have all—*any*—of the facts, wasn't the brightest thing to do.

"I mean, she was there, right?" Brent said, trying to steer the conversation from an admission to a fact-seeking exercise.

"Brent, what happened to Em?"

He shifted his weight from one foot to the other, slowly regretting his idea to confront Ava.

"I don't know, that's the thing. I can't remember."

"But you said you saw her *body*."

Brent licked his lips.

"I just meant I know she was there, but I can't remember anything else. Maybe if you told me a little about that night, I could…" he let his sentence trail off.

"Didn't you get what you wanted?" Ava said, suddenly becoming angry. "You got to keep your circle of friends, and Emily was left with nothing."

"What do you mean?" Brent said reflexively. "She cheated on me. That was her choice."

Something was different about Ava. She'd been sad when her friendship with Emily had been severed, but she'd never held it against Brent.

Until now.

"If I were you, I'd just forget that we were even there."

"Everyone keeps saying that!" Brent nearly shouted. "But *why*?"

They were at Ava's front door now. She opened it with her key and then looked back at him.

"Because if anything happened to Em, it was you who was responsible. *You* are responsible for all of this, Brent."

And then Ava slammed the door in his face.

Chapter 13

"NO, I'M SERIOUS, IT'S THE worst thing you can ever eat. *Ever.*" Felix slurped a strand of spaghetti. "What was it called again, dad? That stinky fish thing?"

"Surströmming," Brad said in what sounded to Chase like a pretty good Swedish accent. "And it's not a stinky fish thing; it's fermented herring."

Felix stuck out his tongue and mimed ramming a finger down his throat.

"Ew," Georgina said. "That sounds gross."

Chase watched as the girl twirled her spaghetti. Georgina superstitiously glanced at Chase, clearly wanting to slurp like Felix, but she resisted the urge. This made Chase smile.

Things were going far better than she could have ever hoped. Sure, Felix was cold when they'd first arrived—*handshake please, no hugs*—but he'd soon warmed up. And they had Georgina to thank for that. The girl had seamlessly pulled Felix into a conversation, dragged him, if not kicking and screaming at least, digging his heels in, by asking questions about what it was like to live in Sweden.

It was good, apparently, aside from the Surströmming.

"You trying to look older?" Brad said, taking a sip of red wine.

"Older?"

"Yeah, your hair."

"Oh, that's… a long story."

"I have time."

"It's also a story for a different audience." Chase gestured toward Felix and Georgina who were giggling about something. "And the beard? That supposed to make you look *younger*? More hip?"

Brad rubbed the stubble on his chin.

"Does it?"

"No."

"Maybe I just forgot then," Brad said with a chuckle.

"Yeah, right. Zero chance of that. Sweden may have changed your dietary and grooming habits, but you'd have to live on Mars to 'forget' to shave."

Brad laughed and Chase felt her cheeks flush. She grabbed her own wine and swallowed a mouthful.

It's just the alcohol, she lied to herself.

It was strange how easily she fell back into a comfortable place with Brad, despite exceedingly uncomfortable circumstances. Before leaving the country, the man had done everything in his power to help her, to keep her afloat, but Chase had been intent on drowning. Eventually, Brad had just broken down. Then, when the job opportunity had arisen in Sweden, he'd taken Felix and left. Brad was a good father and if Felix's attitude and behavior tonight was any indication, he continued to be one abroad. Chase didn't blame the man for wanting to protect Felix and leave. The truth was, at the time Chase had difficulty looking after herself let alone a child.

All this made sense, at least on some level. What didn't compute was why Chase hadn't expended more effort reaching out. How many times had she called them? Five? Six? Surely less than a dozen.

Why?

Chase wasn't equipped to answer this question, this was something that even Dr. Matteo might have had a hard time sorting out, but this realization didn't keep the question from gnawing at her.

You spent all this time and effort on your niece but abandoned your own child.

"Chase? We're both done. Can we get a gumball from the machine at the front?" Georgina tilted her bowl to prove that she'd eaten everything. Felix did the same.

Only the best Italian establishments have gumball machines at the entrance, Chase thought.

"Sure." She hesitated. "I mean, if it's okay with you."

Brad reached into his pocket and pulled out a handful of change.

"Stay out of trouble, you two."

And then they were gone. Chase watched their heads bob away and for once she didn't feel anxious about not having Georgina next to her in public.

"You doing alright?"

Chase looked back at Brad.

"You know what?" she said, opting for honesty instead of lashing out, which was her usual defense mechanism whenever someone asked how she was doing. "It hasn't always been easy, but I think I'm in a better spot now. Thanks."

A different man might be bitter at this, a different man might get their back up, say, *well, I guess you were better off without me, then*. But not Brad. Brad seemed pleased.

"I'm glad. I really am, Chase."

Fuck, why do you have to be like this? Why can't you get pissed off and storm out of here like a normal person?"

"And you? You and Felix?" Just saying her son's name exacerbated her guilt.

"I'm not gonna lie to you, it was tough adjusting to life in Sweden, and," he lowered his voice just a little, "Surströmming is absolutely disgusting—even the smell is enough to make you want to puke. But we manage. And let me tell you a little bit about Felix, he is your son. Stubborn as all hell. But we're doing all right."

Of all things, this made Chase cry. Not sob, but two silent streams dripped down her cheeks. She moved to wipe them away, but Brad beat her to it.

And then he flushed.

"Sorry," he said and started to pull his hand back, but Chase grabbed his wrist. When they'd hugged before, they hadn't made skin-on-skin contact. And, for the first time in a while, she hadn't been thinking about her voodoo.

But now that they'd touched, Chase saw something. A flash, but not of a violent death or crime like she'd seen countless times before. Instead, she saw herself on their wedding day, her head thrown back in laughter, her hair, longer and darker then, swept up in a breeze.

It was beautiful and Chase was helpless to prevent more tears from falling.

"It's okay, you can touch me."

And she wanted him too. She *really* wanted him to, and not just her face, either.

Jesus, what's wrong with me?

Brad grew uncomfortable and he cleared his throat.

"The reason why I came back is that I have a job opportunity stateside. It's in Chicago. Really, really good gig. More money, better hours, and it's what I really wanted to do."

Chase felt butterflies in her stomach.

"Really? What about Felix?"

"You mean how would he feel about the move?"

"Yeah."

Brad shrugged.

"To be honest with you, the schooling that he got in Sweden? He's going to be light years ahead of his classmates here. That won't be a problem. On the social side, he's stubborn as hell, he's got you to thank for that, but adaptable. And he's a good kid."

"You did well, Brad. I can't thank you—"

"I've missed you," Brad interrupted. He was looking down at his half-empty bowl of carbonara, and his hair had fallen over his forehead.

Chase wanted so badly to reach across and brush that hair away. And then she wanted to kiss him. But then she thought of Tate and Rachel and the little life they'd started to carve out together. It wasn't much—she didn't know what it was, not really—but she knew that she didn't deserve either of them.

Dr. Matteo probably thought that cautioning Chase about her coping mechanisms would make it easier for her to recognize the patterns. But how does the Joseph Heller saying go? *Just because you're paranoid doesn't mean they aren't after you?*

Just because she wanted to have sex with Brad didn't mean that her feelings weren't legitimate.

"I've missed you, too," Chase said. This, she concluded, was definitely genuine.

Chapter 14

BRENT HAD NO CHOICE BUT to go back. He had to know if what he saw was real. And he had to get his phone. Nobody would tell him what happened Saturday night—Brent also realized that there were large sections of the preceding week that he couldn't recall—but there might be evidence buried in his photos.

Evidence…

Going back was also a terrible idea. Ava had tried to warn him, albeit in a strange and aggressive way, that if something had happened to Emily, he would be the prime suspect. But he couldn't just leave her. After all, it was inevitable that she'd be found. It was two weeks from prom and everyone in Tenbury's senior class would be at The Shack after a king and queen were crowned. And the idea of their classmates stumbling across her corpse, naked and exposed, was nauseating.

This whole thing was nauseating.

Brent swallowed three times in rapid succession. If he had anything in his stomach other than Zoloft, he might have vomited again.

He kept picturing Emily, lying on the filthy mattress, those dead eyes locking on him.

Not wanting to leave tire tracks, Brent parked on the main road and huffed it on foot to The Shack. It was only about a five or six-minute walk from where he'd left his car, but that proved enough time to make his head spin. He tried to think of something else, anything other than Emily, but this became his pink elephant: tell someone not to think about a pink elephant and they immediately start to picture it. Only, in Brent Matthews' case, his pink elephant was a dead ex-girlfriend.

The Shack was a different place during the day. At night, it was mysterious, with an air of creepiness, a distinct Blair Witch vibe. With the sun still peeking through the trees, The Shack was simply that: a shack, dirty, graffiti covered, and derelict.

Roughly fifteen feet squared, the exterior of the building was a white plaster that was flaking and peeling everywhere. It had what might have been a roof at one time but now consisted of more holes than coverage. The thick, rotted front door hung open and Brent was instantly transported to the last time he'd been there.

He remembered falling out of The Shack and landing on all fours, shouting that she was dead.

Did I close the door behind me?

No, he didn't think so. But it was closed now, sort of—at least, it was closed enough that he couldn't slip through. Had someone else been here?

Brent reached for the door only to stop just before touching it.

Gloves. Why didn't I bring gloves?

He'd had the foresight to park half a mile away but didn't bring gloves. It didn't make sense—his brain still wasn't working right.

Although, as Brent used his boot to wedge the door open, he didn't think that gloves would make a difference. After all, he'd been here, he'd been drinking here, had been hanging out with everyone. His DNA and fingerprints were likely all over The Shack.

The reek of alcohol, cigarettes, and marijuana accosted Brent as he stepped inside. It made him gag and he pulled his T-shirt up over his nose or mouth.

There were bottles everywhere, littering the floor, and cigarette butts covered nearly every flat surface.

Brent wasn't interested in these.

His eyes went to the staircase. His phone was down there.

And so was *she*.

Run—just fucking run. Get back in your car and keep driving. Keep driving and don't stop.

But something compelled him forward. Triggered by the low staircase, memories came back to him. Not a deluge, but more of those irritating flashes.

Ava laughing with Em. Jackson smoking. His own hand trembling slightly as he took a sip of beer.

Eventually these images stitched together into a more cohesive narrative.

Brent saw Em heading downstairs and he followed.

Why?

He hated the creepy basement. He hated the earthen smell; he hated the lack of lights.

Reverie met reality, and Brent descended into a basement that shouldn't even exist. Every step seemed more difficult than the previous, as if his Chuck Taylors weren't made of canvas and rubber, but cement and rebar. By the time he made it to the bottom, his heart was thudding in his chest hard enough to rock his entire body.

Don't look, don't look.

But he had to look. Except, from his vantage point, Brent could only see the half-closed curtain and not inside what once had been destined to be an electrical closet.

He spotted his phone lying in the dirt. It was only about ten feet from him, but those were the hardest ten feet Brent had ever traversed.

Even bending to pick it up seemed a herculean task. But he managed. And with the phone in hand, thankfully not cracked or broken, although very dead, Brent turned his head and saw her.

The Shack might be a very different place during the day, but Emily Dawson was the same: dead. Her eyes were cataractous, and flies buzzed about her face. Her skin was paler now, and there were spider webs of blue veins on her face and chest. Dark bruises on her throat were now clearly visible.

"No," Brent moaned. "No."

The word had just escaped his lips when he heard a sound from behind him. His first thought was that it was the giant rat he'd seen the last time he was here. But no rat was this big. Not even one that had Emily Dawson as a buffet.

"What did you do? What the fuck did you do?" Somewhere in the back of Brent's mind, he registered that this was Carlos's voice, and he remembered the man's threat from earlier in the day.

If you hurt her—if you hurt her again*—I'm going to kill you, Brent.*

But even when the man tackled him, Brent did nothing to defend himself. He couldn't tear his eyes away from Em.

What happened, Em? What happened to you?

Hands wrapped around his throat and squeezed.

Em? I'm so, so sorry. I… I love you.

His vision began to tunnel, bringing Em's features into even greater focus like the moon amplifying the sun's rays during an eclipse.

I love you.

Just before the lights went out, Brent registered another sound. Bottles being kicked and broken upstairs.

Who's that?

It didn't matter. Nothing mattered.

Em was dead.

There was a shout and Carlos peeled his hands off his throat. Brent instinctively sucked in a fresh breath and stars speckled his vision as a surge of blood flooded his retinas.

No, I don't deserve to live.

"Hawkesbury Sheriff's Department! Put your *fucking* hands in the air!"

Chapter 15

"How'd it go?" Tate asked the moment they stepped through the front door.

"Oh, it was great." Georgina answered cheerily. "Felix is so nice. *So* nice. And he has so many stories about Sweden. Did you know that they eat this fish that is, like, rotten?"

"Not rotten," Chase corrected. "Fermented."

"Well, Felix said it smelled rotten, that's for sure." Georgina pinched her nose and Rachel laughed.

"Why don't you tell Rachel all about your dinner as you guys get ready for bed?" Tate suggested.

"Sure. Hey, Rachel, Felix said that in elementary school they spend most of the day outside. They also…"

Georgina's excited voice was drowned out by the sound of the chair lift carrying Rachel upstairs.

When the girls were out of earshot, Tate poured Chase a glass of wine from the bottle that he'd started, and half-finished, before refilling his own glass.

"And? Other than learning about Surströmming, how'd things go?"

Chase had started to bring the glass of wine to her lips when she paused.

"Wait—how do you know about Surströmming?"

Tate smoothed his mustache.

"What can I say, I'm a cultured man."

When Chase waited for a less trite explanation, he shrugged and added, "It's my job to know things."

"Do you also know that Brad has an interview stateside? In Chicago?"

Tate immediately looked away, which was answer enough.

"That's not fair, Tate, looking into him like that. What'd you do? Use FBI computers to investigate my ex-husband? Or maybe use one of Stu's guys to hack into his e-mail?"

Tate ignored the latter two questions.

"I just did a little reconnaissance. Like you wouldn't do the same. Like you didn't investigate my wife? Into Robin?"

He had her there; that was exactly what Chase had done. Tate had told her about the accident, about his wife's arrest and subsequent conviction, but something about it seemed off. Yet, her 'investigation' hadn't revealed any red flags. Robin Abernathy had claimed that the weather was the reason for the accident and not her 0.09 blood alcohol concentration. The judge disagreed and then he'd thrown the book at her.

"That's not the same thing," Chase said. She took a large gulp of wine. "And you know it."

"What I know," Tate countered, "is that I'm enjoying my time with you, Chase. I think Georgina has been a godsend for Rachel, too. So, yeah, when your ex-husband roars into town and you basically sprint to meet him, I did a little research."

"I didn't rush to see him." Chase was becoming defensive now, but she couldn't help it. She thought about how she'd flushed when Brad touched her cheek. Familiarity might breed contempt, but it also brought comfort.

"Okay, maybe not. But when you came through that door less than five minutes ago, you were glowing. I'm not too proud to admit that I'm worried. Especially because you're avoiding my questions about how things went, and I'm not talking about fermented herring. I'm asking about you. I'm asking about *him*."

"But you're not asking about my son, are you, Tate?"

Take screwed up his face. This was unfair, too. It was a lot to put on the man, but Chase was pissed and not necessarily at him.

"Well, your lack of answer is answer enough," Tate said, turning his back to her.

Chase knew she should say something, assuage his concerns, but wasn't sure how. She wasn't like Tate, she couldn't just fake things. She was real, always real.

Painfully real.

After finishing her wine in silence, Chase headed upstairs. Even though Georgina had her own room, she usually slept on a blow-up mattress on the floor beside Rachel. This had dramatically cut down on the girl's night terrors, which had gone from nightly to once every three days or so.

Chase leaned into the room and listened to the girls' giggle for a moment.

"I don't want to interrupt, just wanted to say goodnight to you girls."

"Goodnight, Chase," both Rachel and Georgina said in unison.

"Goodnight, goofballs."

She was about to leave and get ready for bed herself when Georgina called her back.

"Chase?" Her tone was serious.

"Yes?"

"I like Felix. And I like Brad. Are they gonna become part of our family, too? Are they gonna move in here with Rachel and Tate and us?"

The question caught Chase off guard. Someone Georgina's age, especially someone as bright as she was, should probably have a better understanding of a normal family dynamic. But then again, the girl's upbringing had been anything but normal.

She'd initially been raised by her piece-of-shit father and a handful of indoctrinated mothers on an isolated compound. And then she'd moved to rural New York with Chase but pretty much split her time with Louisa and her boys. And then they'd relocated—temporarily—to Virginia with Tate and Rachel.

So, yeah, the question was a valid one.

"I'm not sure, Georgina. Brad is applying for a job, but he won't know for a few weeks if he's going to stay or not."

It was a non-answer if there had ever been one but before Georgina could challenge her, as Chase knew she would, she quickly said good night again and closed the door.

Instead of going to the bathroom to wash up, Chase decided to head back downstairs. She hadn't been fair to Tate. An apology was on the tip of her tongue, but she stemmed it when she saw Tate standing at the bottom landing. Her first thought was that he was eavesdropping, but his expression suggested otherwise. He looked serious, not caught.

"What's wrong?" Chase asked.

"Did you know that during World War One, on the Western Front, the Allied and Central soldiers decided to stop shooting each other during Christmas? It wasn't even a declared thing, it was just a temporary truce."

"What are you talking about?"

"What I'm saying, is that our first fight is going to have to be put on hold for a little while." Tate held up his cell phone. "That was Director Hampton—the CVU just got its first case and we're going to have to leave... *tonight.*"

PART II – The Shack

Chapter 16

CHASE KNEW THE INSTANT SHE laid eyes on Hawkesbury County Sheriff Harold Grimes that they weren't going to get along. He was a big, burly man with a thick mustache that was considerably darker than his short gray hair. The man's face was tough, like worn leather, which was strange given that he was in charge of just under twenty-thousand people who lived in and around the sleepy Pennsylvania town. Chase hadn't had the opportunity to look into Hawkesbury's crime rate but assumed it to be lower, much lower, than the national average. Yet, Sheriff Grimes presented himself as someone who spent his long days chasing hardened criminals and not handing out speeding tickets or citations for the occasional noise violation. After a moment's consideration and given that the only thing Chase knew about the town was that it was home to the prestigious Tenbury Academy, a private high school for the affluent, she added underage drinking to the list.

Tate, who was nearly as adept at sensing impending friction as he was at changing his stripes, took the lead without hesitation.

"Look, I get it, I do, but here's the thing: we," Tate did a little finger wag indicating Chase and himself, "don't get to choose our cases—we just go where we're told. And the boss, well, he started up this new unit, the CVU—yeah, sounds cheesy, I know—and he wants to get the ball rolling. So, we're just here to lend a hand where we can, not take over. And the better we work together, the faster we can get out of your hair and go back to Virginia."

The sheriff bristled and Chase thought that perhaps Tate had made a rare mistake in his approach to the man. But then the big man started to nod.

"Okay, I get it. Just didn't expect two of you or for you to get here so fast."

The man had a bit of a Southern accent, which Chase couldn't quite place. Louisiana, maybe? Kentucky?

"Great. Now—"

"But," the sheriff raised a hand, "your stay might be shorter than expected. The case, as far as I'm concerned, is already solved."

Tate raised an eyebrow.

"Really? You have someone in custody?"

It was as if Chase wasn't even there anymore, which suited her just fine. She kept one ear in the conversation as she surveyed their surroundings. Their crime scene was located roughly ten miles from the center of town, buried in an oak-hickory forest, the location of which reminded Chase a little of her home in New York State. Only, this was more unkempt and organic while hers, like almost everything in New York, seemed deliberate and manufactured.

She liked it.

The building, which Chase had already heard referred to as The Shack on more than one occasion, she did not. Its state of disrepair wasn't the only thing that made it an eyesore. It was the strangeness of it being here, on a narrow dirt path that was well hidden from the main road, which gave her an uncomfortable feeling in her gut. Only bad things happened in a place this isolated.

Chase took a few photos of The Shack's graffiti-covered exterior and then of the dirt lane. There were three sheriff's department cars parked in front of the building, and likely countless other vehicles that had come and gone before they'd arrived, rendering what tire tracks she might be able to identify later probably useless, but it didn't hurt to be thorough.

"His name is Carlos Mendoza," the sheriff continued. "Caught him here with another high school kid. Carlos had knocked the boy down and was on top of him, his hands wrapped around his throat." Chase cringed inwardly when Sheriff Grimes, in exceptionally poor taste, mimed a strangulation.

"Shit," Tate replied. His voice had taken on a bit of a rough edge as well, and Chase once again marveled at the man's ability to seamlessly transform himself into one of the boys. "Carlos... Martinez?"

"Mendoza," the sheriff corrected.

"He, *uh*, from around here?"

The sheriff made a *hmph* sound as they made their way to the front door, which was flanked by two deputies who looked to Chase like part-time bouncers. The door itself, which was made of thick wood that like the rest of the place had seen better days, hung as wide as the rusted hinges would allow.

The men said nothing as they stepped inside.

"From around here? Yeah, I guess."

"Does he go to that fancy school? Denbury University or whatever?"

"Tenbury Academy." Tate had a memory like a steel vice; this error, Chase knew, was deliberate, as was him messing up Carlos' surname. "Yep, he goes there. Scholarship kid."

Chase noted that the sheriff hadn't said that Carlos received a scholarship, but that he was a scholarship kid. This suggested a label and she got the impression that it wasn't a favorable one.

"Scholarship, huh? I'm guessing that Tenbury ain't cheap."

"Don't I know it."

The sheriff followed this up with a dry, humorless chuckle. Just two mustachioed boys shooting the shit.

The Shack smelled as Chase expected it would: damp and moldy with overtones of alcohol, weed, and cigarettes. Bottles and cans littered the floor. The room itself was nondescript. Likely whoever built this cabin had meant for it to be a general living room of sorts. There was what might have once passed as a kitchen towards the back, but the only reason Chase recognized it as such was because of the countertop, which, while heavily defaced and damaged, was mostly intact. The building itself had no power, but the upstairs was well-illuminated, sunlight somehow evading the surrounding forest to bleed in through countless broken windows. Chase spotted a doorway, just an opening behind the kitchen with no actual door to speak of, that led to a descending staircase, where she suspected the light could not reach.

"So, I'm guessing this is where the kids like to come and get away? To let loose a little?" Tate asked as he tapped a beer bottle with the toe of his shoe.

"It's tradition. Tenbury kids come here a couple times a year. Usually, they don't have any problems."

Right. Underage kids drinking and smoking weed in an off-the-grid shack? What could go wrong?

Well, a high school girl strangled to death, for one.

"Does Carlos and… what's the other kid's name? The one Carlos was attacking?"

"Brent Matthews. Good kid—I know his father well."

Chase got the impression that Tate was raising his voice for her benefit, but she thought she'd already heard enough. Sheriff Grimes thought the case was closed and he would present his evidence in a manner that reflected this opinion.

Chase preferred a more unbiased approach.

She slipped away from the two men and headed to the stairway. Unlike the main living area, which at least had a plywood subfloor, the basement ground was just packed dirt. Whoever had excavated it hadn't even bothered with a foundation. Why The Shack had a basement in the first place was also curious.

Chase was reminded of the dirt cages that Brian and Tim Jalston had thrown her and her sister in all those years ago.

Being surrounded by dirt is an excellent way to muffle screams.

Chase shuddered.

"Whoa, whoa, you can't be down here, ma'am. This is a crime scene."

Hawkesbury Sheriff's Department had set up a series of spotlights to illuminate the basement, with a particular focus on a back corner. The voice came from that direction, but when he stepped forward, Chase was looking into the light and could only make out his outline.

"Ma'am?"

Ma'am. Chase shook her head.

"Chase Adams, FBI," she said, whipping out her badge and flashing it. The man continued forward and eventually blocked out enough of the light that she got a better look at his features.

The deputy was young, maybe late twenties, with features that were almost the polar opposite of the sheriff's in every way. He was tall and thin, with a smooth face and almost apologetic eyes.

He gently took the badge from her and inspected it. He seemed impressed as he handed it back.

"Wow, FBI, huh?"

Chase felt no need to say anything, and the young deputy got the idea.

"Sorry." He offered her a boyish grin. "Deputy Jardine."

Again, Chase remained silent. She'd already told him her name.

The deputy cleared his throat and got down to business.

"This area is where we found Carlos and Brent fighting." Chase noted an overturned lawn chair and an area with fresh impressions in the dirt. "And back here, behind the curtain and on the mattress, is where we found Emily Dawson."

The deputy turned and led her back the way he'd come. Chase had to watch her footing to avoid kicking any of the loose bottles and cans as she followed.

"We've tried our best to keep people out, just in case we get good footprints to match to a suspect," Deputy Jardine said, noting her careful movements. "But as you might expect, we don't have high hopes for any of that. Just too many kids have come and gone over the years. Same for DNA, fingerprints, that sort of thing."

The man was right. Finding usable evidence here was going to be next to impossible.

"Emily was in here."

Using a gloved hand, the deputy pulled back a filthy curtain to reveal a small alcove where someone might have had designs to put in a water heater one day. On the ground, lay the mattress. It was so stained that whatever design might have been on it—flowers, stripes, even the coil pattern—was impossible to discern. Equally as clandestine was the original color. Probably white, Chase assumed, but now it was a mixture of brown and yellow, like oxidized mustard.

She had a difficult time imagining who would use such a mattress. People always said that teenagers were disgusting, but even lusty, hormonal drunk rich kids had their limits. This was pushing it.

Ignoring the deputy who continued to ramble on about things of no consequence, Chase got on her haunches and inspected the mattress more closely. She pictured Emily Dawson lying on her back, naked, as she'd been in the photograph that Director Hampton had provided. It was surreal, almost impossible to imagine.

"CSU took some samples, but... yeah, there's a lot of bodily fluid that has accumulated over the years."

Chase snapped a few photos of her own with her cell and then stood, stretching her back.

As much as she didn't want to agree with the deputy, he was right. She wouldn't have been so polite about it, but they weren't getting sweet fuck all when it came to evidence in this shithole.

"What do you... what do you think?"

It was an odd comment and Chase leveled her eyes at the young deputy.

"What do I think?" she repeated. "I think you need to take me to the body—that's what I think."

Chapter 17

IT WAS CHASE'S DECISION TO split up and while it made sense from an investigative perspective, Tate couldn't help thinking that this had something to do with yesterday's argument.

The truth was, it was getting more and more difficult for him to control his emotions around Chase. When speaking to Sheriff Harold Grimes, the big man in the driver's seat, it was a cinch. He knew exactly how people like Harold, or Hal—they'd become so friendly over the last hour or so that the man insisted that he called them Hal—thought. But when talking to Chase... he couldn't lie to her. Well, he *could*, but she'd see right through it.

Tate also didn't *want* to lie to her. She was one of the few people he felt he could be honest with—mostly honest. And she was right, he was jealous. If it had only been her ex-husband, Tate thought he could deal with it. But it wasn't.

It was also her son.

This revelation had come as a shock. Like Chase, Tate had done his research, but nothing he'd uncovered revealed that she had a child. It wasn't this fact alone that was a deal breaker—he had Rachel, after all—but he hated being surprised like this.

I guess we have that in common, too.

"You said you knew Brent well, what about Carlos? Has he been in trouble with the law?" Tate asked as they pulled into the modest Sheriff's Department parking lot.

"*Uh-huh.* Him and his brother always getting into fights. Let's just say that they don't really fit in."

In saying so little, the sheriff revealed so much.

"And now this. Sounds like progression to me."

The sheriff didn't skip a beat.

"That's right. Everyone knew that Carlos and Daniel were bad news. It was only a matter of time before something like this went down."

It sounded oddly personal now.

Hawkesbury Sheriff's Department was exactly what Tate pictured when he thought of small-town law enforcement. Small, one-story, probably most used to house drunks while they sobered up. It had a homely feel, which Tate rather liked. As they stepped through the front doors, a cute-looking secretary on the plumper side said hello. And not, "Good morning, Sheriff," in forced professionalism as was required in larger cities, but more casual with, "How's it going, Hal?"

"Mornin', Francie. This is Agent Tate Abernathy with the FBI."

The secretary's eyes widened a little and Tate felt a hint of pride. Years of fake TV shows about the Bureau had done nothing to minimize its mystique, it seemed. Nor had countless scandals.

"Nice to meet you, Francie."

"Nice to meet you too, Agent Abernathy."

Tate smiled, knowing that he was on the verge of slipping out of character but not minding the attention from the pretty secretary.

"Just Tate, please."

"Tate's part of this new fancy dancy children's unit with the FBI. This is their first case."

"Children's victim unit—CVU," Tate elaborated.

"Right, anyways, Francie can you please make a note for Deputy Dean Jardine that I'd like a word." As he spoke, the sheriff tapped the counter with a straight finger.

Tate observed a shift in the secretary's eyes, and he knew that this conversation, whatever the nature, wasn't going to be as friendly as the current one. Francie apparently recognized this as well.

"Yes, Sheriff."

"Thanks." The sheriff then turned to him. "Carlos is being held in a cell downstairs. Let me take you to him."

***

Carlos Mendoza was slight with dark hair and surprisingly bright eyes. Under normal circumstances, Tate would have passed the young man off as being handsome, but at present, he looked only one thing: terrified.

"Carlos," Sheriff Grimes barked as they approached. "Someone wants to talk to you. This is Agent Abernathy with the—"

"Carlos? My name's Tate. I'm with the FBI." Tate didn't mind playing a role so long as it suited his needs, but appearing buddy-buddy with the sheriff was unlikely to get him the information he needed.

Grimes might be convinced that Carlos had killed Emily, and while Tate wasn't in a position to disagree, he wouldn't mind seeing a little evidence to back up this claim, either.

Carlos, who epitomized the deer in the headlights look, only managed a weak nod.

"Do you have a lawyer?"

The sheriff's posture stiffened, and the man exhaled loudly through his nose.

"I read Carlos his Miranda Rights and offered him counsel," he said defensively. "The man declined. Twice"

"You're eighteen, right?"

Another nod.

"He's an adult," Sheriff Grimes interjected.

Rapport with the suspect trumped rapport with the local law enforcement.

"Right, but Mr. Mendoza, I strongly recommend that you seek counsel. In fact, I insist. Once you do that, I'd like to have a chat with you, if you're up to it."

Tate wasn't bluffing. He had the benefit of being an outsider of this tight-knit community, which the sheriff had not so subtly indicated Carlos had also failed to integrate into and wanted to make this as obvious as possible. It was a simple but often effective tactic, a not-so-brash good cop, bad cop routine. And Sheriff Grimes was playing it perfectly, even if he didn't know it.

"Carlos, I've already informed you of your Miranda rights, but I have no problem repeating them. You have the right to remain silent. Anything—"

"I didn't do anything." Carlos protested, his voice high and tight. "I don't understand why you think I would—"

"Didn't do *anything*?" The sheriff mocked, not quite replicating the man's voice, but coming close. "You were strangling Brent Matthews with your bare hands."

Just keep lobbing me these softballs, Hal.

"But Brent isn't pressing charges, is he?"

Sheriff Grimes made a face like he'd stepped in a steaming pile of horseshit.

"No." The word came out like a curse. "Not yet, anyway. But this isn't about Brent Matthews. This is about Emily Dawson."

Upon mention of the deceased's name, Carlos rose and rushed to the bars. He looked manic now, intense.

Sheriff Grimes smirked.

"I didn't kill Em, I *loved* her." Carlos' voice was even higher now. "Brent was the one who killed her! He fucking killed her, not me. That's why I was attacking him!"

Tate took a step back and observed this interaction closely.

"Right. And why would he do that?" the sheriff said, almost sounding bored.

"Because Emily left him for me! He couldn't get over her. He fucking…" Carlos' voice cracked. "He fucking killed her. Brent killed her."

As much as Tate wanted this display to continue, he had the long game in mind.

"Carlos, please take my advice and get a lawyer."

"That's right, Carlos. Get a lawyer," Sheriff Grimes said, feeling the need to save face.

They left Carlos weeping into his hands, and once out of earshot, Tate preemptively apologized.

"I'm sorry about that, Sheriff. That's kinda the routine that me and my partner use, but she's cuter, so I let her be the good guy. Not really that used to it, so if I came off as condescending, well, I didn't mean it."

The sheriff eyed him and eventually shrugged.

"No big deal. Next time, just let me know. You're probably right, anyway, Carlos is going to need a lawyer."

"You charge him yet?"

"No. Still waiting on the DA. Soon, though."

"Gotcha. Listen, you wanna grab a beer or something?" Tate asked as they walked back toward the front desk.

"Beer?" Grimes chuckled. "You fancy FBI guys drink beer?"

We do, but unfortunately, I noticed something you didn't. And your pint is going to have to wait.

"Sheriff Grimes? I'm sorry to interrupt," a nervous-looking Francie said.

"Yeah? What's up?"

"Deputy Dean Jardine is waiting for you."

Grimes soured.

"Tate, how 'bout a rain check on that beer?"

Tate pulled out his phone.

"Rain check, sure. I should probably meet up with my partner anyway."

"Sounds good."

They shook hands and Tate turned to leave. He walked slowly, listening to the big sheriff with his Batman utility belt jangling as he moved in the opposite direction. Halfway to the door, Tate stopped and made his way back to the secretary's desk.

"Francie? Is there a bathroom I can use? I've been holding it all the way from Virginia, and I'm about to burst."

The woman smiled. She was cute, no doubt about it.

"Yes, for sure, down the hall on the left."

"Appreciate it."

Take followed her finger toward the bathroom but as soon as he was out of sight, he changed course and followed the sheriff instead.

Grimes ducked into a conference room that was already occupied by a thin deputy sporting an even thinner mustache.

Tate, who ironically really did have to use the bathroom, and badly, leaned up against the wall and listened.

Chapter 18

THE DEPUTY, WHO HAD SINCE introduced himself as Deputy Jardine, offered to escort Chase to the morgue. She declined, politely, at first, but when he insisted, she agreed to follow him in her own car.

Chase was pretty sure that the man was flirting with her and while she wouldn't go as far to reciprocate, she didn't shut it down, either. Let Tate have the big grumpy sheriff and let her have the cute, young deputy. Who knows when either might come in handy?

Twenty minutes later, they arrived at a building on the outskirts of town. At first, Chase thought that the deputy was hungry because he pulled into a Subway parking lot. But this wasn't a lame attempt at forcing her into a date; the Hawkesbury morgue was located around back.

Deputy Jardine held the door open for her.

"You have a full-time medical examiner in Hawkesbury?"

"No, not medical examiner—coroner. And, fair warning, while he's competent, he's very… eccentric."

Coroner, meaning no official medical training.

"Is the coroner still here?"

The hallway was dark and appropriate for a morgue. Hard walls, harsh lighting, and hollow echoes.

"Yep, I called him to let him know we were coming. His name is Arthur Ramos, by the way."

"Thanks."

The deputy stopped outside an unmarked door and Chase, not wanting to experience any sort of awkward chivalry, reached for it.

"Wait. Arthur doesn't like it when people barge in. He gets a little skittish, if you know what I mean."

Chase put her hands up and stepped back. Deputy Jardine then knocked three times, paused, then knocked twice more. This odd sequence reminded her of what children might do to gain access to an exclusive treehouse. And then things got stranger still. The deputy retreated two paces, bowed his head, and folded his hands in front of him.

What the fuck is this?

Thirty seconds passed before the door opened a smidgen and a single eye peered out from behind a bifocal lens.

"Deputy Jardine," the man said and eased the door a little wider. He was sporting a worn Oakland A's baseball cap that failed to contain a head of thick gray curls. "Who are you?"

"Chase Adams, FBI."

It felt good to say that again. It shouldn't, not really, but it did.

"Badge?"

Chase rolled her eyes but produced it. Arthur leaned close and tilted his head upward so that he could read it through the glasses that rested on the tip of his beak-like nose.

"Hmm." Apparently, he approved. "Arthur Ramos."

"I'm here to see the body."

"Indeed."

Only now did Arthur let them enter the claustrophobically small room, which was barely large enough for the three of them, let alone the coroner's table of tools, and the single gurney.

Why the hell did it take him so long to get to the door?

Arthur leaned into the hall, looked both ways, before closing the door and locking it behind him.

What the fuck.

"Emily is over here."

At least he was direct.

Arthur yanked the sheet atop the gurney back like a magician removing a tablecloth from a set table, revealing Emily Dawson's naked corpse. Chase had seen many bodies in her time, some younger than the girl before her now, some in much worse shape, but something about Emily's bluish flesh made her grimace.

"I'm still finalizing the report but cause of death was manual strangulation. There is clear petechial hemorrhaging in both eyes and the hyoid bone in her throat is broken. You can see bruising here on her neck." Arthur indicated these injuries with a pencil.

Even in death, Chase could see that Emily had been a pretty girl. Dark hair, full lips, big, blue eyes.

"Time of death?"

"Liver temp suggests sometime late Saturday night or early Sunday morning. Blood settled in her back, suggesting that she died the way she was found and it's unlikely that she was moved postmortem."

"Anything else you can tell me?"

"I'm still finishing my measurements. I believe that the person who strangled her had thumbs measuring between three and a quarter and three and a half inches long."

Chase looked down at her own hands.

"That's quite large. Are we thinking a man's hands?"

"Most likely," Arthur confirmed.

Chase cocked her head and examined Emily's corpse in greater detail. The girl was fair skinned and now her veins stood out prominently, making it difficult to ascertain what was normal and what was pathological. She thought she saw some bruising under her left breast and perhaps on her right hip.

"So, the FBI..." Arthur said, leading.

"Part of a new branch," Chase answered, eyes still locked on the corpse. "The CVU—Children's Victim Unit."

"Well, Emily Dawson is not a child. She was 17 years old and six months at the time—"

"Yeah, I know."

Arthur harrumphed and pushed his glasses up a little.

"Yeah," Deputy Jardine said, trying to keep the peace, "my brother reached out to the FBI, thought they might be able to help. Get things wrapped up quickly, you know? Especially given how well liked Emily was."

"Ah, I see. Well, if there's anything—Agent? Agent, you need to put on gloves before you—please! Please, do not touch the body!"

But this, like most of what had come out of the annoying coroner's mouth went ignored. Chase had already gotten everything she could out of inspecting the body, leaving only one thing left to do.

Touch Emily's skin and see through her eyes.

***

The world is made of wavy lines... but I'm not sure if it's because my head is moving in a circular motion or if the Earth is suddenly spinning on a new axis.

A face emerges from the darkness, close to mine, but then it recedes. A moment later it returns.

Rhythmic, here now, gone, back again.

And the sound... a tired grunting, almost bored.

In, out, in, out.

It's not just a face now, but a piston between my legs. Firing home.

In, out, in, out.

Darkness envelopes, darkness overcomes.

And then I feel rough hands encircle my throat and begin to squeeze...

***

The imagery was so vivid and powerful that Chase's own world began to spin. She was reminded of the first time she saw through the eyes of the dead, years ago in Alaska.

I need to get out of here... I have to get out of here, now!

"Agent Adams?" someone said, but Chase barely heard them.

In her rush to get to the door, she banged into the gurney, rocking Emily's corpse.

Rhythmic rocking... thrusting... in, out, in, out.

"Agent Adams?"

Chase somehow managed to unlock the door and then she stumbled into the hallway.

The air wasn't much fresher here than in the morgue, but she placed her hands on her knees and inhaled, anyway.

Halfway through the deep breath, Chase gagged and sputtered. This eventually degenerated into a cough. A hand came down on her back, but she slid away from the touch.

Five seconds passed, then ten. At around fifteen, Chase managed to stand up straight. Both Arthur and Deputy Jardine had joined her in the hallway, and both were asking if she was alright.

Chase ignored their queries and resisted the urge to apologize or explain her actions.

"She was raped." Chase sucked in another lungful of air. "You need to do a rape kit on Emily."

Arthur pursed his lips.

"There is no evidence of vaginal bruising or tearing. What I was about to tell you before you touched the body is that I performed a swab, and it came back positive for the presence of semen in her vagina. Emily had intercourse very near to the time of her death. Whether that was consensual or—"

"It wasn't," Chase snapped, regaining most of her composure. "She was raped. Bruising or no bruising. I think she might have been drunk or drugged."

"*Hmm.* Well, about that, I sent a blood sample for toxicology. Should find out what was in her system in a few hours."

"What about DNA from the semen?"

"Running it through the system."

Chase nodded and then regretted it. The motion was too similar to her vision.

"If you don't get any hits, I'll run it through the FBI database. What about an autopsy?"

"Needs to be ordered by the Sheriff's Department," Arthur told her. "And that needs to be performed by a Medical Examiner, which—"

"I'm in charge here—do it. I want a full autopsy. Get an ME here as fast as you can."

Arthur looked to Deputy Jardine, who shrugged.

"It's her case. Full autopsy, it is."

"Of course. Right away."

But despite these words, the man didn't move.

"Now!" Chase shouted.

Arthur startled and his hat shifted. He tucked his curls back in best he could and then returned to his sweaty office.

"He'll do it," the deputy told her.

"Good. I want a list of all Emily's friends, anyone she could have been with at The Shack. Actually, no, I want a list of everyone who knows about The Shack."

Deputy Jardine shifted his weight uncomfortably.

"What?"

"Well, that's gonna be a lot of people. All of Tenbury Academy, past and present, going back at least six years. Including yours truly."

"You went to Tenbury?"

Deputy Jardine nodded.

"Me and my brother both."

"Fine. Just her friends and classmates, then."

Unlike Arthur, the deputy didn't hesitate.

"Of course, I'll get right on it."

He left and Chase pulled out her cell.

Her partner answered on the first ring.

"Tate? Where are you right now? We need to get together and talk. *Now*."

Chapter 19

CHASE SPOTTED TATE LEANING UP against the exterior wall of the Hawkesbury County Sheriff's Department. She pulled up next to him and opened the door. Even before he was entirely inside the vehicle, Chase was off again.

"Emily was raped," she said flatly. "And whoever raped her also strangled her." No need for preamble; they had to move quickly on this. Once this information got out, and it would, the rumor mill would start churning. In a town such as this one, it would spread faster than any virus and make it impossible to determine what was real and what was rumor. "I've got one of the deputies, Deputy Jardine, looking into Emily's friends, who she hangs out with, and who might have been at The Shack on Saturday night."

"Deputy Jardine?" Tate sounded incredulous.

Chase was annoyed that he was focusing on this of all the things.

"Yeah, Deputy Jardine. Why?"

Tate pointed at the building that was quickly fading in the rear view.

"Because I just eavesdropped on Sheriff Grimes berating Deputy Jardine in there."

"What? Now's not the time for games, Tate."

"It's not a fucking game. I saw them, they were arguing. Pretty heated, too."

"About what?

"Us—the FBI being involved in the case, I guess. Couldn't really hear that great. The walls in there must be solid concrete."

"I don't—" Chase suddenly remembered something. "Wait, what is Deputy Jardine's first name?"

"Dean."

"Fuck. Mine was Tim. They're brothers."

"Only in small towns."

"No kidding. Anyway, my guy said it was his brother who called in the FBI."

"Someone's not happy about us being here, that's for sure," Tate remarked. "So, Emily was raped and then strangled? Any luck with DNA or fibers? Any evidence?"

Chase was embarrassed that she'd been in such a rush to get out of there that she forgot to ask.

"They're working on it." Not quite a lie. "But I'm not hopeful. You saw it: that place, The Shack, is a cesspool of DNA and fingerprints. They did retrieve semen from the victim, however, and they're running it now."

"Okay."

"What about you? Find out anything?"

"I found out that Carlos Mendoza, the kid they have pegged for murdering Emily because he was strangling Brent Matthews three feet from her corpse, doesn't even have a lawyer."

"You're joking."

"I wish. Good ol' Hal thinks that this is a slam dunk. Apparently, Carlos isn't the most popular kid in town. But they're not asking the right questions."

"Which are?"

"Why the fuck were either of them there in the first place? Oh, and Carlos says that Brent killed Emily because she left him for Carlos, by the way."

Chase tried not to picture the bruising and indentations around Emily's throat.

"Maybe they left some evidence behind."

"They?"

Chase had meant either of them, but Tate's question gave her an idea.

"Or, maybe they worked together to kill Emily. Wouldn't be the first time. Then one of them gets cold feet and heads back to the scene. They're intercepted and… well, you know the saying: two people can keep a secret if one of them is dead."

"I guess…"

"Don't do that. If you want to say—"

"It's just that I didn't get the impression that Brent and Carlos were best buds. Although, if Carlos really was dating Emily, then maybe."

"Yeah, you're right, it's kind of dumb. But—" Chase reached over Tate's lap and popped the glove box. She pulled out the case file and tossed it at him. "—there's one way we can find out. Where does Brent live?"

Tate found the information in the file and relayed it to her, which Chase promptly inputted into Waze.

"Ah, would you look at that, it's not far from here. Small towns, after all."

***

"Jesus, check this place out," Tate said.

The Matthews home was impressive, as were all of the homes on his street. Two stories, big bay windows, Corinthian columns out front. It wasn't anything close to Stu Barnes' place in Vegas, but this was Hawkesbury. And it was in stark contrast to The Shack where Emily had been murdered.

There was an older BMW parked in the driveway, but it was the official vehicle parked at the curb that got Tate's attention.

"That's the sheriff's car."

To Chase, it looked just like every other Hawkesbury Sheriff's Department vehicle.

"You sure?"

"Yeah, I'm sure."

"How did he get here before us? Don't tell me he has a brother, too."

"*Ha*, naw, I just think he must know some back roads that Waze doesn't."

"I'll tell you what, since you guys are best friends, you keep Sheriff Grimes at bay and I'll talk to Brent," Chase suggested.

"Sounds like a plan."

The closer they got to the house, the more Tate's posture changed. It was subtle but real. He started to stoop a little and become less formal.

The sheriff answered the door.

"Tate?" Grimes said, clearly surprised to see them there.

"Hal. We just wanted to have a chat with Brent. I thought you were back at the station."

"Actually," Grimes held up an empty evidence bag, "I was just bringing Brent his phone back."

"What phone?" Chase couldn't help herself.

"Brent's—it was on the ground at The Shack and one of the deputies scooped it. Just returning it now. Not related to Emily's death."

Maybe someone more impartial should be the judge of that, Chase thought. *Like, someone who isn't the sheriff and performing house calls at one of two persons of interest in this case.*

"You think maybe we can take a look at it? Just in case?" Tate asked, clearly thinking the same thing she was.

"Can't hurt to ask—but you know teens and their phones." Sheriff Grimes opened the door all the way. "Come on in."

This felt strange and Chase wasn't sure how to proceed. Did the sheriff have the authority to invite them in?

"Are Brent's parents home?" she inquired.

"Naw, Mrs. Matthews died almost a decade ago. Robert won't be home for another hour or so."

Chase looked at Tate who made a face that could only mean one thing: small towns.

"Hal, did you tell Brent about Emily?" Not accusatory, just curious.

"Yeah," Grimes admitted. "Took it pretty hard—I think he's still in shock. They used to date."

That's one for Carlos, Chase thought. She'd hoped for more time before people found out about Emily but… small towns.

"Brent, can you come down here, please? Some people want to talk to you."

They were standing in a grand foyer and Chase let her eyes drift first to the wide staircase on the left then to the closed doors on the second floor.

"Brent?" the sheriff yelled again.

The third door opened and a pale kid who looked closer to 13 than 18 stepped out. He was wearing a blue polo shirt and faded jeans. In his hand, he held a cell phone, and despite being called out of his room by the sheriff, his eyes remained locked on the screen.

"See what I mean?" Sheriff Grimes nudged Tate playfully. "Brent, these FBI agents want to speak with you."

At the mention of the FBI, he finally peeled his gaze away from the screen. He wasn't just pale, Chase realized, but nearly translucent.

"Come on down, Brent." No more joking around for Sheriff Grimes.

Brent needed to hold the banister to steady himself and Chase wondered if this was because he'd just found out his ex-girlfriend was murdered or because he'd killed her.

Chapter 20

WHILE TATE DISTRACTED SHERIFF GRIMES—Chase wanted them to leave the house entirely, but the sheriff wasn't having any of it—she had a conversation with Brent Matthews. He was young and scared, but an adult, which was good, and she made it clear that he wasn't in trouble. Chase just wanted to learn about Emily Dawson.

"First, I just want to say how sorry I am for what happened to your friend Emily. I can't imagine what you're going through." Brent nodded appreciatively and Chase continued. "You guys dated, right?" Another nod. "For long?"

Now he sniffed and rubbed his eyes like a child up past their bedtime.

"Brent, I'm part of a new unit in the FBI, called the CVU. We specialize in crimes against young people, like Emily. I just want to learn about her, get to know who she was, what she was like. I told you earlier that I couldn't understand what you're going through, but that was a lie. I've lost someone close to me, too, and if there's one piece of advice I can give you, it's that even though just thinking about her hurts now, the more you talk, the better you'll feel. I mean that." Brent looked like he was about to open up, so Chase added, "And this is your home. If you don't want to say anything, you can just ask us to leave. You're not under arrest and you have no obligation to answer our questions. But, like I said, you will feel better. So, do you want to talk?"

"Yes," Brent said meekly.

"Good. So, did you and Emily date long?"

Brent wiped away silent tears.

"About a year and a half." His voice hitched halfway through the sentence.

"A year and a half? That's a long time. When did you guys break up?"

The way Brent winced when Chase said 'break up' meant something, but it wasn't until the kid answered her question that she realized its significance.

"Three months ago, maybe a little longer. We were still friends though."

That was a lie. Their break up wasn't amicable, as much as Brent might have wanted it to be. But Chase sensed that if she challenged him on this, he was likely to shut down completely, so she let it go for now. Referring to Emily in the past tense was also unusual. Most people took months to speak of someone they loved who had died in anything but the present tense.

"Did Emily have a group of friends that she always liked to hang out with?"

Brent shrugged.

"She was popular. Everyone loved Em."

"Right, but when I was in high school, me and three friends were inseparable. Wendy, Corinne, and this goofy guy we called Archie even though his name was Chris—don't ask—went everywhere together," Chase lied. This was actually something that a suspect had told her when she'd been a Narc in Seattle. She was surprised that this insignificant nugget of information stayed with her, especially considering how messed up she was around that time. But memories were strange like that. "Literally everywhere. Did Emily have a crew like that?"

"Y-yeah." Brent looked down. "We had a group; me, Ethan, Theo, Ava, Laura, Natalia, and of course Emily. We hung out all the time."

"Even after you broke up?"

Brent grimaced.

"That's all right, I get it. You guys were friends after the breakup, but it was dicey. When you guys hung out, though, did you guys go to The Shack for drinks? That something you might do?"

Brent shook his head emphatically.

"Tenbury seniors only go to The Shack three times. It's a tradition, you know? Once during spring break, once after prom, and once before Uni."

"But everyone knows where it is, right?"

"Sure."

"So, you could go there any time, right?"

Brent looked extremely uncomfortable now.

"I guess, but, like, we didn't. No one did. Only those three times."

Chase sighed and finally picked her spot.

"Except that's not true, is it, Brent?" Her tone was so soft, but the accusation, as well as her stare, were both firm.

"What? What do you mean?"

"What I mean, is that you're not telling me the truth, are you Brent?"

"Wh-what?"

"Three times—you only go to The Shack three times, you said. Before spring break, after prom, and before uni. Is that right?"

"Yeah, just three times. Everyone knows that."

"Agent Adams, maybe—"

The sheriff was apparently listening, after all. She tried to wave him off without looking at the man, but she sensed him moving closer.

C'mon, Tate, keep your dog back.

"But that's a lie," Chase insisted.

"No, I mean, like—"

"It's a lie, and I know it's a lie, Brent, because the coroner told me that Emily was murdered Saturday night. He also told me that she was not moved after she was killed." Chase paused for effect. "The thing is, my niece is on Spring Break now, but she's only in elementary school and that's in New York. I did a little research before coming here and, what do you know, your Spring Break was almost two months ago. And prom isn't for another, what, two weeks, am I right?"

"More like three, but, yeah. I don't really know—"

"That means that Emily went to The Shack outside of those three occasions, am I right? Do you agree?"

"I-I-I don't know." Brent's gaze darted toward the sheriff, but Tate expertly slid between them not allowing them to lock eyes.

"What don't you know?" Chase said.

"Agent Adams, I think—"

Chase quickly cut the sheriff off.

"I just told you that she was there on Saturday night. You think I'm lying to you?"

"N-no."

"Then why can't you admit that seniors go to The Shack at other times in addition to the three you mentioned."

"Well, I don't know what Em was—"

"What I'm really interested in, Brent, is who was with her on Saturday night?"

The kid's eyes bulged.

"I-I have no idea."

"Really?"

"Really, I swear. I don't know why she was there, and I don't know who she was with."

"You sure about that?"

"Yes!"

"But there was someone with her. I know this, and it's not because she didn't strangle herself, Brent. It's because someone raped her. Someone raped Emily and then they murdered her."

"Ah, Jesus, Agent Adams, this is taking things too far," Sheriff Grimes said. "This boy has been through—"

The front door suddenly blew open and all eyes turned to look at the man who entered. Chase, Tate, and the sheriff went for their guns, but didn't draw.

"Hal? What the hell is going on here?" The man's dark eyes fell on chase and Tate, "And who the hell are they?"

Chapter 21

IT TOOK A FEW MINUTES for Sheriff Grimes to calm the man down, and the way he did it, by speaking softly to him and squeezing his shoulder, suggested that they had more than just a professional relationship. The sheriff introduced him as Robert Matthews, Brent's father, which Chase had already deduced by the way the man had come into the home and she'd overheard the sheriff refer to him as Rob twice. Tate did the honors of reciprocation. Unlike Deputy Jardine, Robert didn't seem impressed by the FBI gracing their small town with their presence.

"We were just asking Brent a few questions about Emily," Tate said, being deliberately aloof as neither of them was sure how much the man knew of what had happened at The Shack, both on Saturday night and earlier today. "Your son told us that they were dating for quite some time."

Robert shrugged this off.

"They did, but they're just teenagers. Still, this is tough— Em... she was a great kid and I know her parents well. Everyone in Hawkesbury knows the Dawsons. I still can't believe it. I—I just can't believe that this happened. *Here*. It's like a fucking nightmare. Sorry, excuse the language, but this is a terrible shock."

So, he knows. Wow, news travels faster here than I even thought.

"We understand. I think we're just about done here. Agents?" Sheriff Grimes was clearly trying to protect his friend and his constituent.

"In a minute," Chase countered, trying to sound casual. If nothing else, Robert's intrusion acted as a sort of reset, an opportunity to build the tension again before blowing the powder keg. "I was asking Brent about The Shack when you entered. Are you familiar with it?"

Robert looked at her as if she had three heads.

"Of course, it's been a long-standing tradition for all seniors of Tenbury Academy to visit it a couple of times a year." Robert suddenly remembered who he was speaking with. "I am aware of the rumors that alcohol is consumed on the premises, which, for the record, has no official affiliation with the Academy, and I have never witnessed it myself. That being said, until recently, in addition to being a tradition, it's also been considered a safe place for the seniors."

Chase almost lost it. An image of the isolated, ramshackle building tucked away in the woods, littered with bottles and butts and roaches came to mind.

A safe place? A safe *fucking* place?

Chase had heard about parents who, under the guise of wanting to create a safe space for their children, allowed them to drink or smoke weed at home while underage. They often claimed that this was better than them imbibing in a stranger's house or going to drink somewhere even more clandestine. They could keep an eye on them, monitor the children, make sure they didn't do something stupid like overdose or drive. But in Chase's experience, these people were trying to relive their own youth and were attempting to befriend their children rather than parent them. And, sometimes, their motivation was even more nefarious.

Did Emily Dawson consider it a safe place when she was being raped and gasping for air?

"Right," Chase said, struggling not to take her feelings out on Robert. She cleared her throat. "I get it. And we're not concerned with underage drinking. We only want to figure out what happened to Emily."

"What happened to her?" Robert glanced at the sheriff.

Ah, so he's getting his information directly from the source. Interesting.

"I thought you arrested Carlos Mendoza?"

Sheriff Grimes was clearly embarrassed by the leak because he couldn't bring himself to look at either Chase or Tate.

"Carlos is under arrest for Emily's murder—we just have to present our case to the DA."

It was almost as if Grimes was apologetic for judicial course.

What kind of dynamic exists in this town where the sheriff bows down to—

Chase realized that she didn't know what Robert did for work.

"Right, and we just want to make sure that there are no questions when this thing goes to trial," Tate said, filling the silence that was eking toward an end to the conversation. "You know, the FBI can fast track things like DNA evidence and use special software to lift fingerprints, even palm prints from human skin."

This was pure bullshit and anyone with knowledge of the science behind crime scene analysis would know it instantly. Even someone with common sense might be able to sniff out the lie. But perhaps not a kid who grew up watching hyper-saturated episodes of CSI where PCR is performed on a DNA sample in mere minutes and the results are perfect each and every time.

Chase watched Brent closely, but the kid remained stoic. Either he was calling Tate's bluff, or he had no concern of being caught.

There was a third alternative, of course: he wasn't involved in Emily's murder.

Chase was on the fence.

Did you kill, Brent? Did you rape Emily and then wrap your hands around her throat because she left you for someone else?

"Right, sure," Grimes said.

"But I realize that this must be very difficult for you, Brent," Tate's eyes moved to Robert, "for the both of you. We're probably going to have some more questions in the coming days but for now—"

Tate was wrapping things up, but Chase wasn't quite done yet.

"Actually, I just had one more question for you, Brent, if that's all right?"

Playing the good guy card now, making it seem as if she were asking permission when Chase was doing nothing of the sort.

"Yeah, sure," Robert answered a little hesitantly. He still wasn't sure what to make of the young, sparkplug of an FBI Agent with light gray hair.

Chase was like a mangy dog on a scrap of meat. Just one sniff and it had to be hers. And once it was hers, you weren't getting it back.

"We've established that Emily was at The Shack Saturday night, which means that sometimes kids go there outside of those three occasions you mentioned." The word occasions was framed by air quotes and accompanied by quick glare in Robert's direction.

"Y-yes."

"Good. Now, I just need you to admit that you were there, too."

"*Nooo.*" The word was like a moan. "I wasn't there, I don't—
"

"Agent Adams," Grimes warned but it was getting easier to ignore the brash sheriff.

"You misunderstood my comment," Chase said dismissively. "You were there another time... Brent, you were there today when the Sheriff's Department arrived."

"He was accosted by Carlos Mendoza," Robert reminded them. He had been standing behind Brent, but now he stepped forward and placed a comforting hand on his son's shoulder. "Listen, Brent was ill today, and he left school early. I don't think now is the time—"

Chase often got tunnel vision when interviewing a person of interest. Sometimes, like now, this was beneficial—she could shut out everyone but herself and the interviewee. Other times, like when she was with Brian Jalston, she got so locked in that she put herself in danger.

"Like I said, just one more question: why were you there today, Brent? Why did you go to The Shack at all? If, as you claim, you had no idea that anything had happened to Emily Dawson, why'd you go there? Was it just a big ol' coincidence that your ex-girlfriend happened to by lying dead in the basement when you decided to investigate The Shack's architecture?"

Brent looked like he was going to be physically ill.

"I'm sorry, but I'm going to have to end this here," Robert Matthews said, squeezing his son's shoulder hard now to prevent him from answering.

Chase rose and offered Brent a weak smile.

"Of course, I'm sorry that your tummy is upset, Brent. And... you don't need to answer, because I know why you were there. You were there because of your cell phone... you were there because you left your cell phone at The Shack on Saturday night, didn't you?"

Brent looked like a tortoise trying to pull his head back into his shell.

Chase turned to Grimes and was about to ask a question, but Tate beat her to it.

"Hal, I know that you returned Brent his phone already, but I was hoping that we could have a look at it?"

Chase was certain that Sheriff Grimes would object, but he didn't, and Brent surprised her by pulling the cell phone from his pocket. With a trembling hand, he held it out to her.

"No, actually, I think this interview is done," Robert Matthews stated, this time with confidence. He pressed a palm on Brent's forearm, forcing the boy to lower the phone. "Maybe after he gets some rest, we can resume this interview."

A lot had happened in the past few seconds that Chase was still processing. She wanted the phone, yes, but not getting it wasn't their main objective.

"Yes, of course. I'm very sorry about what happened to Emily," Chase said.

Grimes shook Robert's hand, the kind of knowing shake where you grab them near the elbow with your opposite hand, and then he joined Tate and Chase outside.

"Brent seems like a good kid," Tate remarked, falling back into his role. "Scared, but who wouldn't be."

Sheriff Grimes removed his hat and wiped sweat from his forehead.

"Yeah, I think you're barking up the wrong tree there."

The comment was directed at Chase.

"Oh, no, I'm just asking questions. I've got a… well, I can be aggressive sometimes. Didn't mean to come off as callous or uncaring."

Tate gave Hal a look in response to this, the meaning of which was clear even to Chase: *told you.*

This made Chase wonder what the hell the two men had talked about.

Mustache wax and pussy?

"So? What's next for you guys?"

Tate checked his watch.

"Probably going to stop in and see Emily Dawson's parents. I assume that you've broken the news?"

"*Uh-huh.* Sent one of my deputies over there as soon as she was pronounced. They, *uhh,* they're pretty beaten up."

Hidden meaning: maybe you should wait before you put them through the ringer. Especially if you're going to be aggressive again.

"It's just that school's out and we wanted to speak to some of Emily's classmates together."

"Really?" Grimes craned his neck to look back at the Matthews house. "Well, I guess you'll be seeing Robert Matthews sooner rather than later, then."

"Why's that?" Chase piped in.

Grimes' brow lowered and he focused his attention on her. He had a *you don't know?* expression on his wide face.

"Because Robert Matthews is the principal at Tenbury Academy. Anything that happens there goes through him."

Chapter 22

"WELL, THAT WAS... INTERESTING," TATE offered as they drove. In the rearview, Chase spotted Sheriff Grimes leaning against his car, cell phone pressed to his ear. He looked troubled. "You pissed that you didn't get the phone?"

"Not really," Chase replied absently. She was still mulling over what had happened and was only listening to her partner with half an ear.

"Why?"

"Because Brent was about to hand it over, that's why."

"I'm not following."

The in-dash GPS instructed them to turn right. They were just under eleven minutes away from the address they'd inputted before leaving Brent Matthews and his father.

His *principal* father.

Chase still didn't know what to make of that, but it did explain some of the mysteries of this place. The sheriff didn't want to piss off the principal of the town's really only draw. Tenbury Academy was expensive and expensive meant rich parents had to pay for it. Rich parents meant campaign money and the Hawkesbury sheriff was an elected position.

Fucking small towns.

"Brent was ready to hand his phone over, which means that if there was anything incriminating on there, he'd already deleted it. Otherwise, he would have fought tooth and nail to make sure that we didn't get it."

"But Sheriff Grimes couldn't have been there more than five minutes before we arrived. You think that in that short a time Brent managed to delete everything incriminating? Dick pics included?"

"Give a teenager a cell phone and two minutes and they can probably hack into the Pentagon."

Tate smirked.

"Probably right. I'm guessing that our buddy Hal made a big show of returning the phone himself to save face with principal Rob."

"Yep."

"Small towns."

Even though this was exactly what Chase was thinking, she was starting to have second thoughts.

"You get the impression that there's something rotten here in Hawkesbury? Something that runs a little deeper than Emily's murder?"

When Tate didn't answer immediately, Chase glanced in his direction. He was deep in thought.

"I... don't know. Something definitely isn't normal about this place, but I can't tell whether it's just because the sheriff is trying to calm a brooding storm and keep his job or there's something more to it than that."

"Brent seemed shell-shocked but he's just a kid. The sheriff and the principal, on the other hand... I mean, they said all the right things, but they don't seem all that upset that a popular high school girl was brutally raped and murdered in their town."

"Devil's advocate?"

"Sure."

"The sleepy Pennsylvania hamlet surrounded by beautiful greenery has no history of violent crime," Tate said in a British accent. He went back to his normal voice. "They're still processing, trying to avoid panic and not look stupid in front of the feds. Besides, they've already got their guy and that's good enough for them."

It made sense but they were making assumptions and Chase didn't like assumptions.

"Is there no violent crime here in Hawkesbury?"

"Good question. I'll find out." Tate fired off a text just as they arrived at the Dawsons' address. "Wow."

It was more an estate than a home and it dwarfed the Matthews' place. Three stories, large windows that were so clean that the reflection of the late afternoon sunlight was almost blinding.

"You wanna take the lead on this one, or should I?" Tate asked.

"Let's play it by ear."

As they walked up the long and impressive path that funneled them toward massive double doors, Chase couldn't help but think about Floyd. Floyd and his PTSD from having to break unthinkable news to a parent who lost their child. This wasn't exactly the same thing—according to the sheriff, Emily's parents had already been informed of their daughter's death—but it still made Chase very uncomfortable.

Sheriff Grimes had subtly suggested that she take it easy with the Dawsons, handle them with baby gloves, so to speak, but she never set out to be aggressive. While Chase suffered no delusions that she was a compassionate shoulder to cry on, she believed she was fair. But once someone started lying or obscuring the investigation? All bets were off.

Catching a killer trumped massaging feelings all day, every day.

The woman who answered the door looked so much like Emily that Chase was momentarily taken aback. She had the same big lips and blue eyes, same chestnut hair. She had lines on her face and was obviously less pale. But the resemblance was striking.

"Mrs Dawson?" Chase said after collecting herself. "My name is Agent Adams, and this is my partner, Agent Abernathy. We're with the FBI, a special division that investigates crimes against..." She stopped herself, hating the acronym CVU and knowing that saying the words didn't make sense, either. Emily wasn't a child, she was a teenager, pretty much an adult. "Crimes against children and young adults. We're very, very sorry to hear about what happened to your daughter Emily."

A man appeared behind Mrs. Dawson. It was clear that Emily had gotten her looks from her mother. Mr. Dawson was short and stout, shaped like a bowling pin. What little hair he had was thin and dyed a matte brown.

"They're with the FBI," Mrs. Dawson said told her husband. "Agents..." She tried to come up with their names but when she couldn't, she just threw her arms up. "Oh, I don't know..."

"Adams and Abernathy," Chase repeated. The woman retreated and the man stepped forward, holding out his hand. Tate, knowing her dislike of handshakes, did the honors.

"Carl Dawson, and my wife's Jennifer."

"Is it alright if we come in?" Tate asked. Now he was the empathetic law enforcement agent the Dawsons needed.

"Sure, come in."

Unlike the Matthews' place, which was sparsely decorated, the interior of the Dawson home was as impressive or even more so than the exterior. Oil paintings by real artists, Chase assumed though didn't know for sure, hung from most walls and the furniture looked expensive but classy. Chase and Tate followed Carl and Jennifer around a spiral staircase towards a sitting area. There were two cups of coffee sitting on opposite ends of a table and Chase knew exactly what the Dawsons had been doing before they'd arrived: nothing.

Absolutely nothing.

They were just staring at their coffee and imagining a time when their daughter wasn't dead.

"Would you like a coffee or something?" Jennifer Dawson whispered.

"No, we're fine. Thank you," Chase answered. "Mrs. Dawson, would you mind showing me Emily's room?"

***

Chase expected her feelings of dread and despair to increase upon entering Emily's room, but the opposite happened. It was as if whoever had decorated the room had done so by typing 'Teenage girl's room' into Pinterest and replicating the first image they'd seen: the walls were painted a light lavender; a massive four post bed was placed against one wall; and a clean, white desk with a closed laptop sitting on top of it against another. There were a handful of hanging framed pieces of art, but they were all generic—a feather, a silhouette, an artistic quote—and revealed nothing of the person who used to live here.

"I still can't believe Em's never gonna sleep here again." Chase didn't know what to say so she remained quiet. "I guess she didn't have that many nights left, anyway. Em was going to Penn in the fall."

The rationalization of Emily's murder stung Chase.

"I'm sorry. We're going to do everything we can to find out what happened to her."

One corner of the creme-colored bedspread had been pulled back. Jennifer fixed it then smoothed the fabric with her palms. Chase casually walked over to the girl's desk. In addition to her computer, she spotted several notepads. One had 'Story Planner' written on the front and she picked it up.

"Mind if I take a look?" she asked, holding the book for Jennifer to see.

"Em was going to Penn for creative writing. She loved to read and to write."

Chase took this as a yes and thumbed through the pages. She was impressed at the cursive writing that filled each sheet. Most girls Emily's age who were inclined to write, and not wasting time ever-scrolling on their phones, would have preferred to type their work. Not Emily. Most of the writing was just musings about a particular character along with the occasional poem. Towards the back of the book, one of the more recent entries looked more long-form, likely the start of a novel.

"Mrs. Dawson?"

"Please, just call me Jennifer." The woman was speaking softly and with disinterest.

"Okay, Jennifer, I know this is hard but it's important for us to move quickly. The better I understand who Emily was, the easier it is to piece together exactly what happened. Can you tell me a little bit about her friends? Boyfriends, maybe?"

"I heard that they have somebody in custody. Do you know who—"

"That's the sheriff's investigation, not ours. We're the FBI so we do things a little differently. Please, anything you can tell me about Emily and her relationships will be a great help. Brent Matthews said that they were close, that he and Emily used to date."

"Yes, that's right."

"Do you know why they broke up?"

Jennifer shrugged.

"Em said they just started to grow apart. They dated for a while but, to be honest, I don't think that it was ever that serious."

"Emily was a teenager—everything is serious when you're a teenager."

The grieving woman smiled at this.

"You're right. As for friends, Emily was close with Ava, Natalia, and Laura. But..."

"But what?"

Another smile, this one tired.

"Let's just say that Em was excited about a fresh start at college."

Chase read between the lines. When things had gone south with Brent, Emily's relationship with her friends also took a hit.

"Jennifer, do you know a boy named Carlos Mendoza?"

No smile at all now.

"Yeah, he was part of a scholarship program at the school. I heard he was a nice enough kid. His brother, Daniel, not so much. Why are you asking about Carlos?"

Chase focused on the narrative.

"Did Emily know Carlos?"

"Sure, they're both seniors."

Present tense.

"And did they date at all? Emily and Carlos?"

Jennifer looked insulted.

"Dating? No, they didn't date. Why are asking about him? Did he have something to do with Emily's death?"

Chase was at a crossroads. If she lied about Carlos' arrest, Jennifer would find out—small towns and all that—and that would ensure that this was the last good-natured conversation they'd have. Probably the last without lawyers present, too.

"To be honest, Mrs. Dawson—sorry, Jennifer, my partner I just got into town just a few hours ago. We like to keep a little distance between us and local law enforcement, you know? Try to be as impartial as possible as we collect facts. We work together when we have to, but what the Sheriff's Department is doing and what we're doing aren't always the same thing." Chase was being so ambiguous that she was starting to annoy herself. "I just have one more question for you."

People loved *one last question*. It put a time limit on things, but it was almost never used literally.

"Yes?"

"Are you familiar with a place called The Shack?"

"Of course. Everyone knows about The Shack. Seniors go there—"

"Three times, I know. Did Emily mention going there any other time?"

"No."

The lack of emotion in Jennifer's voice suggested that she wasn't aware that her daughter was discovered there.

"What about Saturday night? Did Emily say where she was going?"

The one last question tally had reached four now.

Jennifer exhaled loudly and her shoulders rounded.

"She said… Em said she was going to the movies alone. A movie… this all seems like a movie. Or a nightmare. A terrible nightmare. My Em, gone. Gone forever." Jennifer sobbed. "She'll never see another movie again. And I'll never see her…"

Chapter 23

As soon as the FBI agents left, Brent broke away from his father and ran upstairs. He barely had enough time to lift the toilet seat before vomiting. His body clenched, ridding itself of seemingly every ounce of fluid he had left in his stomach, intestines, anywhere. And then, when all of his efforts turned his purging into a dry cough, he rested his sweat-slicked forehead on his forearm over the bowl.

"Brent? Brent, you okay? Need anything?"

Yeah, I need this to all go away. All of it. I need to go back to three months ago when I was sitting with Em, and she told me she didn't love me. I need to go back before the slap.

"Fine. Just sick." He wasn't sure how he managed to say even this.

"Okay. I put a Gatorade and some Pepto outside the door, alright? And when you're feeling better, we need to talk, okay, son?"

Brent heard his father lean up against the door, but he knew that the man wouldn't open it. The sad truth was that they had never been particularly close. There had been time, shortly after his mother died, that they'd tried to connect on a deeper level, but it always felt forced and didn't last. Brent didn't hate his father, nothing like that, but the man just worked so much and stressed so hard about money that there was little time or mental energy left for love. Being the principal at Tenbury didn't help things, either; Robert couldn't risk being even accused of a hint of favoritism, so he pushed hard the other way.

"Love you, Brent."

Brent didn't answer and after a ten count, he heard his father walk away.

After catching his breath, Brent popped two more Zoloft. They were nearly impossible to swallow, but he choked them down by scooping water from the sink with a cupped hand into his mouth. They were already half dissolved.

The FBI… the fucking FBI was here. And they'd asked for my cell phone. Did they know what was on it?

The Burt Reynolds-looking agent with the mustache had said the FBI had all sorts of special tools. Could they use it to hack into his phone?

Had they seen the pictures?

When Sheriff Grimes had stopped by to give his cell back to him, he'd wanted to talk, too. Brent had said that he'd left school because he was sick and needed to lie down—both true. But he also needed time alone with his phone to see what was on it.

And Brent had no problem finding what he was looking for: a single photograph taken at 12:34 a.m. on Saturday night.

Brent also believed that it was the last photograph taken of Emily while she was still alive.

It was the seven of them—Ava, Laura, Natalia, Jackson, Ethan, Theo, and Em—and of course him, but Brent was taking the picture and wasn't in it.

They had their arms wrapped around one another and all were smiling. Brent zoomed into Em's face and felt his cheeks become damp with tears—apparently, his vomiting hadn't rid him of all fluid, after all.

Like the rest of them, Em was smiling. But he knew her smile and this one was fake. It didn't reach her eyes.

What happened? What the fuck happened?

The photo was taken at The Shack, no doubt about that—Brent could see the bottles on the ground behind them and the ruined counter in the background.

But he couldn't remember taking it. And he'd couldn't believe she was actually dead. It seemed impossible. Here Emily was fake smiling in a photo he'd taken less than three days ago.

Now she was gone.

His mind wasn't processing this information properly, he knew that. It was making him physically ill.

If only I could remember, that would make things better.

This didn't make sense, but Brent was desperate. And he was in a sort of fugue state when he sent the message to everyone who had been there.

"The Shack. Meet me at the Shack at 12:34 tonight. If you don't show up, I'll tell everyone you were there on Saturday."

And then, just in case they thought he was bluffing, Brent attached the photograph to the message.

It was read by everyone almost instantly, but nobody replied. It didn't matter. He knew they would show.

That was when the doorbell rang. Brent didn't know who it was, but knew it was for him.

His decision to delete the photo and the message he'd just sent wasn't to cover his own ass, at least not entirely.

If they arrested him, he might never find out the truth.

With great effort, Brent managed to peel himself off the bathroom floor, driven by anger at himself and at his friends.

Then he stared down at his hands.

There is no way I killed Emily. His lips pulled back in a sneer. *But you slapped her, didn't you? You slapped her—Brent, is it so hard to believe that you could choke her, as well?*

"Impossible."

Yet there was that inkling of doubt driven by his memory gaps. Was this his mind's way of shielding it from the horrible truth?

Brent's teeth started to chatter, and he thought about Carlos Mendoza of all people. Carlos, the prick who was fucking *his* girlfriend, was convinced that Brent had killed Emily.

If I did it, I'll turn my ass in, Brent decided at that moment. *I don't care what happens to me. If I killed her, I will drive my ass to Sheriff Grimes' house and demand he put the cuffs on me.*

But first, he had to find out what happened Saturday night.

And he would.

Tonight at 12:34 AM.

Brent popped another Zoloft.

Until then, he would sleep, because something told him he was going to need it.

Chapter 24

"**It doesn't get any easier**, does it?" Tate asked.

"No, it doesn't," Chase admitted.

Before starting the car, Chase tossed the Story Planner on Tate's lap.

"What's this?" He picked it up and started to open it. "This Emily's?"

"Yeah. She had a laptop too, but her mother didn't know the password. If we really wanted to, we could send it back to Quantico and get them to jail break it, but I'm pretty sure that this book is going to tell us everything we need to know about Emily Dawson."

Tate nodded.

"What about her cell phone? Anyone find it?"

"Not so far as I know. Wasn't at The Shack and her parents don't know where it is. Whoever killed her probably has it."

"Number?"

"Should be in the file."

Tate swapped Emily's notepad for the case file and then made a call on his phone.

"Hey, think you do me a favor? No, just a small one this time. Need to see if you can track this cell. Number is…" Tate found the number, read it off, and then hung up. He noticed Chase staring at him and said, "What?"

"Nothing."

"Oh, you're doing that thing now?"

"Fair enough—it's just that I'm surprised people at the Bureau still talk to you. Normally, when an agent finds out that you've partnered up with Chase Adams, your ability to call in favors dries up real quick."

"You really think highly of yourself, don't you?" Tate joked.

"Yeah, saying that coming close to me is like catching the Bubonic Plague is an ego flex if I ever heard one."

"Well, the good news is that I'm pretty sure I'm immune. At least for now. Truth is, I've been in this game a long time, Chase, and there are a bunch of people that I've helped out over the years who owe me. *Really* owe me. I think we're going to be okay for the time being. You find out anything from Mrs. Dawson?"

Chase relayed the information about Emily's close friends and Jennifer's almost visceral denial of her daughter being involved with Carlos.

"Could be nothing, but could be a motive," she said.

"Go on."

"Tenbury princess engaged to the prince but leaves him for the jester. The court isn't too happy about it."

"I never pegged you as a medieval poet. But in this hypothetical scenario, do you think that the court would completely abandon the princess?"

Chase decided to drop the analogy.

"If Emily cheated on Brent with Carlos, the outcast scholarship kid? It's possible."

"*Tsk, tsk.* And here I was, thinking that the maligned Chase Adams was above stereotypes."

"Oh, I am. Trust me. But you know who might not be?"

"People who live in multi-million dollar homes in Hawkesbury County?" Tate suggested.

Chase recalled the way Jennifer Dawson had cringed at just the mention of Carlos' name.

"Bingo. What do you think we stop by the Mendozas' and get their side of the story?"

"Sounds like a plan to me, my liege."

***

Carlos Mendoza lived at the opposite of town to the Matthews and the Dawsons in a cute, one-story bungalow. It was well-maintained, the lawn recently cut and the gray paint on the fence outside couldn't have been more than a year old, but there was no denying that it wasn't close to being in the same tax bracket as the other two.

From the file, they knew that Carlos lived with his mother, Sylvia Mendoza, but she wasn't the person who answered the door. Instead, it was a young man who appeared to be in his early twenties. He was shirtless, showing off his tanned, but skinny body, and he had dark hair and darker eyebrows. He was drinking a glass of water.

"Hi, we're with the FBI," Chase said. "Your mother wouldn't happen to be home, would she?"

"Ma's gone to talk with Carlos." The kid looked at them with disdain. "Cuz you arrested him for hurting that girl, which is bullshit. He didn't hurt her, why the fuck would he do that?"

Well, the cat was definitely out of the bag now. Just to be sure…

"You mean Emily?" Chase asked.

The man's scowl became something closer to a snarl.

"Yeah, Emily. Who the fuck else?"

"Were your brother and Emily dating?"

"You sure you with the FBI? Like you ain't some junior detective or some shit?"

"Easy now," Tate cautioned.

Chase replied by showing her badge. Carlos' brother didn't even look at it.

"Let me ask you again, were your brother and Emily dating?"

"Yeah, they was dating. And let me tell you, lady, them gringos in town didn't like that one bit."

"Were they together long?"

The boy shrugged. Some of his anger was starting to dissolve. That was the thing about being incensed: it always passed. Only sometimes, what it left in its wake was worse. Guilt. Despair. Loss.

Loneliness.

"Coupla months. They was both going to Penn in the fall."

"What's your name?"

He gave Chase the old up-down.

"What's *your* name?"

"Chase."

The immediacy of her answer seemed to break down the tough guy facade that kept creeping up.

"Daniel."

"And you're Carlos' older brother?"

"Yeah."

"Do you also go to Tenbury Academy, Daniel? Or *did* you go, I mean?"

"Naw, I ain't got the grades like Carlos. And we can't afford it no other way."

"Did you meet any of Emily's friends?"

"Friends?" Daniel shook his head. "Nah. Like everyone else in this fuckin' town, she don't want nothin' to do with the token Mexican family. Not in public, anyway. She'd come over after dark."

"You don't seem all that upset about Emily having been killed?" Tate said.

Daniel shrugged dismissively.

"I ain't happy she dead. But I ain't gonna lie to you, Carlos was better off before he started dating her."

"How so?"

"Let's just say that I was happy when people left us alone. But after he started dating her, shit started happenin'. I come outta work, my tires are mysteriously flat. And then there was a coupla broken windows—that shit's expensive to fix. Then one day, Carlos comes home from school with a black eye. He ain't never told me who did it, but I know. And let me tell you, anybody who fuck wit' my brother fuck wit' me."

"Who was it?"

Daniel let out a humorless laugh. Despite not being a fan of his callous nature, Chase understood where he was coming from. It must have been hard for them as outcasts to live here without the drama of Carlos stealing Brent's girlfriend, if that's really how things went down. And then the 'accidents' and now this: Carlos being accused of her murder.

"Was it Brent?" Tate asked. "Did Brent attack Carlos?"

Daniel laughed again but this time the sound was laced with mirth.

"Brent? Brent Matthews? You gotta be kidding me. I heard that he used to be this big lacrosse player, but now he's just a skinny little prick. Couldn't hurt a fly."

"Then who?"

"That prick Jackson," Daniel said without hesitation. "But don't worry, I got him back."

"Jackson?"

"*Shiiit*, you guys really are junior detectives, ain't ya?"

Chase felt Tate tense and she held her hand out at her side to indicate for him to stay quiet. After a moment, Daniel sighed.

"Jackson Grimes, the sheriff's son, that's who. It was that motherfucker who slashed my tires, broke my window, and punched Carlos in the face. So, I go and confront him, right? And he attacks me. I shit you not. Alls I'm doing is defending myself but then cops show up and Jackson, you wanna know what he did? Planted some shit on me. Some drugs. I don't even know what the fuck it was, can't even pronounce that shit. But I go down for it. Of course, I do, cuz his daddy don't want nobody to know that a spic kicked his son's ass. His sheriff daddy's been covering up for that degenerate for years." Daniel paused to take a deep breath. His face had turned red. "Cuz y'all are just junior detectives or some shit, I'ma help you out a bit: if you want to know who really killed Emily—and it ain't my fuckin' brother, that's for sure—I'd start looking at Jackson Grimes."

Chase didn't want to glance over at Tate but couldn't resist. And although no words passed between them, two of them went directly from her brain and into his.

Small towns.

Chapter 25

THINGS WERE COMPLICATED *BEFORE* CHASE got the call at dinner. Tate did a shallow dive into Jackson Grimes, mostly limited to a background check. There was no way to corroborate anything that Daniel Mendoza had told them about Jackson, but they didn't expect to find much if anything. The man's father was the sheriff and as they'd already found out, things worked a little differently in Hawkesbury than they would in, say, New York City or even Stafford County.

Jackson was squeaky clean.

Daniel, on the other hand, was not. There were three arrests on his record, two for assault and one for drug possession. There was no plaintiff listed in either assault but if Chase had to bet, she would have gone all-in on that being Jackson. The drug arrest was even more damning. The compound that Daniel claimed not to even know how to pronounce was Rohypnol, more commonly referred to as the date rape drug.

In… out… in… out… everything moving in strange wavy lines…

Chase had been eager to chat with Daniel again after learning this tidbit of information, but Tate had dissuaded her. They were just doing preliminary recon for now. Second visits would come but at a later date. The plan was to corral Brent's posse tomorrow at Tenbury and see what they knew about last Saturday night. They were high school kids and if there were no secrets in a small town then there were fewer in the classroom, so Chase guessed a lot. Getting them to talk would be the difficult part. After that, they would track down Jackson Grimes and attempt to have a chat with him. Convincing the sheriff's son to talk would be next to impossible, but they had to try.

During the consumption of surprisingly good homemade hamburgers at the local diner, and sucking back cold draft beer, the call came in.

"Am I speaking with Agent Adams of the FBI? Of the Children's Victim Unit?" Chase, who had been chuckling at Tate's imitation of Director Hampton, immediately grew serious.

"Yes, this is Agent Adams. Is this Arthur Ramos?"

She wanted to put it on speaker so that Tate could listen in, but the restaurant was too loud.

"This is he, the Hawkesbury coroner. I wanted to let you know that toxicology results came back on Emily Dawson. Now, normally I would never do this over the phone—"

"What did the tox screen reveal?"

Arthur cleared his throat, a reminder to Chase of how much he hated to be interrupted. And how strange the man was in general.

"Yes, as I was saying, something has come up and I'm unable to meet you in person this evening. Given the sensitivity of this matter, I thought I would call you to update you on the findings."

Oh, get on with it, for fuck's sake.

"Yes?"

"We discovered high levels of flunitrazepam in Miss Dawson's blood."

"Flu-*what*?" Chase blurted.

The man laughed. He *actually* laughed.

What the fuck is wrong with him?

"Yes, well, flunitrazepam is more commonly known by its trade name, Rohypnol. It's a benzodiazepine and is—"

"I know what it is." Chase no longer cared about interrupting the strange man. "Anything else?"

A long pause.

"Hmm, yes. In addition to the flunitrazepam we also found human chorionic gonadotropin in Emily Dawson's blood."

Oh, Jesus, what the fuck is that, now?

"What?"

"Hmm." It sounded like Arthur was getting off on this.

Oh, look, the big city FBI agent doesn't even know what human chronic gonadshit is.

He'd lost the plot. A high school girl had been raped and murdered.

Chase was prepared to remind him.

"Arthur, you need to—"

The man just spoke over her.

"Human chorionic gonadotropin is more commonly known as HCG, and it's produced by trophoblast tissue."

HCG, Chase knew, of course.

"She was pregnant," Chase breathed.

"Yes, Emily Dawson was pregnant at the time of her death."

Tate, who was only hearing her side of the conversation, gawked.

"How far along was she?"

"Between three and six weeks."

"She probably knew," Chase whispered. "Arthur, who knows that Emily was pregnant?"

"Well, as you just mentioned, it is likely that Emily noted her missed monthly menstrus, so—"

"No, I meant who have you told that she was pregnant?"

"Nobody," Arthur said quickly. "I called you first."

"And you know that the CVU has taken over this case, correct?" Not technically true, but the coroner didn't know that.

"I thought that the FBI was working in tandem with the Hawkesbury Sheriff's Department."

Okay, maybe he did.

"Arthur, I'm telling you right now, that the FBI is taking over this case."

"Did I do something wrong?"

"No, on the contrary, you've done great. I appreciate your expediency and now I'm asking for discretion." Normally, this is where Chase would have left it, her not saying the words more impactful than spelling things out. Except, Arthur Ramos clearly wasn't normal. "I don't want anybody to know that Emily was pregnant. And I mean nobody, including the Sheriff's Department and Sheriff Grimes. Do you understand me?"

"Yes, of course."

"Good. Just one more thing, Arthur. Can you get a DNA profile of the fetus for the purpose of identifying the father or do we need to call a medical examiner in for that?"

"As per your request, I have called in a medical examiner to perform an autopsy, but they're backlogged. It won't be—"

"Can you—"

"—another week or so until they can come in. However—"

"Arthur, is there—"

"*However*, I have already managed to isolate fetal cells from Miss Dawson's blood. Creating a DNA profile is something that I am capable of doing, but our resources are limited, both financial and technological."

Chase remembered Tate and his favors.

"That's not a problem. We can get you an address to overnight the samples to. You will be well compensated for your time, as well, Arthur. Again, I would like to stress that this should be kept between the FBI and yourself."

"Understandable. Forward me the address and I'll ship the sample out as soon as possible. Tomorrow morning, most likely, because as I said, something has come up and—"

"Thanks."

Chase hung up and then gently laid the phone down on the table beside her plate of leftover fries. She stole a few breaths while waiting for the information to sink in.

"Well?" Tate said, hands out.

Chase leaned forward and lowered her voice in case others were listening, which of course they were.

"Emily was dosed with Rohypnol, and she was pregnant. That weird coroner is willing to send fetal DNA to one of your contacts to see who the father is." She expected Tate to insert a witty remark, but he remained stoic.

"Not a problem."

Chase pushed her plate of fries away—she wasn't hungry anymore—and then drank a large gulp of beer.

Tate made a quick call, got a name, and passed it on to her. In turn, Chase relayed the address to Arthur. She was amazed at how quickly Tate got things done. It almost made her second guess all the decisions she'd made over the years to piss people off.

"You think it's gonna work? You think this Arthur guy is going to be able to keep this between us?"

"Honestly? No shot. I just hope that we get a couple days before it's the most talked about thing in town."

"Yeah, small towns," Tate said, this time without humor. He'd lost his appetite as well. They both finished their beers, then he said, "Let's get out of here."

***

Maybe it was learning that Emily was pregnant or maybe it was because Chase felt guilty for leaving Felix so soon after finally being reunited. Whatever the reason, she was compelled to call both her niece and her son as soon as she got back to the hotel. The conversation with Georgina went predictably well, the ebullient girl speaking excitedly about the day that she'd spent with Rachel and with Felix as well. Apparently, Brad had taken the day off from preparing for his interview and had teamed up with Marguerite to take all three of them to a local art fair. This choice struck Chase as odd because Brad was never into art—he was more a numbers guy—and she didn't think Georgina would be into it, either.

She was wrong.

Georgina couldn't stop raving about a man who painted a cosmic space theme using only a series of bowls and cans of spray paint. Brad had bought her one of these paintings and she was excited to show her when she got home. Naturally, this led to the question of *when* Chase would be returning home.

She opted for the classic—and obtuse—*I won't be gone long.*

Conversely, her conversation with Felix had been strained. It was like pulling teeth with the ten-year-old boy and she ended up having to reference things that Georgina had told her to keep things going. All told, they managed to suffer through roughly five minutes of this before Felix handed the phone back to Brad. Chase explained that she was on a case, that it was a sensitive matter, and that she hoped that it wouldn't take more than a few days. Brad sounded agreeable enough, but Chase didn't know how to interpret this reaction. There had been a time when he would complain about her working too hard, becoming too involved in her cases, but not anymore. It simply wasn't his place. Next, Rachel came on the line and Chase passed it off to Tate.

All of this was surreal. Chase partnering up with her current boyfriend, housemate, live-in boyfriend, whatever you call him, to form a new FBI unit. Her biological son and her ex-husband hanging out with her niece, for whom she was the legal guardian and her boyfriend's daughter... it was enough to make anybody's head spin.

Her life had always been complicated but this was taking it into new territory.

Tate said goodnight to his daughter and handed the phone back to her. They both sat in silence for a while, digesting what had just happened.

"Sounds like they had fun today," Tate remarked.

Chase thought of how she'd felt with Brad at the restaurant, at how comfortable she'd been. How she'd nearly overstepped that boundary, the one that she'd leaped over when she'd been married to Brad too many times to count. How things had changed... now he was on the other side.

"Yeah... hey, what happened with Daniel Mendoza?" she asked.

"What do you mean?"

Chase wasn't sure where this had come from—she'd just wanted to change the subject. But now that she thought about it...

"You almost lost your cool there. I've never seen you like that in front of a suspect or a witness or whatever you consider Daniel to be."

Tate pounded his chest with a closed fist.

"He make fun of woman. Me no like when he make fun of woman."

Chase was unimpressed by this act.

"He really upset you that much? A pissed-off twenty-year-old called me a... I don't even remember. Rookie detective?"

Tate rubbed his mustache across his lower lip. He wasn't joking now.

"Junior detective. I thought maybe he'd be amenable to a little pushback."

"No, you didn't," Chase challenged. "You didn't think that at all. I *didn't* think that. Daniel Mendoza is a pissed off young man with a chip on his shoulder. You push him, he just shoves back even harder. *That* even a junior detective could see. I don't need you to stand up for me, Tate, protect me or whatever you think you were doing."

"Chase, come on."

Tate looked hurt, which hadn't been Chase's objective. Hell, she hadn't even planned to bring the Daniel thing up. But now that she had, Chase felt a strong compulsion to keep going, to not let it go.

Dr. Matteo had warned her that she had a propensity for self-sabotage. When things were going well, she would do something that would fuck everything up. She knew he was speaking the truth and she even knew why she did it. Things had been going smoothly with Tate, and besides the hiccup with her son, things with Brad were copacetic, as well.

And that wasn't good.

That wasn't good because Chase didn't deserve things to go well.

Stop it, Chase, a voice in her head warned. But the voice belonged to her prefrontal cortex, and it was too easily bullied by her limbic cortex.

"No, I'm serious. I don't want you to stick up for me, okay? I said it before but here," she indicated the room that they were in, including the two of them, "we're partners. That's it. We're gonna have each other's backs, we're gonna complement each other's work, but we're not gonna let this, whatever this is, get in the way of the job."

Tate grumbled.

"Whatever *this* is?"

Not fair, that stupid voice told her. *You're not being fair.*

It took everything she had not to answer.

"Okay," Tate said with a sarcastic nod, "Okay, I see where you're coming from. Just partners, right? So, I guess that means that this," he made a circle with the thumb and forefinger of one hand and then used the pointer of his other to rhythmically pump it in and out, "ain't gonna happen."

Chase hated the crude gesture, hated this version of Tate.

"No need to be crass."

"No need? Really? But we're just partners, right? If you're *just* my partner, then I'm going to treat you that way. You should have heard the shit I used to tell Floyd—would make you shit your pants."

By the end of the sentence, Tate's face had reddened considerably. He got to his feet and went to the door wanting— *begging*—Chase to tell him that he meant more than just a partner.

But she couldn't do it.

"Where are you going?"

"For a walk."

Tate slammed the door behind him.

What's wrong with me? Just when things were going good, you had to fuck it all up again.

Chase was exhausted—it had been a long and emotionally draining day and an even longer and more emotionally draining week. But she knew she was far off. She didn't suffer from the extreme insomnia that Tate did, but whenever her mind was reeling like this, she found it almost impossible to settle down.

Instead of fighting this losing battle, Chase grabbed Emily Dawson's Story Planner from the nightside table, lay down, and started to read.

Chapter 26

THEY WERE ALL THERE. AVA, Natalia, Laura, Theo, Ethan, and even Jackson.

Brent arrived first but he didn't enter The Shack. He'd stood in the shadows and watched and listened. No one said much—not even Laura, who normally couldn't keep her mouth shut. He couldn't tell if they were scared or if they were hiding something. There was a mention of a video—Ava brought it up, he thought—but Laura told her not to say anything.

Jackson came last, pulling up in his Chevelle, the engine rumbling, the tire sinking deep into the earth. The second he got out of the car, he shouted, "Where is he? Where the fuck is Brent?"

Brent waited a beat before he stepped forward.

"I'm here."

Jackson walked aggressively in his direction and Brent cowered, but Ava got in his way.

"I fucking told you to keep your mouth shut, Brent. I warned you!" Ava tried to calm him down, but Jackson was too geeked up for that. "You shouldn't have sent that picture!"

"And you should have told me the truth!"

"The truth? The fucking *truth*?"

"Yeah!" Brent's anger was rising now, too. "The truth!" Aside from Jackson, everyone else looked tired and ashamed. "She was our fucking friend! And—"

"You told us she cheated on you," Ava said softly. "You made us push her away."

Brent growled.

"So, what? We had our problems, yeah, but she's dead. She's *fucking* dead!" Tears filled Brent's eyes and he made no move to brush them away. "And none of you—" he pointed at them individually, "—seem to give a shit!"

"Oh, I care! I care!" Ava protested, tears running down her face. "We all care!"

"Then why won't you talk about what happened Saturday night!"

"You really don't remember?" Theo asked.

"No!" Brent threw his hands up. "No! I don't remember anything!"

"It was your idea." Laura was staring at her feet as she spoke. "It was your idea to bring her here."

"What?" Brent balked. "What are you talking about?"

"You saw Em with Carlos at school on Friday, saw them holding hands," Laura continued. "I don't know if you wanted to teach her a lesson or if you really thought that you could bring her back into the group, get her to leave Carlos. You just said you wanted to bring her here and that we should party like we did back on spring break."

"No, I didn't."

"Yes, you fuckin' did," Jackson countered.

"But... I don't—"

"You know what? I'm getting pretty tired of this I don't remember bullshit."

"Yeah, it's getting old," Ethan said, backing up Jackson.

"But it's true! And if you don't tell me what happened, I'm going to the cops. I'll show them the picture," Brent bluffed. He didn't actually have the picture anymore, but they didn't know that. "I swear I will."

Ava got out of Jackson's way and the man stepped forward. He had a strange expression on his face.

"You really want to know what happened?"

"Yes! Fucking tell me! I want to know!"

"You sure about that?"

Brent hesitated, remembering his promise to himself, his promise that if he hurt Emily, he'd turn himself in.

"Yes," he repeated, less emphatically this time. He reached for his Zoloft. "Tell me."

"How about I show you."

Leering at him, Jackson produced his cell phone.

"Jackson, don't," Ava pleaded softly. "Please."

Jackson tapped his screen.

"No, he wants to know. He wants to know, so I'm going to show him."

Show me?

Brent's heart started to race.

What the fuck happened?

Ava stepped forward and tried to grab Jackson's arm, but he just shrugged her off.

"Ava's right, maybe we shouldn't," Natalia protested.

"Fuck him." Jackson suddenly thrust the cell phone in Brent's face and that was the end of the discussion. It took a few seconds for his eyes to focus on the video, which was dark to begin with.

But when Brent finally comprehended what he was seeing, he wished he was blind.

"No," he moaned. "No, please… this… this… isn't real."

"Oh, it's real, Brent. You wanted to fucking see! So, *look!*" Jackson screamed. "You're telling me that you don't remember this!"

Brent was bawling now. He tried to turn away, but Jackson moved the phone in front of him so that he was forced to close his eyes to make the horrible video stop.

"You're telling me that you don't remember *raping* Emily?"

Someone—probably Ava—sobbed.

"You made this up... it's a fake. It's a fake video. This... this never happened. I'm... I'm going to the cops. Fuck this."

"No, you're fucking not."

Brent's eyes were still closed when the first blow struck him. It was hard, harder than almost any hit he could remember taking on the Lacrosse field.

And he dropped like a stone.

He wasn't even sure where he'd been struck, just knew that it was somewhere around his head.

"Jackson!"

"Fuck him. He was going to the cops."

Another blow, this time to the ribs. Then another to his legs.

"Stop, please."

In his mind, images of his and Emily's naked bodies on the mattress flashed.

I didn't rape her.

I didn't.

I wouldn't.

The blows were coming nearly continuously now.

You slapped her, is it too hard to believe that you could rape her? That you could **kill** *her?*

"Stop! What do you think is going to happen when he wakes up? He's still going to go to the cops! And then we're all fucked. All of us, including you!"

The beating paused.

"Then we have to get ahead of it, control the narrative."

"How?"

"We send the video ourselves—anonymously."

Brent groaned and tried to roll over. A foot came down on his surgically reconstructed shoulder, sending pain shooting down his spine to his lower back and pinning him in place.

"To the cops?"

"No, not the cops. To the school, to every student in the school."

A gasp but no argument.

They can't be serious. They can't send this to the school. Please, Brent wanted to shout, but his body had stopped responding.

"Brent wanted to see it, now everyone is going to get that chance."

"But Emily—"

"Emily's gone."

"Send it, Jackson. *Do it.*"

Something struck Brent in the face, a boot or a fist, and the power was suddenly cut off from his brain and everything went black.

PART III – Tenbury

Academy

Chapter 27

CHASE DIDN'T REMEMBER FALLING ASLEEP, but she shook out of her slumber with a start.

The book on her chest fell to the floor and she opened her eyes.

Tate was there, not sleeping, the man never slept, but typing away on his phone.

"Morning," he said, rising to his feet. Chase noticed that he was already dressed in his work attire, a different outfit but almost identical to yesterday's. Tate's style was conservative, reserved, chinos rather than jeans, and a shirt that was usually white or off-white and had buttons. "You want to get ready while I grab some coffee?"

"Sure," Chase said, sitting up. She had fallen asleep in her clothes. "What time is it?"

"8:15."

"Shit." Chase got out of bed and went to the bathroom. "What time does Tenbury Academy start?"

"First bell is at 8:45."

Chase looked at herself in the mirror. Her hair was a mess from having slept on it and her face looked pale and drawn.

She barely had time for a shower, but she had to make herself presentable. The younger Chase appeared, the more relatable she would be to high school kids.

"You get any sleep?" she asked as she started the shower. When there was no answer, Chase leaned out into the hotel room proper.

It was empty—Tate was already gone on a coffee hunt.

Chase shook her head, disgusted with the way she'd acted yesterday.

An apology was in order, not for what she said—Chase would stand by her words, at work they were only partners—but how she said it. There was such a thing as tact, after all. But for now, shower time.

Five minutes later she was out, clean, her teeth brushed, and her hair combed. The gray color wasn't doing her many favors in the looking younger department and until now she hadn't considered doing anything with it. It just wasn't a priority. Besides, she kind of liked it. Chase tied it up in a loose bun and then applied some makeup, going a little heavier than she normally would.

She couldn't pass as a teenager like she could when she'd been a narc for Seattle PD—her body had some tough miles on it—but she was petite and fit, which helped.

Chase was waiting outside the room when Tate returned with two coffees. He handed her one and they went to her car with only a polite 'thank you' passing between them. Twice, Chase opened her mouth to apologize, only to close it again. She justified the delay by citing the fact that they were technically on the job.

Oh, and Chase didn't have any clue how to broach the subject.

Their plan was to go to Tenbury Academy and ask Principal Robert Matthews to round up Brent's crew: Brent, Ava, Theo, Ethan, Natalia, and Laura, and sit them down. They were gonna play them off one another, find out who was closest to Emily, and pressure them. Let the kids do most of the talking. If one or more had been at The Shack on Saturday night, it would come out.

Chase wouldn't leave until it did.

The only sticking point in their plan was principal Robert Matthews. There were no legal issues speaking to the students, they were all adults, but Matthews could make things difficult for them.

Tate's cell phone rang, and he showed her the call display: Deputy Dean Jardine. He put the call on speakerphone.

"Morning, Deputy Jardine."

"Anything but, Agent Abernathy. Anything but." There was a heaviness to the man's voice, a voice that Chase found uncannily similar to the Deputy Jardine she'd met.

"What's up?" There was Tate, keeping it casual, keeping it small town.

"Brent Matthews was just admitted into the hospital. He's in some kind of mess."

Tate pointed at the GPS display screen, but Chase was already on it. She zoomed out, moving away from the blue line that was directing to Tenbury Academy, and instead rerouted them to the 'H' on the map.

"What happened? Was he in an accident?"

"Don't know," the deputy said. "Swelling on the brain, multiple contusions, bruises all over."

"Is he conscious?"

"Not anymore. He kinda just stumbled in. The doctors put him in an induced coma, trying to relieve the swelling in his brain."

"Ah, shit, okay, we'll be there shortly."

"See you soon."

Tate hung up and looked at Chase.

"Fucking hell—you think it was Daniel?"

That was exactly what Chase was thinking. That, or maybe Jackson. She didn't know what would be worse. The brother of the man charged with Emily's murder assaulting her ex-boyfriend or the son of the sheriff doing the beating.

Chase couldn't think of a solid motivation for either without working some mental gymnastics, but she had to remember that they were dealing with teenagers.

She parked in the ambulance bay and got out.

"That's the sheriff's car." Tate pointed to one of two other vehicles parked in the tow-away lane. "And I think I remember that car from when we left the Matthews' house. Probably the principal's."

"Yeah, I think you're right."

"This might work out in favor. Both the sheriff and the principal are here at the hospital..."

"... which means that I can go speak to the kids without interference."

"Exactly."

It made sense, but she couldn't help but feel a little strange about splitting up again. But it was the right call.

Professional, keep things professional.

"Sounds good—keep in touch. When you're done see if you can hitch a ride with someone to the school."

"If not, I can just hitchhike. Toodles."

Chase rolled her eyes and got back into the car. She watched Tate enter through the hospital's automatic doors, admiring the way he slipped back into character.

She was nearly at the Academy when she received a call from the *other* Deputy Jardine, Tim.

Fucking small towns.

"Agent Adams."

"Hi, it's Deputy Tim Jardine, I've got something you're gonna want to see."

Chase was only half-listening. She was ducking down and peering through the windshield to get a better look at Tenbury Academy.

What the hell?

Tenbury looked less like a high school than it did a smaller version of Yale. The main building was constructed of thick gray bricks and there was a huge clock tower in the center. Ivy climbed up the East side of the building. The student parking lot was full of foreign cars.

Daniel wasn't lying when he said this place was for the privileged.

"I'm actually just pulling up at Tenbury Academy now. Can this wait?"

"Definitely not," the deputy said. That's when she spotted his car. "But the good news is, I'm already here. I'll meet you at the main entrance."

Chapter 28

TATE MET DEPUTY JARDINE IN the hospital lobby and shook his hand.

"We've got Brent on security walking up to the hospital, staggering, really, but that's about it. No idea how he got here or what happened to him. No car accidents reported, at least not in town."

Tate looked over his shoulder toward the entrance. It was a surprisingly modern and upscale hospital for a town of this size.

"Are there red-light cameras around here? Anything like that?"

"Not sure, I'll double-check."

The hospital seemed to be located in a new part of town almost as if someone had the hopes of building this area up. New infrastructure was more likely to have red light cameras.

Deputy Jardine got on his walkie-talkie and asked Francie back at headquarters to see about acquiring footage from red light cameras in the area. This seemed to Tate to be more a job for someone like a deputy, but they were already spread pretty thin.

Also, this is a—

Tate stopped himself from thinking those two words. It was getting annoying.

"C'mon, I'll take you to Brent's room. Sheriff Grimes is already here and so is Brent's father, Robert."

The way Deputy Jardine said Robert's name gave Tate the impression that he wasn't too fond of the man. That was alright, because Tate felt the same way.

Even without the deputy's help, Tate would have no problem finding Brent's room. He was on the first floor and all he had to do was follow the commotion. The closer they got, the more Tate made a deliberate effort to move in front of the deputy. He had established a rapport with Sheriff Grimes and didn't want to jeopardize that.

In the end, it didn't really matter because the sheriff and Robert Matthews were in a heated argument and didn't notice them approaching. Once again, it appeared that the balance of power was in the principal's favor, as Robert was pointing an angry finger at Grimes' chest.

"Get control of your town, Hal. Things are getting—"

"Sheriff? Mr. Matthews?" Tate said, announcing his presence. They stopped arguing and looked at him. Tate addressed Robert first then shook Hal's hand. "I'm sorry to hear about your son. How's he doing?"

"Stable," Robert said.

Tate walked up to the glass window and looked inside. Deputy Jardine wasn't lying; Brett's face was an absolute mess. There were bandages covering his forehead and part of his skull, and his nose was off center. His eyes were both swollen, and his lips were three times the size of yesterday.

A myriad of medical equipment was hooked up to Brent and surrounded his hospital bed.

This was no common high school scrap. This was violent and brutal. There was a purpose behind this attack.

"They've induced a coma to keep his brain from swelling," Sheriff Grimes said, joining Tate by the glass. "Three broken ribs, a fractured orbital bone, concussion, broken nose, two lost teeth, and a split lip." It was like he was reading off an ingredient list.

"Shit," Tate said under his breath. "Any idea who might have done this to him?"

"Yeah, I know *exactly* who fucking did it," Robert interjected. "The apple doesn't fall far from the tree, right, Sheriff?"

At first, Tate thought that Robert was talking about the Sheriff's son, Jackson. Tate even started to move between the two men in case they started to come to blows. But then Grimes rubbed his mustache.

"I've got men heading to the Mendoza house right now."

"You think Daniel is behind this?" Tate deliberately dropped the man's first name. So far, they'd been running this investigation in parallel. Maybe it was time to bring things together.

"Damn right, he is. First Carlos murders Emily Dawson and then his brother nearly kills my son! They're a bunch of fucking savages."

"Robert, please," Grimes said, trying to calm the man. "Like I said, we have men heading out there now."

"To arrest him, *right*?"

"Please. Let me do my job."

"Then fucking *do it*! First Emily and now this? What the fuck is happening to Hawkesbury, Hal?"

Sheriff Grimes looked at Tate, his face red. It was clear he was used to this sort of berating, but he was embarrassed that this was happening in front of the FBI.

"Cool it, Robert. We'll find out who did this to Brent and we'll arrest him. These things just take time."

"Time? *Time?* My son is in a fucking coma!" The sheriff's lapel squawked. "Don't you answer that. Hal! *Hal!*"

But Grimes had already answered.

"*Goddamn it!*"

Tate backed off, preferring to be a passive observer.

It didn't last long.

"What?" Grimes shouted.

"Yeah, you need to come to Tenbury now. There's a video of Emily Dawson going around. A video from Saturday night." The voice coming out of the sheriff's mic sounded exactly like Deputy Dean Jardine, who Tate had forgotten was even there.

"I'll be there as—"

Robert's face drained of color and to Tate's surprise, the man turned and started to run.

"Robert! Hey!" Grimes called after him. "*Robert!*"

But Robert had no intention of stopping.

"Fuck," the sheriff cursed under his breath. Then he clicked the mic again. "Robert's coming in. Who do you have with you there now?"

"Just me. Oh, and the FBI lady is on her way."

FBI lady.

Grimes looked at Tate and he forced the scowl that was forming on his lips away.

"Yeah, my partner's already there. Agent Adams."

"And I have my other two deputies at Daniel's house. Shit." Grimes appeared to mull his options over. "Okay, Tim, you go to Tenbury and meet up with your brother. Tate, you want to come with me?"

"Yeah, sounds good."

This confirmed Tate's suspicion that the Hawkesbury Sheriff's Department was spread woefully thin.

He recalled what Chase had told him about what Jardine had said, and under his breath, Tate told his Jardine, "Thank goodness you called us in."

The deputy gave him a strange look and then turned and followed after Robert without a word. Tate clapped his hands.

"Alright, let's go have another chat with this prick Daniel Mendoza, shall we?"

Chapter 29

Deputy Tim Jardine was flanked by two men who looked like security guards. Chase suspected that they worked for the school.

She skipped pleasantries and got straight to instructions.

"I want Laura, Natalia, Ava, Ethan, Theo and—" she almost said Brent but then stopped herself. "I want the five of them in the principal's office now."

The security guards turned to the deputy, who Chase initially misunderstood as looking for confirmation. She was about to snap at them when the deputy quickly spoke up, reciting the students' surnames from memory.

"Ethan Saunders, Theo Blackwood, Ava Morency, Natalia Delarosa, and Laura Malone."

The two guards hurried off.

"What's this video you mentioned?" Chase asked when they were alone.

The deputy reached for her lower back, intent on guiding her to somewhere more private than the middle of the hallway, but Chase slid out of range.

"Sorry, I… it's sensitive."

"Does it show her murder?"

Deputy Jardine was surprised by her frankness. FBI Agent or not, she could tell he still harbored some generalizations about her based on her gender and stature.

"Not exactly. But I really do think we should go somewhere—"

"Take me to the principal's office," Chase ordered, knowing that Robert Matthews was still at the hospital.

The two of them walked with purpose down the double-wide hall. Much like the exterior, the inside of Tenbury

Academy reminded Chase more of an old French Chateau, something taken out of a fairy tale and transposed in Hawkesbury of all places, rather than a high school. Sure, the walls were adorned with trophy cases filled with an equal number of athletic and scholastic achievements, but even these were crafted out of rich mahogany and, although they were clearly new additions, they didn't detract from the illusion.

The only thing that was out of place was the frosted inlaid glass with the word Office written on it that Jardine stopped in front of. Chase was inclined to knock, influenced by the formality of their surroundings, but Jardine just opened the door.

They entered a waiting area that held a handful of chairs—plastic, not at all part of the facade—and a U-shaped secretary desk. Behind the desk sat a woman with round features and heavy eye makeup.

"Principal Ma—"

Chase didn't even let her finish the sentence.

"We're using his office." Without waiting for permission, Chase walked to a second door with the same frosting as the first, only this one was adorned with the word 'Principal'.

It was locked.

Chase grunted.

"Do you have a key?"

"Yes, of course."

The secretary rifled through a drawer full of junk, mostly staples and pencils and pens. She found a single key and started to rise. Chase grabbed the key from her with a quick, "Thanks," and then opened the door to Principal Robert Matthews' office.

It was impressive. Not overly large, about twelve feet wide and eight feet deep, but everything was made from dark wood, from the built-in floor-to-ceiling bookcase behind the massive desk to the desk itself. Robert's chair was made of some top grain leather, the kind that didn't crack when it aged but acquired a patina that just exuded class. Even the two chairs across from the desk, those nearest the door, were leather, although not quite as impressive as the principal's.

Chase shut the door behind them.

"Okay, let's see it," she said, gesturing for Jardine to get his phone out.

"Yeah, sure, but, trigger warning here, it's graphic."

Trigger warning.

Chase shook her head in annoyance and just held her hand out. The deputy scrolled for a second and then held his phone out. Chase took it and watched.

The man's warning was well served but it wasn't the graphic nature of the video that made Chase uncomfortable, it was the strange duality of the experience; she felt as if she'd already seen it—the rape. Only, in the coroner's office, she'd seen the rape through Emily's eyes, staring out at her then unknown assailant, her head bobbing back and forth with every thrust.

This was different. Someone had taken the video from behind and above the mattress.

And it showed everything.

Brent was lying naked on top of Emily, his cheek resting on the top of her head on account of their height discrepancy. He took his time as he thrust into her, moving slowly. Emily, whose eyes were unfocused, stared at nothing and her mouth hung open slightly. Brent took his time with her, a fact that Chase registered immediately. Most rapists, especially first- or second-timers, worked furiously, not trying to savor the moment, but just trying to get off as quickly as possible, their fear of getting caught fueling their desire and arousal.

The video ran for fourteen seconds before it stopped abruptly with no change in the scene.

Chase chewed the inside of her cheek as she played the video a second time. It was just the two of them, Brent and Emily, and that filthy mattress in the frame.

"No audio?"

Deputy Jardine shook his head.

"No audio. Just the video."

"Where did it come from?"

"I forced a student to send it to me."

"Her name?"

"I think her name was Corinne or something like that. She's a junior."

Chase was surprised that the deputy didn't know her surname like he did the others.

"How does she fit into the picture?"

Deputy Jardine cocked his head, not understanding the question.

"How does this Corinne or whatever know Emily and Brent?"

"Oh, no, sorry, she has nothing to do with the case. Everyone in the school was sent the video early this morning. It came from an anonymous number."

Chase mulled this over.

"No way to trace it?" she asked, even though she already knew the answer.

"We tried, but no luck. We can reach out to the phone company, ask them to help and if they don't comply, we can get a warrant, but in my experience, anyone who sends this sort of material usually uses a masking service and a VPN. I doubt the phone company can even trace it."

"Yeah, you're probably right. Might be worth—" Something occurred to Chase, and she stopped midsentence. "You said that this was sent to the entire school, like, every student?"

"Yep. First thing I did was hop on the PA and tell them that if anybody is seen playing or even in possession of the video, then they will face criminal charges."

That was good—not enforceable but sometimes a threat was as effective as the succeeding action—but it wasn't why Chase was asking.

"I don't know much about Tenbury, but I'm guessing that a master list of all students' cell phone numbers isn't something that would be readily available, would it?"

"Very doubtful."

"So, who would have access to that list?"

Deputy Jardine shrugged.

"The principal, maybe some teachers." He hooked a thumb over his shoulder. "Prolly Mrs. Story."

"Brent." The word just escaped her lips—she hadn't meant to say it out loud.

"Yeah, I mean, if he could access his father's computer, I'm sure he could find it."

"But why would he send it?" Tate and Stitts, maybe even Floyd, would have recognized her tone and known that she was musing to herself, but not Jardine.

"Maybe he was showing off."

"Showing off?"

Another shrug.

"Sometimes it's not enough to get away with raping someone, sometimes you need others to know about it, know it was you behind the crime. Like the serial killer who taunts the police, you know? It would explain someone kicking his ass, too."

Chase did know, but it didn't make sense. It sure as hell didn't look like Brent was showing off in the video—there was no taunting to the camera, no whooping and hollering, sound or no sound. In fact, it didn't even look like Brent was enjoying it. If anything, he, like Emily, appeared out of it. Even more confusing is why he would send it and then stick around town. Brent didn't strike Chase as someone who was so desperate for attention that they would resort to such extreme measures.

"The sheriff," she said, once again thinking out loud.

"I suppose if the sheriff wanted to, he could gain access to the list, sure."

Chase was about to say that by applying the same logic as they had with Brent then Jackson Grimes would also have access, but she was interrupted by a knock at the door.

"Yeah?"

A security guard opened the door and nodded at her. He held it open as he ushered five extremely frightened students into the office. They had their heads down and entered single file. They naturally formed an organized suspect lineup, which was fitting because that was how Chase had intended to address them: as suspects.

"My name is Agent Chase Adams and I'm with the FBI," she said in a loud, clear voice. "As I'm sure you are aware, a video of your friend Emily Dawson being raped by Brent Matthews is being circulated around the school." One of the girls, the thinnest of the three, whimpered but Chase continued, unabated. "I brought you in here today because I only want to know one thing: Which one of you savages was the one who recorded it?"

Chapter 30

"HE'S GOT A KNIFE AND he refuses to come out of the house," a deputy Tate didn't recognize informed the sheriff.

"How long has he been in there?"

"We got here about twenty minutes ago. Knocked on the door, announced that we were with the Sheriff's Department and Daniel opened it. Flashed the knife, then went back inside and locked the door. I've got Deputy Lane 'round back just in case he tries to slip out and make a run for it."

"Did you mention why you were here?" Tate asked.

"I'm sorry, who are you?"

"He's with the FBI."

The deputy, whose name, at least according to the tag on his breast, was Barill, stiffened.

"No, sir, like I stated, we just went to the door and announced Sheriff's Department."

"He knows why we're here, alright," Sheriff Grimes said under his breath.

Tate didn't necessarily agree. Daniel had been pissed off yesterday, pissed off at the sheriff, at the sheriff's son, at Chase, pretty much at everybody. The sheriff showing up now might have just tipped the scales. It wasn't, in his opinion, indicative of involvement in Brent's attack.

"Does Daniel work?" Tate asked.

"Yeah, he works nights over at Lou's Garage," Grimes answered.

"Anybody reach out to Lou and see if he was working last night?" Blank stares. "Oh, allow me."

Tate backed away from the front stoop and found the number for Lou's Garage in town. He asked to speak to a supervisor and then explained who he was and that he wanted to know if Daniel had been working last night. As he spoke, Tate observed Sheriff Grimes in action. The man was barking orders like they were planning to apprehend Osama Bin Laden and not a skinny Latino kid with a knife locked inside his home.

"Thanks," Tate said after the supervisor had supplied the information he'd asked for. "Sheriff?"

But Sheriff Grimes couldn't hear him over his fists pounding on the door.

"Daniel Mendoza, come on out with your hands up. If you do not comply, we will break this door down."

Tate heard something in Spanish—*ventana* and *coño* and something else he didn't recognize—shouted back.

"Danny Mendoza, you're under arrest for assault and battery."

The sheriff drew his gun and tipped his cap toward Deputy Barill.

What the fuck is going on here?

So far as he knew, no judge had issued a warrant for Daniel Mendoza's arrest, let alone for search and seizure. And what, exactly, did 'flashing a knife' mean? Had he tried to stab one of the deputies? Unlikely—they probably would have led with that. What if he was just chopping up some tomatoes?

This had degenerated quickly, and Tate thought that things would only go downhill from here.

He hurried up the steps to meet the sheriff.

"I just got off the phone with Daniel's boss. He was at work all night—just got home two hours ago."

Tate was trying to diffuse the situation, but it was obvious that he was wasting his breath.

"And Brent rolled into the hospital about an hour ago," the sheriff countered.

Tate glanced at the driveway—there was no car.

"Does Daniel have a car? And where's Lou's Garage from here? The hospital is at least—ah, fuck it."

This was going nowhere.

"Stand back," Sheriff Grimes warned. Another nod in Deputy Barill's direction and the man kicked the door in. It was flimsy and hollow core and the frame flexed. The second kick blew it inward.

Sheriff Grimes stormed into the home, leading with his gun. A shirtless Daniel Mendoza was near the back, in the kitchen. He was holding a knife, but he wasn't waving it around. He wasn't cutting tomatoes, either; on the cutting board was a sliced banana.

"Drop the fucking knife," Grimes ordered, raising the gun and aiming it directly at the center of Daniel's bare chest.

There was always a moment during every standoff where Tate envisioned the worst possible scenario. This was no different. In his mind, he pictured Daniel raising the knife, maybe taking a step forward or two, maybe not, and then somebody, probably not Grimes but a less experienced deputy, would fire. The sound would be deafening in the confined space and the charred smell of gunpowder would fill the room.

But thankfully, this didn't happen.

Not today.

The knife fell from Daniel's hand and clanged on the floor. The sheriff holstered his weapon and charged, while Barill kept his gun trained on the kid.

Tate watched from the doorway, torn between two courses of action. He could step up, claim a higher authority, and take Daniel into Federal custody. Or he could do nothing and let Grimes handle this.

He opted for the latter. If he intervened all of his hard work forming a relationship with the overweight sheriff would be for naught. And he needed the man. Grimes knew everyone in town and, perhaps more importantly, he knew how things worked in Hawkesbury.

Shit.

Grimes tackled the much smaller man hard—*too* hard. Daniel was winded as he was taken down, his face red as Grimes flipped him over. With a knee pressed into the back of Daniel's neck, his hands were wrenched behind him, and he was cuffed.

The curses came as soon as Daniel was able to breathe again.

"Shut up," the sheriff growled. He got off the suspect and yanked him painfully to his feet.

Tate had to step out of the way to avoid being bowled over by the two of them as they exited Daniel's home.

It was as if he wasn't even there.

And then the sheriff was barking orders again as he shoved Daniel Mendoza into the back of his car.

Tate watched in fascination. And then, before he could register what was happening, everyone was gone.

The sheriff and the two deputies left him there, standing in the smashed doorway to Daniel's home, alone, with his dick in his hand.

"What the fuck?"

Tate looked skyward and then made a call.

"Hey, Deputy Jardine, think you can pick me up? I know, I know, you're probably not even at the school yet but I could really use a ride."

And a drink. And a *fucking* drink.

What is wrong with this place?

Chapter 31

NOBODY ANSWERED, NOT THAT CHASE expected them to. But all five kids went from indigestion uncomfortable to shitting in your pants uncomfortable.

"Oh, maybe I made a mistake. Maybe one of you didn't take the video." Their relief was palpable. "Maybe it was more than one. Was it three of you? All five?"

Eyes dropped, weight shifted, sweat broke out on noses and brows.

"Here's the deal. I know that you're friends with Brent and I know that you used to be friends with Emily. Believe it or not, I was in high school once. But then something happened, right? They broke up and you had to pick a side?"

Still nothing.

"The questions are only going to get harder. And if you don't start answering I'm going to split you up and take you down to the station. It's not fun there, trust me. You'll sit in this square room for hours, thinking about—"

"She cheated on him," one of the boys said. He was on the thicker side.

"No," a girl countered. Chase knew that this had to be Ava. "No, that's not it." She glared at the boy. "Brent hit her."

"What?" the other boy this time. "What are you talking about, Ava?"

"Hold up," Chase intervened.

"It's true! She told me—" all of sudden, Ava stopped speaking and lowered her head again.

"Just keep your mouth shut," the skinny boy warned.

"Hey, what's your name? You?"

"Ethan."

"Ethan, you tell Ava to shut up again, and I'm going to have Deputy Jardine drag your ass to holding. Got it?"

Ethan sucked his teeth.

Normally, a threat such as this one to a rich, entitled prick would instantly make them go flaccid. But not Ethan. He didn't look hardened, though, despite his best efforts. No, he was brave because he was friends with the sheriff's son.

"Okay. Good. Now, Ava, please tell me what happened. Brent hit Emily? Open hand, fist, what?"

Ava's voice was but a mere whisper.

"Brent slapped her. She said it was no big deal but…"

"It's always a big deal, okay? *Always.*" Chase waited for Ava to acknowledge her comment before continuing. "So why did you—all of you—choose to stay friends with Brent when he assaulted Emily?"

"I didn't—I didn't know about this," one of the other girls pleaded. "This is the first I've heard of him hitting her." She sounded appalled.

"I didn't know about this, either," the fat boy chimed in.

They could be lying, but Chase didn't think so.

"Why would you keep this to yourself, Ava?" she challenged. Ava was Emily's best friend and Chase suspected that she was also the weakest link of the group.

Ava looked up and her eyes went wide.

"I only just found out! I didn't—she just told me—"

This time, when she stopped speaking, Chase filled in the blanks.

"Saturday night, right? That's when you first found out about Brent hitting Emily? She told you then?"

Chase saw it in the girl's face; this was exactly what happened. If only she could get Ava to say it.

She sighed and interlaced her fingers.

"Guys, let me explain something to you. I saw the video, and I know that at least one of you guys recorded it. Which means that you were there, and you did nothing to stop the rape." Ava started to shudder and cry. "Let me explain something to you: let's say you're the getaway driver for a bank robbery. Nobody sets out to hurt anyone, but things go sour and someone in the bank gets shot. Now, you never actually left the car, but because someone was killed during the commission of a felony? That doesn't matter. Every single person involved in the robbery, including the talking head who planned it, will be charged with murder. And you want to know what class of crime rape is? Hmm? Yeah, you guessed it, a felony. So, even though you might not have stuck your dick in—"

The door flew open so powerfully that it smashed into one of the security guard's sides and he bent over in pain.

"What the hell is going on here?" Principal Matthews demanded. He glared Deputy Jardine. "Deputy? Who let—"

"I'm in charge here," Chase said. "And I'm asking these lovely students who took the video of Emily being raped."

"What video?"

"Mr. Matthews, I think you should contact a lawyer."

"What? Why?"

Under other circumstances, Chase might have felt bad for the guy. After all, his son had been brutally attacked and was in an induced coma. But then she remembered what Brent had done to Emily.

The principal looked at his son's friends for an answer, but their running shoes were suddenly the most interesting things in the world.

"The video of your son raping Emily Dawson," Chase said with finality. "So let me repeat myself: go get a lawyer."

Chapter 32

"I THOUGHT YOU WERE WITH the sheriff?" Deputy Jardine asked as Tate got into the passenger seat of his car.

"I was." Tate buckled up. "I'm not anymore. Sorry for making you drive me around like Miss Daisy."

The deputy peered past him to the open front door.

"What happened?"

"Sheriff Grimes happened."

This was evidently sufficient for Jardine, which was telling in and of itself.

"Where to?"

Tate wasn't sure. He was tempted to follow the sheriff back to the Department, speak to Carlos again, and maybe talk with Daniel, but perhaps it was better to let them all cool off—the sheriff included. There was the hospital, but the doctor had promised that if there were any changes to Brent's condition, he'd give him a call. That left the Academy.

"You know what? Take me to Tenbury."

"Sure thing. Oh, by the way, I might have found something. There's no red-light camera around the hospital, but I managed to snag footage from an ATM of what I *think* is Brent's car. Take a look."

Deputy Jardine tossed his cell phone to Tate, and he watched the preloaded video. It did indeed look like Brent's black BMW he'd seen in the Matthews' driveway. The video was grainy, designed to pick up the person using the machine, and maybe someone behind them if there was a robbery, and not traffic from the nearby street.

And this didn't make sense, because the car wasn't at the hospital. They'd had security check every license plate in the lot.

"Someone else must have been driving," Tate said, stating the obvious. He pinched the video and zoomed in. Then he slowed it down to half speed. He only saw one person in the car, the driver. But the windows were tinted, and the angle was such that if there was someone in the back, he probably wouldn't have been able to tell. Tate focused on the driver. It appeared to be a woman, a woman with narrow features.

"Hey," Tate said, focusing his attention on the video, "can you have someone swing by the Matthews house and see if Brent's car is there?"

"I'll try. Might take a while, though, everyone's all tied up."

"Yeah, that's the impression I get. Hey, let me ask you something, between us?"

"Sure."

"Why did you call in the FBI?"

The deputy didn't say anything.

"Ah, I get it. Don't want to speak ill of your boss. Another question for you: is he dirty? Is Grimes dirty?"

Tate observed Jardine closely. He still didn't say anything, but the muscles in his jaw tightened a little.

"Okay, point taken."

Tate whistled at the sight of Tenbury Academy. It was more impressive than he'd imagined, though he knew, based on the price tag to send your child there, that it was going to be a sight. What he hadn't expected was the mass of students congregated out in front of the school.

Having been born and raised in Chicago, his mind immediately went to active shooter, and he reached for his gun. This instinct faded when Tate noticed a couple of security guards directing traffic, telling people to go home. They were agitated but didn't have that iconic 'holy fuck, we're going to die' look of inexperienced people who were being shot at.

"What the hell is going on?" Tate asked.

"Don't know—didn't even get here yet when you called to come and get you."

Deputy Jardine got on his radio and inquired about what was happening at Tenbury. The answer was immediate, and the voice was familiar.

And that must be Deputy Jardine #2, Tate thought.

"They're sending everyone home. There was a video that surfaced, and… Dean, just get your ass over here."

"I'm here, I'm here."

Tate leaned over and said, "Deputy, this is Agent Abernathy, can you keep the three girls… *uh, uh...* Ava, Natalia, and Laura around?"

Static and then: "They already left—Principal Matthews instructed them to get a lawyer. Ethan and Theo, too."

"Shit. K, thanks."

"Just pulling up now," Deputy Jardine informed his brother.

Tate spotted Chase at once, although, if it had been for her recognizable gray hair, she would have easily blended into the crowd of students.

She appeared to be arguing with Principal Matthews who was half in and half out of his car.

"Can you take me to my partner? She's there, up front—"

The angle was perfect, identical to that in the ATM video he'd just watched. The car was different, that one had been a dark BMW, this one a light gray Tesla, but Tate had no doubt in his mind that the driver was the same.

"Hey! Get in front of that! Don't let it leave the parking lot!"

Deputy Jardine didn't ask *why,* he just *did,* swerving in a way that almost made them T-bone the other car.

Tate could see the driver go into panic mode and he jumped out and ran up to the window.

He pressed his open badge against the glass.

"Ava, can you please turn the engine off and kindly step out of the vehicle, please and thank you."

Chapter 33

IT WAS STRANGE SEEING BOTH Deputy Jardines together, the only thing really separating the twins being Dean's mustache, a weak one, but a mustache, nonetheless. Chase suspected that this was the purpose behind it; to tell them apart.

It was no comparison to Tate's lip warmer.

"What's going on?" Chase stepped away from Robert Matthews and watched as Ava stepped out of her car. Her cheeks were still damp with tears.

Tate nodded at his Jardine, and he put the cuffs on Ava.

Okay…

Chase had noticed the near accident and it had pulled her away from Robert. He used the distraction to finally get into his car and close the door.

Damn it.

She let him go and walked over to her partner.

Tate saw her approach and preemptively said, "Ava is under arrest for assault and battery."

"What?" This was as much a surprise to Ava as it was to Chase. The former tried to twist around to look at her accuser, but Dean Jardine held her firm.

"Yep," Tate confirmed, "Ava here was the one who drove Brent Matthews to the hospital in the wee early hours of the morning. Got her on video."

"I—I didn't—I didn't hurt him!" Ava protested. "I mean, I dropped him off, but I didn't hurt him! What the hell!"

"Don't say anything until you speak to your lawyer, Ava."

Chase whipped around. Robert Matthews had an apparent change of heart and had reemerged from his car. And now he was interfering.

"What are you doing here, anyway?" Tate challenged, clearly annoyed by the interruption. "Shouldn't you be in the hospital with your son?"

"Yeah, you seem to be right keen on helping everyone but Brent get a lawyer, and he needs it more than anyone," Chase said.

"Ava, lawyer," Principal Matthew reiterated.

Chase could see that Tate was more than annoyed now but before she could calm him down, Dean Jardine took the helm.

"Mr. Matthews, don't you have other business to deal with?" Deputy Jardine gestured toward the crowd that instead of thinning had grown around them. "After all, school's out for the day."

Robert Matthews scowled but he heeded the deputy's advice... only after offering a stern nod in Ava's direction.

"Deputy Jardine, please take Ava to holding," Tate instructed.

"No! I didn't hurt him! *Please.*"

"Come on, let's go," Jardine pulled Ava toward his car. "You going to be alright for a ride this time?" he smiled. "Or am I going to have to turn around and pick you up in ten."

"I'll be fine, thanks."

Deputy Jardine loaded Ava into the backseat and was off.

Chase looked around and found the man's twin.

"Can you, Deputy Jardine, please pay our friend Brent Matthews a visit to the hospital?" She could see Tate's eyebrows rise. "I don't care if he's still in a coma, I want you to cuff him. Got it?"

"Yes ma'am."

She cringed at the word ma'am but let it go.

Chase stood beside Tate as they helped the security guards clear out the rest of the students. When they were all gone, he said, "What now?"

"Now, we go for lunch and *ketchup*."

Tate laughed.

***

"Fuck," Tate cursed. He handed the phone back to Chase. "Why do we do this? I'm going to be rail thin if we keep talking business, watching videos like this, at lunch."

Again, they'd both lost their appetite.

"Yeah, pretty brutal," Chase said dryly. She took a sip of water, trying to moisten her throat.

"And do you think that one of Emily's five friends took that video?"

"Six," Chase corrected.

Tate counted the names off on his fingers.

"Laura, Ava, Natalia, Ethan, Theo. Who am I missing here?"

"Jackson Grimes."

"Ah. The only person who *doesn't* go to Tenbury Academy. I would love to have a chat with him."

"Me, too. And now might be the time, seeing as the sheriff is preoccupied with Daniel. How did that go, by the way?"

Tate scoffed.

"Terribly. I don't know Daniel from Adam, but everyone in this town, including the sheriff, has a hard-on for them. Grimes just busted down his door and yanked him out."

"Because they think that he was the one who beat Brent?"

"Right. *Think*—without evidence, mind you."

"Sounds familiar," Chase said, her mind going to Carlos Mendoza. "And now we have Ava driving Brent to the hospital. I can't see her and Daniel working together, not after what the kid had to say when we visited him at his house."

"Me neither."

"Then who the hell beat Brent? You can't honestly think that Ava did that."

Tate shook his head.

"No chance. She's, what? Ninety pounds soaking wet? Brent's no hulk but…"

"What if one of the guys, Ethan, Theo, or even Jackson, found out that Brent had slapped Emily and decided to give him a piece of his own medicine," Chase suggested.

Tate turned his hand over.

"Maybe? We can't forget that Daniel was arrested for possession of Rohypnol and Emily had some in her system when she was raped."

Chase was starting to get a headache.

"None of this makes sense. Why would Daniel drug Emily and then Brent rape her? Brent has to hate Carlos because he stole his girlfriend."

"And Daniel didn't exactly have glowing words to say about Brent, either."

"This fucking town," Chase said, a little more loudly than she'd wanted to.

"I got one more for you," Tate said. "I've been watching the way that Grimes and Robert Matthews interact, and the principal tells the sheriff where to shit."

"And yet the deputy tells Robert to fuck off and he doesn't say boo."

"Exactly."

Chase sighed and drank more water. Tate took out his phone.

"Who are you calling?"

"Just doing my Maury Povich thing."

"Your what?"

Tate held up his finger, and Chase rolled her eyes.

"Hey, you get that sample? The one sent from Hawkesbury?"

Ah, so he's figuring out who's the father of Emily's unborn child.

Chase felt a little useless—Tate had his contacts, his people, and she had nothing. No one.

Except that wasn't exactly true.

Chase made a phone call of her own.

"Agent Adams, to what do I owe the pleasure?"

"Stitts, how long have you been waiting to say that?"

"Which part? The Agent Adams part or the what do I owe the pleasure part?"

"Both?"

"A good six months. What's up, Chase? How is your first case treating you? Director Hampton give you a softball?"

Chase closed her eyes and pictured Emily lying naked on the filthy mattress.

"I wish. Look, I know it's not your purview, not your expertise, but if I sent you a video, you think you can try and extract some information from it?"

"You're right, that's not my area of expertise. But I can have Floyd take a look. What do you want to know?"

Chase pondered this.

"I'm not really sure. A time and date maybe?" She changed her mind, not sure how that would be helpful. "What about who recorded it? And maybe there's audio that has been deleted or muted? I don't really know."

"We'll give it the good ol' college try."

"Just a warning, Stitts, it's pretty graphic."

"Figured as much."

Chase saw Tate wrapping up his phone call and decided to end hers, as well.

"Thanks. Just... if you find anything, please give me a call. I appreciate it."

"No problem. Take care of yourself."

Chase hung up and sent the video through a secure channel and Stitts wrote back with 'received'.

"What was that about?" Tate asked.

"You're not the only one who can call in a favor."

Tate smirked.

"Let me guess, he's a member of a new unit in the FBI, a cold case unit and he also happens to have the initials JS?"

This annoyed Chase and she did her best to ignore it.

"They get a DNA profile of the father?"

Tate stopped joking.

"Yeah—they're running it through CODIS now. Not sure what we can learn, though, given that neither Brent nor Carlos are in the system."

"You know who is, though?"

It took Tate a moment and then he snapped his fingers.

"Shit, you're right. Daniel should be in the system because of his Rohypnol arrest."

"And if we get a partial match, we can link it to Carlos."

Chase's phone buzzed and she frowned.

Not even Stitts worked that fast.

"Hello?"

"It's Deputy Jardine. I did what you asked, cuffed Brent to the hospital bed."

"Good, thank you. Is he still in a coma?"

"Yeah, they still have him conked out. But I spoke to the doctor, and he said he ran some tests on Brent's blood."

"And?"

"And I thought you wanted to know that Brent had fluniza… *uh*... flunitra…"

"Flunitrazepam?"

"Yeah, that's it. Brent had the date rape drug in his system. A lot of it, too."

Chapter 34

"YOU KNOW, WHEN I WAS younger, sixteen, seventeen, something like that, I went on this backpacking trip through Europe. Hitchhiking, hostels, that sort of thing, it was kind of a rite of passage, you know?"

They were on their way to the Sheriff's Department when Tate had broken into story. She thought that maybe it was meant as a distraction, to avoid having to talk about their own issues again. It was also technically a personal tale, and they were on duty, but she let it pass.

"Yeah, and?"

"And, well, I met up with these other travelers, a couple from Australia and a single guy from Canada. So, we go out one night and get absolutely wasted, I'm talking stagger back to the hostel kinda drunk. But the thing is, there aren't enough beds for everyone—in fact, there's only one. As gentlemen, we give the couple the bed and me and the Canadian sleep on the floor. I forgot to mention, we're in Portugal and it's stinking hot out. We leave the windows open and pass the fuck out. In the morning, there's this terrible buzzing sound in the room and there are thick flies everywhere. I wake up, all hungover, and then it hits me: the smell. It smells like someone took a big shit in the room. And they did… in the bidet. It's horrible but nobody owns up to it."

"Is there a point to this engaging tale?"

"Oh, there is. Just let me finish. We draw straws to see who has to clean it up. Of course, I get the short straw. I cut one of those big plastic coke bottles in half and I'm bent over to scoop it up. Overnight it hardened a bit—"

"Gross."

"—but now that it's disturbed, revealing the molten center, it fucking *reeks*. Like, it absolutely stinks."

Chase's lips turned downward as she waited for the punchline. It never came.

"That's it?"

"That's it."

"What the hell, Tate? You doing that thing that you used to do with Floyd, just to prove a point? You used to gross him out and now you're doing the same to me?"

Tate chuckled.

"No, you don't get it."

"No, I don't get it," Chase parroted.

"Although he didn't explicitly say as much, Deputy Jardine #2 told me that something in the Sheriff's Department stinks."

"And?"

"And I think we should stir things up and see what real smells we can unearth."

Tate clearly wanted a big 'aha' from Chase, a nice analogy, but she refused to give it to him. Instead, she said, "So, you told me this weird story about some holiday in Portugal and a mysterious turd just to suggest that we ruffle some feathers?"

"Well, yeah. I mean, it was a little more eloquent and engaging than that but… yeah."

"Why didn't you just say that?"

Tate hesitated.

"Well, it's a true story."

"True or not, it's gross." Chase sighed. "Do me a favor, Tate? I know I said I wanted to keep this professional, but keep these gross stories to Floyd or some of your drinking buddies, okay?"

Tate sulked.

"I thought it was a good story." He pressed his head against the glass. "Also, we're being followed."

"What?" Chase blurted.

"We're being followed. Black Chevelle, about two blocks back."

"For real?" Chase glanced in the mirror but didn't see the car.

"Yep. You see, I have a tie-in with my story about that, too, because we drove into Portugal in a—"

"Tate."

"Sorry," he grumbled.

"Are you sure we're being followed?"

"Definitely."

Chase turned into the Sheriff's Department parking lot.

"Well, I may not be the expert storyteller that you are, Tate Hemingway, so I'll just say this straight: I am an absolute expert at stirring shit up."

***

"Why is Ava Morency here?" Sheriff Grimes asked the second he became aware of their presence. "And what is this I hear about Brent Matthews being arrested?"

Chase stood up tall, even though she barely came up to the hollow of the sheriff's throat.

"Ava Morency is under arrest for assaulting Brent Matthews."

"What?" The sheriff balked. "What are you talking about?"

"We have video of Ava driving Brent's car with him in it. She dropped him off at the hospital."

Chase waited for this to sink in.

"I mean, even if this is true," Sheriff Grimes began, "she can't weigh more than a hundred pounds. There's no way that she did that to Brent."

Chase shrugged, knowing that her nonchalance would only serve to infuriate the man further.

"I mean, I don't weigh more than a buck fifteen and I can deliver one hell of a punch. An even better kick."

"What?" The sheriff looked incredulous as he turned to Tate. "Tate, can you please—"

"Agent Abernathy," he corrected. Unlike Chase, he saw eye to eye with the sheriff.

"What?" Now the man just looked confused, and Chase took a petty bit of pleasure in this.

"You will address me as Agent Abernathy, Hal. And as for your second question, the reason why Brent Matthews is being arrested, is because he raped Emily Dawson. And that, by the way, is probably why Ava kicked the shit out of him." He waved his finger in an obnoxiously small circle. "Full circle."

Grimes' face was beyond red now; it had gone purple.

"I've seen the video and all I can see is two kids making a sex tape."

That was the wrong thing to say.

"Really?" Chase got right in the man's face. "That's what you see?"

Grimes didn't back down.

"That's what I see."

"You want to know what I see?" Tate tried to pull Chase back, but she remained rooted. "I see a woman who was roofied and then raped while his friends recorded it."

"Well, I—"

"And then I see that same woman with hands around her throat choking her to death."

Finally, Grimes had a change of heart. Not about the charges but at least about challenging Chase.

"Well, it's not enough evidence to warrant an arrest. A full investigation, sure, but—"

"What evidence do you have that Daniel Mendoza was involved in Brent's assault? The fact that he... refused to answer the door when you knocked?" Tate intervened.

"It's not—look, that family has been nothing but problems. Carlos and his brother always getting into fights and—"

"Yeah, with whom?" Chase prodded.

"Doesn't matter," Grimes snapped. "They've just been a problem. Oh, that reminds me, you're talking about date rape drug... well, Daniel Mendoza has a prior for possession of that drug. And don't forget that his brother is currently under arrest for Emily's murder. So, maybe now you understand when I say that they've been less than stellar members of the Hawkesbury community."

The man seemed pleased with himself, like winning this argument negated the fact that they were investigating the rape and murder of a seventeen-year-old. As for the Rohypnol, Chase had read the case report. Daniel was caught with one vial of the substance and vehemently claimed it wasn't his, which wasn't uncommon for someone facing jail time. There was also the curious fact that Brent *also* had Rohypnol in his system, which the sheriff seemed unaware of, and something that Chase was still trying to wrap her head around.

"Guess you just figured it all out, huh?" Tate remarked, moving forward. Chase stopped him. They'd already stirred the shit and it would do them no good to come to blows.

"Anyways," Chase said, "it's getting kind of late, and we have three interviews to conduct today: Ava, Carlos, and Daniel."

"I think I'll stick around," Grimes said. "In fact, I think I'll join you."

"I don't have a problem with that," Chase said. "Do you, Agent Abernathy?"

"Nope, no problem at all."

"Except, of course, you can't be there when we interview your son, Jackson Grimes. You know, conflict of interest and all that."

Chapter 35

CARLOS MENDOZA HAD TAKEN TATE'S advice and lawyered up. Still, he agreed to speak to them, and it took only seconds into the interview to realize why.

"You gotta let my brother go," Carlos pleaded, his eyes darting to Sheriff Grimes who was standing behind Tate who was, in turn, standing behind a seated Chase. The sheriff's arms were folded atop his large gut. "He didn't do anything. He... he's never done anything."

Carlos was afraid to say what he really meant, what Daniel had already told them: Jackson Grimes had set him up and the sheriff had put him down.

"We're going to go speak to him next, but I want to focus on your case for now," Chase said.

"About that," Carlos' lawyer began. Judging by the man's suit, he was court-appointed, which made sense for a scholarship kid. "When are you going to drop these trumped-up charges? My client didn't kill anybody, let alone the woman he loved. He's grieving and holding him here on with no evidence is cruel. Cruel and, honestly? It's also shameful."

"Mr...?"

"Dawson."

Shock showed on Chase's face.

"*What?*"

"No relation—just a coincidence."

Fucking hell.

"I'll tell you what, Agent Adams, Carlos is willing to plead to misdemeanor assault on Brent Matthews. But, given Mr. Matthews' recent complications, I think a fair punishment for my client is probation. As I've said, Carlos is grieving."

Part of this interview was a fishing expedition; news spread fast in Hawkesbury, but Chase wasn't sure *how* fast.

Was this complication the lawyer was speaking of the beating Brent had taken, which was ten times more severe than when Carlos had attacked him, or the rape video?

Chase assumed the latter. If Carlos was aware of the former, she suspected he would be incensed as opposed to depressed.

"Unfortunately, the charges were laid by the Hawkesbury Sheriff's Department so at present, they are the only ones who can drop them."

"Bullshit," the lawyer muttered under his breath.

"But—*but*, you help us out, give us something, and I promise you I will do my best to make sure that you get fair treatment here."

Carlos huffed.

"Besides, don't you want us to find out who did this to Emily?"

"Of course."

"Then start by telling us about your relationship with her."

Mr. Dawson leaned in and whispered something into Carlos' ear. He nodded.

"I love Emily—*loved*," he corrected, his voice hitching. "I *loved* Emily. I really did. And she loved me."

"What about Brent? What happened there? They dated for a while and then…"

"And then they broke up."

"Amicable?"

Now Carlos scoffed.

"No. He was *pissed*. He was pissed and then he turned everyone against her with his lies. Said that she cheated on him with me. But she didn't—we waited."

No mention of the slap, which meant that Carlos likely didn't know about it. Chase was beginning to think that only Ava was aware that Brent had hit Emily—if it had happened at all—and even then, she was convinced that the girl had only just found out about it.

"They dated a long time, though, much longer than you two."

"Yeah, so what? She didn't love him. They were pushed together, you know? By their parents? Mostly by Brent's dad. He said they were," Carlos made air quotes, "good for each other. Good for the," more air quotes, "community."

"Really?"

"Yeah, really. Principal Matthews did whatever he could to push them together. Fucking a-asshole." Another hitch.

Chase was surprised that the kid was keeping it together this well.

"What about Emily's friends? What can you tell me about them?"

"Like I said, they abandoned her, sided with Brent. Assholes, all of them."

"Really? I can't picture the girls being assholes. Especially not Ava. She seemed sweet."

Carlos leaned forward and glared at Chase.

"She's the worst of them all. Supposed to be Em's best friend and just cut her off completely."

"I can only imagine how upset this made Emily."

Carlos seemed to be sizing Chase up now, trying to get ahead of the narrative. But he was just a kid. A hormonal teenager trying to deal with an incredible loss that he probably hadn't even started to digest yet.

"Yeah, at first. But she had me. We were happy. Happier than she ever was with *them*." Carlos practically spat the last word.

"I don't doubt that." Chase took a deep breath. "Now, I want to ask you a question and if you can, I want you to try to keep all emotion out of your answer and just say the first thing that comes to mind. Do you think you can do that?"

"Yeah."

"Okay—I get that Em was happy with you, but you have to admit that she probably missed her friends, at least a little. Especially Ava."

A noncommittal shrug.

"If they called her, I mean if Ava called Emily and said, hey, let's get together tonight, do you think she would go?"

A slight hesitation.

"No. No way."

He was lying. Chase could see it in his face. If Ava called and asked to meet up, even if it was at The Shack, Emily would lie to her mom, tell her she was going to the movies, and go see them in a heartbeat.

"Okay, you've been really helpful. One last thing?"

"Yeah?"

Now Carlos' lawyer leaned forward, and Chase saw him extend his hand, just a little, just in case he had to reach over and stop his client from answering.

"Would you be willing to give us a sample of your DNA?"

The lawyer did just as Chase suspected: he put his hand on Carlos' shoulder, effectively silencing him.

"And what good would that do? We're not contesting that my client was at The Shack—we readily admit that he was there on two separate occasions. I would be surprised if his DNA *wasn't* present at the scene."

Chase almost said it—she almost said it had nothing to do with Emily's murder but to determine if the fetus in her womb belonged to him—but something stopped her.

The teenager was keeping it together for now, but Chase got the impression that Carlos was like an amateur tightrope walker: seemingly calm but literally teetering on the edge.

She didn't want to push him over.

Normally, nothing would stop Chase from getting to the truth.

Am I getting soft? Maybe. But soft can be good, right? Soft can polish stones whereas hard can only smash them.

"Carlos?" Chase probed one final time.

"I've got nothing to hide," Carlos said, but then his lawyer promptly whispered something into his ear. "But I'm going to have to decline on my attorney's advice."

Tate leaned forward, but Chase waved him off.

"Thank you, Carlos," she said, rising to her feet. "And, if I didn't say it before, I'm very sorry for your loss."

Chapter 36

UNLIKE CARLOS, HIS BROTHER, DANIEL Mendoza, had declined a lawyer. Unlike Carlos, Daniel wasn't calm.

He was pissed.

Pissed at Tate. He was pissed at Sheriff Grimes, too, but the man had opted to stay behind the glass for this one, a decision that would quickly turn out to be well-warranted.

"Daniel, I'm Agent Adams and this is my partner Agent—" Chase couldn't even get through one sentence before being interrupted.

"Don't you think it's kinda fucked up that you come to my place one day, then the next come *El Jefe* kicks down me door? Look what the fuck he did." Daniel pointed at his nose which was caked with dried blood.

"I saw," Tate admitted.

"Yeah, I know you saw. And you did nothin'."

"Daniel, I know you're upset," Chase intervened.

"Wow, you're a fucking genius, too. The junior detective is a fucking genius."

Despite their earlier conversation, and Chase's warning, Tate scowled and looked ready to pounce.

Don't blow this, she thought.

"I'm trying to help you. You don't believe it, but I am. I don't think you beat up Brent Matthews. I think you were at work."

Daniel crossed his arms over his chest and stared at her defiantly.

"I was—I didn't touch that fucking kid. Besides, the only person whose ass I want to kick is that motherfucker Jackson Grimes."

"Why all this hate for Jackson Grimes? How do you even know him? He went to Tenbury, you didn't."

"Really?" Daniel shook his head. "Because he's a fucking prick, that's why. Gets away with everything. Planted that drug on me…"

Chase waved her hand.

"I know all that, but there had to be something that started this feud."

"Something other than the fact that everyone in this shitty town is a racist asshole?"

"Other than that."

"Ah, well, how about this? As soon as Carlos starts dating Emily, he mysteriously starts showin' up with black eyes, sore ribs, that sort of shit. It was Jackson. That Brent guy probably put him up to it, cuz he's a skinny little bitch." Daniel leered at her. "Like you."

"*What?*" Tate came forward.

"It's okay. I know you don't believe this, but I'm here to help you, Daniel." Chase shot daggers at Tate. "Thing is, I can't do that if you keep acting up. So, let me get this straight: Emily and Carlos start dating, and someone starts harassing him at school."

"You deaf, too? Is the junior detective deaf?" He looked around the room as if playing to an audience. "Not *someone*, but Jackson Grimes. He was beating on my brother."

"Call her a junior detective again and I'll —"

Daniel suddenly jumped to his feet. Chase pushed her chair back and Tate moved in front of her.

God damn it, Tate.

"What you gonna do about it? Huh?" Daniel threatened. "You motherfucking cops think you're so tough with your guns. How about you fight with your bare hand?"

"Guard!" Chase hollered. "*Guard!*"

She wondered what was taking so long. Grimes was watching—why didn't he send someone in?

And what the fuck was Tate's problem? Her partner's hands were balled into fists, and he was bringing them up as if ready to strike. He couldn't be that stupid, could he? Could Tate really take the bait and get into a fistfight with the accused?

"C'mon, c'mon."

Daniel wasn't making fists. Instead, his hands were outstretched, his fingers straight.

That's when Chase noticed the tiny smirk beneath Tate's mustache.

Daniel followed Tate's gaze and suddenly realized how this all looked. He immediately dropped his hands to his sides.

"Nah, man. Nah, I didn't do that." Daniel shook his head. "I didn't do that to that girl."

But that's exactly what it looked like. It looked like Daniel was ready to strangle Tate.

The door opened and a grinning Sheriff Grimes stepped into the interview room.

"Thank you, Agents," he said. And then to Daniel, "Looks like when you get angry, you like to squeeze something, don't you?"

"I didn't do that and neither did my brother. I didn't do nothin'."

Chase hated the look on Grimes' face but couldn't deny that this looked bad.

Really bad.

"Daniel, I'm going to give you the same advice I gave you brother," Tate said, now the epitome of calm. "Get a lawyer."

***

"Tate, what the hell happened in there?"

Tate was acting as if nothing had happened.

"I wanted to see just how angry Daniel can get. Just how angry he really was that his life had been flipped upside down because of his brother and Emily's relationship. I wasn't mad that—"

"I know, I get that now, but you never told me that was the plan. I had no idea that was what you were doing." Chase's words came out harsher than intended and she glanced around. They were back in the hallway, getting ready to head into their third interview of the day. Deputy Jardine and Sheriff Grimes were there, too, but they were in their own world, laughing about some inside joke.

Tate ran a hand through his hair. It stayed upright and, realizing this, he brushed it straight with his palm.

"I had to make it look real, Chase. I wanted the man to show his true colors and he did. You saw him. You saw the way his hands were out like that. I mean, it's not like a smoking gun but…"

"You could have told me."

Chase was more hurt than anything else. Hurt that her partner didn't trust her to be able to keep up the charade.

Did he not know? Did Tate not know that I was a high-functioning heroin addict for years? I should get a fucking Oscar for my performance.

Still, she saw the value of what he'd done.

Recognizing her discomfort, Tate suddenly reached over and wrapped his arm around her shoulders. Chase wanted to pull away, shake him off, remind her partner again that they had to keep it professional. But she was tired, and it felt good to be held. She'd spent so much of her time fighting stereotypes that she'd completely forgotten that even the toughest person needed to be comforted every once in a while.

Tate brought her close, squeezed her, then planted a quick kiss on her forehead.

"Sorry," he repeated. Tate pulled back just enough to lift her chin and was about to lower his lips to hers when someone approached.

"Don't mean to interrupt," Deputy Jardine said, "but Ava's lawyer is yelling for her to be let out. Yelling a whole bunch of shit about a lawsuit against the Sheriff's Department and, well, her family and the sheriff…" he let his sentence trail off.

"Yeah, sorry," Chase backed away from Tate. She pictured Ava as she'd been in Principal Matthews's office: terrified, ready to open up with the right prompting. And Chase had a pretty good idea what that might be. "I'm pretty sure this will be over quick."

Chase glanced at her partner, wondering if he had something else up his sleeve and if he did, if he would say anything to her. But Tate just held his hand out, indicating that she was up now.

It was her turn.

Which was good, because while Tate might know how to break Daniel, Chase knew exactly how to make Ava Morency crumble.

***

After Ava's lawyer, who was wearing a suit that probably cost more than Carlos Mendoza's attorney's car, said his spiel, protracted and laced with threats, Chase finally got her turn to speak.

"Ava, right now, you are being charged with assault and battery."

"This is—"

"—going to go badly if you keep interrupting," Chase warned the attorney. He frowned but said no more. "Good. So, as I was saying, we have video of you driving Brent's car and dropping him off close to the hospital. We have also acquired additional footage of you returning his car to his house."

"As I stated previously," the lawyer said in the most boring tone imaginable, "my client admits to driving Brent Matthews' car. Instead of arresting my client, you should be thanking her."

"And why is that?" Tate asked.

"Because if my client hadn't taken Brent to the hospital, he might very well have died. Ava saved Brent's life."

This was a far more reasonable assertion than Ava, rail thin, pale as a sheet of paper, beat the shit out of Brent. Brent wasn't a big man, but he was much larger than Ava. But the truth was, Chase didn't care who beat the rapist up.

What mattered was who killed Emily.

And her unborn child.

"I would buy that," Chase said honestly, "but you need to give me more. Where did you find Brent? Did you just stumble across him bleeding in a field? In a shopping mall? And why did you drop him off half a block from the hospital instead of taking him in? Were you concerned that Brent wouldn't hit his ten thousand steps for the day?"

"No, that's not—" the lawyer silenced Ava with a look.

"Ava, I know your lawyer already told you this, and you heard it when the deputy read you your rights: you don't need to speak to us. And I'll be the first to admit that it'll be a hard sell to any jury that you actually beat up Brent." Chase flipped her cell phone around and showed the pre-loaded picture of

Brent's swollen face, his eyes completely shut, his nose crooked, his lips caked with blood. Ava predictably inhaled sharply. "But look at his face. Someone did this. Someone dangerous."

"Agent Adams, is this really necessary?"

Chase scrolled to the right, but another image of Brent's face didn't appear. Instead, a video started to play, and Ava gasped.

"Oh—oh, I'm sorry, this isn't Brent. Wait, it *is* Brent, just not from his beating."

"Agent Adams, this is uncalled for." Ava tried to avert her eyes, but Chase kept moving the phone in front of her face. "I will be reporting both of you."

Chase paused the video and laid her phone face up on the table. By sheer chance, the frozen frame clearly showed Emily's face, her eyes rolled back, her mouth slack.

"As I was saying, you'll probably beat the assault case." She nodded as if agreeing with herself. "Yeah, you'll beat it. Even if you don't, I would be very surprised if you got more than just probation, six months of community service *max*. But for raping Emily? I think you'll get fifteen years. The judge—"

"Okay, this interview is over," the lawyer said, starting to rise.

"—will throw the book at you, considering how well-liked Emily was in the community and the fact that you used to be best friends. I'm thinking fifteen years sounds about right."

"Agent Adams, this—"

"I'm almost done, just a sec." Chase looked from the lawyer to Ava. "And if you go down for rape, you'll go down for murder, as well."

"I'm filing a complaint with the bureau."

"I'm sure you will. Good luck with that." Chase almost grinned, thinking about what Director Hampton's response would be. "Oh, I made a mistake. I said *one* murder, but I meant to say *two*. And Pennsylvania has the death penalty, last time I checked." An eerie silence blanketed the interview room. "Wait—you did know that Emily was pregnant, didn't you?"

Chapter 37

"**NOW IT'S MY TURN TO** tell you a story," Chase said.

Tate adjusted himself in the passenger seat.

"Okay, but, fair warning, I got a weak stomach."

"Don't interrupt. So, this story is about a girl who falls in love with somebody on the wrong side of the tracks. This guy is a criminal, been to jail twice, but his crimes aren't violent in nature, he was just trying to protect his family. The girl was from a very affluent neighborhood, and she couldn't really talk to anyone about her relationship. They have to meet each other in secret. Sooner or later, though, someone finds out and her family forces them to split up. But, as you can imagine, they continue to see each other—they're in love! Then the girl gets pregnant, and she has no choice but to tell her parents. They freak out and even though she insists that everything was consensual, they are convinced that she was raped. No way their precious daughter would sleep with *him*. Then they do the unthinkable; they hunt him down and kill him. Distraught, heartbroken, the girl flees and raises her child alone far, far from her parents."

Chase stopped speaking and waited for Tate to say something. It took him a few moments.

"And?"

"And that's it. That's the story. I warned you I wasn't very good at this storytelling thing."

"Well… okay, I'm trying hard here to figure this thing out. It sounds like Carlos and Emily but in this story, Carlos is killed and not Emily. And there's not a real rape? Hmm… is this—is this one of those re-imagining-type stories? Like a Tarantino version of the Holocaust?"

"Try again."

"Okay, is this like a version of what could have been, if Emily hadn't been killed? Help me out, I'm struggling here."

Chase was done with the charade.

"I read this story in Emily's notepad last night. She got the punch line wrong, but all the elements are there."

"Shit, that's fucked up."

"Yeah, it is." Chase took a deep breath. "But at least it helps clear something up. Emily knew she was pregnant, and she really did love Carlos."

"Unfortunately, it doesn't help us figure out who actually killed her unless you think her parents did it out of shame?"

"No."

"Didn't think so. Was there a mention of being drugged anywhere in Emily's story?"

"No."

"We have to talk to the doctor again, figure this Rohypnol thing out. Why was it in Brent's system? Did he drug himself by accident?"

Chase chewed the inside of her cheek.

"What about on purpose?"

Tate made a face.

"Why would he do that?"

"Maybe he knew he was fucked, knew that the video was going to surface, and decided to confuse the narrative."

"And the beating? You think he pulled an Ed Norton from 25th hour?"

"Come again?" Chase didn't know the reference.

"It's a movie where Ed is facing a long prison term for some drug charges, I don't remember exactly what. He's a pretty boy and doesn't want to go in like that so he hires his friends to beat him up. They beat him up good. Not a bad film."

Chase considered what her partner was telling her.

"You know, you could be right."

"But? It sounds like there's a but coming."

Chase smiled.

"But… Brent Matthews does not strike me as this… I dunno… *orchestrated.*"

"We'll see—maybe he's awake and we can ask him."

The car fell silent for a moment and Chase caught Tate shifting uncomfortably in her periphery.

"What?" she asked, not taking her eyes off the road.

"*Uhhh…*"

"Oh, for fuck's sake. I hate when you do this."

"You're the one who told me not to bring up personal shit while at work!" Tate protested.

"It's better than watching you squirm like you shit your pants back in Portugal."

"*What?* First of all, nobody shit their pants. They shit in the bidet. And it wasn't me."

Chase rolled her eyes.

"Yeah, sure. Look, if you have something on your mind, just say it, *please.*"

"Fine. I'm just wondering why you brought up the pregnancy with Ava but didn't do it with Carlos. To be honest, I think it would have been more effective—no, not effective but more *necessary* with him than her."

Because it would have broken him. Carlos hasn't done anything wrong. Ava, on the other hand… Ava abandoned her friend and Ava was most likely there when the video was taken. Which means that if she wasn't involved in the rape, she was at least complicit in it. Same goes for her murder.

Sorry if I have less compassion for Ava than I do Carlos.

Chase timed her response perfectly with parking in the hospital lot.

"You were right, you shouldn't ask personal shit while at work."

Unlike yesterday, the hospital was anything but quiet today. Outside Brent's room, they found Robert Matthews and Deputy Dean Jardine in a heated argument.

"Let him go! The sheriff *ordered* you to let him go!" Robert shouted in the other man's face.

"You better step the fuck back, Robbo."

"Hey, what's going on?" Tate said, trying to diffuse the situation.

A snarling Robert Matthews turned.

"The sheriff ordered that my son, who is still in a *coma*, be released from handcuffs. And this deputy is refusing to listen to his superior."

"The sheriff ordered you to remove the handcuffs?" Tate asked Deputy Jardine.

"He did, but I told him, just like I told Mr. Matthews here, that the FBI ordered the arrest so only they—"

"Who gives a fuck who made the order? The sheriff told you to release my son so you *fucking do it!*"

Jardine's eyes became slits.

"Mind your tone."

"Mind my—" Robert growled and threw his hands up in frustration. Then he backed away.

Chase, who had been seeing this from a distance, made a snap tactical decision.

"You know what? Deputy, you can uncuff Brent. His charges are still pending but he's not going anywhere."

It was Deputy Jardine's turn to scowl.

"You sure?"

"Yeah, remove the cuffs," Tate confirmed.

Jardine glared at Robert and then ducked into Brent's room.

Tate's right, there is a strange dynamic at play here.

Chase barely had time to catch her breath before Robert came up to her. He was still angry but at least he'd stopped shouting.

"I saw the video," Robert spat. "I saw that video of my son and I want whoever took and whoever sent it arrested *immediately.*"

The man's mouth underwent so many convolutions that it reminded Chase of a cartoon.

"Mr. Matthews, your son—" Chase began but stopped speaking when Robert closed the distance between them.

To his credit, Tate didn't intercede. He made his presence known but didn't say anything.

"Is a victim of a brutal shaming attack. That private video should have never seen the light of day."

Chase couldn't believe what Robert was saying. He didn't really believe that his son was the victim, did he?

"Your son raped Emily Dawson."

"Keep your voice down," Robert hissed.

And now Tate came forward not because he was afraid that Robert would do something, or that Chase couldn't protect herself if the man did.

It was because Tate was worried she was going to do something.

All she could picture was Emily's head lolling back and forth as Brent pumped into her.

"All right, Mr. Matthews, I think it's time for you to take a walk."

"Take—"

"The cuffs are off your son, you got what you wanted. Take a *fucking* walk."

Chase knew that Tate was practically begging the man to take a swing at him, but cooler heads prevailed. Robert stormed off and then, probably because he deemed that the course was finally clear, Brent's doctor materialized out of nowhere.

"Just the man we were looking for," Tate said, inexplicably calm.

Chase was still struggling to lower her heart rate.

"Hmm?"

"You're Brent's doctor, right?" Tate asked.

"Dr. Coblentz, yes."

"Agents Adams and Abernathy. Listen, Deputy Jardine called me earlier, said that you detected Rohypnol in Brent's blood."

It looked as if the doctor was going to refuse to reveal any patient information, but Jardine exited Brent's room and gave him an approving nod.

"That's right. Not trace levels, either," Dr. Coblentz confirmed.

"Any way to know when the drug was ingested?"

"If we knew what dose he'd taken."

"But we don't know that."

"No, we don't."

"Hmm. Well, best guess?"

The doctor again looked at Deputy Jardine.

"It's fine, they're helping with the case. Anything they need to know, you're clear to share."

Dr. Coblentz nodded.

"Okay, well, we ran the test about an hour ago, but Brent's blood was drawn earlier this morning. The half-life of Rohypnol is about sixteen hours, give or take."

Chase didn't hear an answer to Tate's question, so she asked it again.

"To be frank, it's impossible to tell whether Brent had ingested a very large dose on Saturday night or early Sunday morning or multiple smaller doses late Sunday or Monday. He could have just as easily taken a medium dose more recently."

"Can't give us anything else, doc?" Tate asked. "Best guess?"

"Off the record?"

"Off the record."

"Well, let me put it this way: nobody micro doses Rohypnol."

"Got it, thanks."

Dr. Coblentz excused himself and headed into Brent's room, leaving Chase and Tate with Deputy Dean Jardine.

"And thank you for keeping your cool," Chase said to the deputy.

The man nodded.

"Robert knows his place."

"Right. Even though Brent isn't cuffed, in case he wakes up, I don't want him going anywhere. I also don't want any of his friends to visit," Chase said. "It's okay if his father and his attorney speak to him, but that's it. Can you keep an eye on him?"

Jardine smiled.

"It would be my pleasure."

Chapter 38

"**ARE YOU GONNA TELL MRS.** Dawson that her daughter was pregnant?" Tate asked.

Chase answered the question with a question of her own.

"What are the odds she already knew?"

"Given the general dislike for Carlos Mendoza in this town? I would say very low."

"You're assuming that Carlos was the father?"

"You're not?"

"I think it's the most likely scenario, but it could be Brent's. Or someone else's. You never know."

"Except we *will* know—soon. It shouldn't take more than a few hours to run the DNA profile through CODIS."

"Yeah."

Tate put an end to their speculation by knocking on the Dawsons' front door.

The first time they'd come, Jennifer Dawson had thrown the door wide almost as if she expected her daughter to be standing there, that the Sheriff's Department had just played a horribly cruel joke on them. This time, it was opened just an inch.

A single, red-rimmed eye peered out.

"Mrs. Dawson, can we have a word?" Chase was so convinced that the woman would open the door that she actually started forward and almost bumped into it when it stayed put.

"I'm sorry, but I have nothing else to say to you."

Chase's eyelids retracted.

"Excuse me?" She wasn't sure she'd heard correctly.

"I really don't have anything else to say to you. I'm sorry." Her voice was low and grainy. Tate slid his foot inside just before the door could be closed on them.

"Maybe you don't remember us, but we're with the FBI. We're trying to find out what happened to your daughter."

"I know what happened to my Em." The woman sniffed. "Carlos Mendoza murdered her. I think... I think you should just go back to wherever you came from and leave us alone."

Shit.

"We're still investigating—"

"The Sheriff's Department told us that Carlos murdered her, and that Carlos' brother nearly killed that nice boy, Brent Matthews."

Fucking Sheriff Grimes. Tate's right, this town is rotten to the core.

Chase leaned forward.

"Jennifer, despite what the sheriff might have told you, your daughter's murder is still an ongoing investigation. There are things we don't know."

"I'm sorry, please remove your foot from the door."

Tate frowned but pulled his foot back. Jennifer Dawson promptly closed the door in their faces.

"What the fuck was that all about?" Chase asked.

"That was about Sheriff Grimes being pissed off. That was about him flexing on us, reminding us that Hawkesbury is his town."

They walked back to Chase's car.

"Maybe we shouldn't have stirred the shit," she remarked.

"Too late now."

"Too late now." Tate paused, then added, "Fucking small towns."

They were driving for five minutes before Tate crouched down and looked in the side mirror.

"The Chevelle's back, following us again."

Chase nodded. She'd actually made it half a block ago. The driver wasn't even trying to stay hidden.

"I'm getting a little bit tired of this place. How about you Chase?"

"Sick and tired."

Chase made a quick left and then an immediate right.

"Hold on."

Wrenching the wheel hard, she whipped her BMW into a tight U-turn, forcing herself against her window and Tate against the center console. As expected, the driver of the black Chevelle feared losing them and had sped up.

They barely managed to slam on the brakes in time to avoid a head-on collision.

The front windshield was illegally tinted, giving them no idea who was inside.

Chase pulled her gun and approached the vehicle.

"Get out of the car."

Tate moved to the passenger window and tapped the glass with the barrel of his own weapon.

"Get the fuck out," he said.

The Chevelle's engine revved, and Chase took a cautious step backward.

"Get out of the car or we smash the windows."

The car remained running but the door slowly opened.

Chase wasn't surprised by the young man with wavy dark hair and a square jaw who stepped out. And while she'd never actually seen a picture of Jackson Grimes, she knew in an instant that this is who it was. He was like a younger, slimmer version of his father.

"The fuck do you want?" Jackson said, eyeing Chase with a sneer. He didn't even acknowledge Tate as he made his way toward the front of the car.

Jackson's birth certificate said he was only twenty, but he looked a hell of a lot older.

"What the fuck do I want?" Tate snapped. "I want you to stop following us."

"It's a free country and I'm just going for a ride." Jackson was only looking at Chase when he spoke.

Ride… ride…

The word triggered something in Chase. She recalled the thick tire marks left outside The Shack.

They looked a lot like the Chevelle's tires.

Chase leaned down and snapped a photo of the treads.

"Fuck you doing?"

"Free country, just taking a picture," Chase replied.

"Well, fuck off."

"Easy now," Tate warned.

Jackson's eyes finally flashed over to him.

"The fuck you gonna do?"

"You know I'm a federal agent, right? You know that I'm with the FBI?"

"I don't give a fuck if you're Goddamn president."

Tate's mouth became a thin line beneath his mustache.

"Calm down," Chase said, annoyed by the dick measuring competition. "Both of you just calm—"

"Why don't you shut the fuck up, bitch?"

Chase recoiled. This Jackson Grimes was one hell of a piece of work.

"Hey!" Tate shouted. "You kiss your daddy with that mouth?"

Chase noticed that Tate had put his gun away and thought back to what Daniel had said when he and her partner had almost come to blows.

You motherfucking cops think you're so tough with your guns.
How about you fight with your bare hand?

He couldn't seriously be thinking about fighting this twerp, could he?

"Tate—" but once again Chase was interrupted. Even though Tate was standing between them, the man was looking over his shoulder at her.

"Nah, I don't kiss my daddy, but he gonna kiss you, lady. He gonna kiss you, and he gonna fuck you good."

Tate shoved Jackson backward. The kid put his hands up as he struggled to stay on his feet. He was grinning, now.

"Tate, he's baiting you," Chase warned, trying, and failing, to pull her partner back. "He wants you to do something so that they can force us out of Hawkesbury County."

Her words fell on deaf ears.

"Sheriff Grimes gonna fuck you good, just like Brent fucked Emily."

Chase saw red. She lunged at Jackson but thankfully Tate was standing between them. Perhaps this was intentional, perhaps not. But it likely saved their jobs.

Tate grabbed her and picked her up before she collided with Jackson. The kid didn't even move, just stood there, egging her on with a lascivious grin on his prematurely weathered face.

Tate carried her like a possessed cat back to her car, suffering multiple minor scratches in the process.

"Calm down." He gripped her tightly around the waist. "Like you said, this is what he wants. The sheriff wants us out of his town, and if you keep going on like this, we'll have no choice but to leave. Then Carlos is going to rot in prison or get the needle for a murder he never committed."

"He gonna fuck you good!" Jackson taunted, laughing now.

Chase made one final effort to break free, but Tate expected this and threw her into her car.

"You're going to get what's coming to you, Jackson," Tate said as he walked around to the other side of the vehicle.

"Bring it on." Jackson mimed come here. "Bring it *on.*"

"Oh, I will," Chase heard Tate whisper. "That's a *fucking* promise."

Chapter 39

TATE KNEW THAT CHASE WAS fuming, but he also knew that she was madder at herself for losing control than at what Jackson Grimes had said. He knew because he felt the same way.

But they'd stirred the shit and they couldn't rightly be mad that they now had to endure the smell. He figured that after pissing off Sheriff Grimes he'd instructed his son to tail them. And Grimes must have known that Jackson would have done what Jackson did best: piss people off and get into fights.

"We should have just hauled ass in," Chase said between clenched teeth. "The tire marks at The Shack were his and they were fresh. He was there Sunday."

"I don't doubt it, but you know what would have happened if we decided to slap the cuffs on him right there on the street?"

"What?"

"He would have fought us. He would have fought us and in the process, he'd end up getting hurt. And the story would be that we beat Jackson up. I know, dumb, right? But I bet the Jennifer Dawson types would back that story, and Robert would claim we were harassing students. It's better we did nothing."

"It just doesn't feel right, letting him go free. Let's imagine that Daniel is telling the truth about Jackson planting the Rohypnol on him. I mean, at the time, Daniel had no idea about Emily being raped or having been drugged, right?"

"Right."

"So, imagine this, Jackson is pissed off because he hates Carlos and his brother. Been fighting with them for years. He says to Brent, I have an idea. Let's convince Emily to come out to The Shack—she loves Carlos, but she misses her friends, too, you know? You wine and dine her—if necessary, I persuade her with a little roofie action—and next thing you know, I'm taking a video of you fucking her. You can show Carlos and he'll be so pissed they'll break up. Then you and Em can get back together."

Tate was cringing.

"I mean, it's a fucking insanely stupid idea… but I get the impression that that's right up Jackson's alley. Possible."

"Possible," Chase concluded. Not necessarily plausible, however.

"Oh, by the way, I got a text from a buddy. He said that there hasn't been a murder in Hawkesbury in more than six years. Last one was some guy from out of town, broke into a house and they got into a shoot-out. Both ended up dead."

"Great," Chase grumbled. "All of these grassy knoll theories might be for naught. Maybe the Sheriff's Department is just so damn inexperienced that they are fucking by accident."

Tate laughed.

"Oh, got another text."

"How many friggin' buddies do you have?"

"What can I say? I'm just super popular. Anyway, Emily's phone arrived in the area of The Shack at eleven on Saturday night and clicked off around two in the morning. No ping since."

"Someone pulled the SIM and powered it down?"

"Most likely."

"Any other tidbits of information you want to share?" Chase inquired, tongue-in-cheek.

"Yeah, I got a video of Jackson Grimes strangling Emily."

"*What?*"

Tate immediately sucked in a breath.

"Shit, sorry, bad joke."

Sheriff Grimes gonna fuck you good, just like Brent fucked Emily.

There was something wrong with Jackson Grimes, there was no doubt about that. But in Chase's experience, most men who talked big acted small.

Tate, who had taken over the driving duties after Chase's meltdown was curiously quiet.

"Why do I get the idea that you're coming up with one of those secret plans again?"

"I'm not coming up with it, Chase, I already have it. But this one? This one, you're not gonna want to know beforehand. Trust me on this, Chase."

***

They actually managed to finish a meal this time. No vile videos or images or commentary to nerf their appetite. And the food wasn't bad; it served its purpose. Tate hadn't realized how hungry he'd been. Afterward, they headed back to the hotel room.

Then they waited.

Tate waited for sundown and for Chase to fall asleep, while she waited for a call from Ava's lawyer that never came. She believed that the pressure they'd put on Ava in the interrogation room, along with the parting bomb that Emily had been pregnant when she'd been killed, was enough to get her to open up about what had actually happened Saturday night. Tate was on the fence about whether she would break.

Tate checked in with his contact at the FBI to see if there was hit on the paternal DNA from the fetus on CODIS. Unbelievably, the entire system had crashed. Even the fucking FBI wasn't immune to the blue screen of death, it appeared. They were hoping to be back up again tomorrow.

The only thing left to do was to speak with Jackson. He was the missing link. They'd poked and prodded everyone else in this case.

Jackson was the last one.

Which brought him to his present plan.

"Just some light reading?" he remarked as Chase slid into bed, Emily Dawson's Story Planner in her hands.

"You know, Emily Dawson wasn't a bad writer. Check this out." Chase read a passage from one of the girl's short stories.

"Not bad," Tate said but Chase could see right through him.

"Not much of a reader, huh?"

"No, not really," he admitted.

Chase smiled. She looked so pretty lying with a book in her hands, so normal.

Could she ever live a normal life? Tate wondered. *Can either of us?*

The real question was whether two traumas negated one another or if they multiplied.

Only time would tell.

"You going to get any sleep tonight?" Chase asked, lowering the notepad.

"I'm exhausted, so yeah, maybe I will."

It was a lie and both of them knew it. Yet, Tate actually felt himself drifting off, falling into that strange purgatory between sleep and wakefulness, but the moment that the Story Planner drooped to Chase's chest, he was wide awake again.

And ready to hunt.

Chapter 40

TATE WASN'T SURE IF HIS tail had gotten better or if they were just lazy.

He spent a good twenty to thirty minutes driving around aimlessly, going close but not too close to Tenbury, the Sheriff's Department, principal Robert Matthews' house, the lights of which were on even though it was after two in the morning, and Jennifer Dawson's place. For good measure, he even went around the Mendozas' block. Eventually, he spotted the black Chevelle in the rearview.

Tate slowed, his turns becoming more deliberate, telegraphed. Eventually, he made his way near the hospital, making sure not to pass in front of the ATM that had picked up Ava driving Brent's car.

He didn't have a specific destination, just an idea of where to go: a subdivision that was still being built. The roads hadn't been paved yet and the tires of Chase's BMW slipped on the loose gravel.

This is going to work well, he thought. *Really well.*

Tate deliberately pumped the gas while turning, sending the car into a tailspin. He gripped the wheel tightly, spinning it in the direction of the spin, the opposite of what everyone is taught to do in driver's ed.

He almost pushed it too far, almost lost complete control.

"Sorry about your car, Chase!"

The vehicle skidded and something flashed in Tate's mind.

A rainy night, his daughter screaming. His wife…

The car skidded into a dark blue dumpster on the driveway of a shell of a home. It struck the passenger door, but not hard enough to cause the airbags to pop.

Knowing that he didn't have much time, Tate forced thoughts and images of the accident that had robbed his entire family of a normal life.

He jumped out of the car, closing the door behind him. While ducking behind the dumpster, Tate pulled the black ski mask from his pocket and put it on. Next, he adjusted his black leather gloves, squeezing between the fingers to make sure there was no chance they could slip off.

The black Chevelle took the final turn too quickly and even its thick tires couldn't keep it on the road.

It was barreling toward Chase's BMW, out of control.

"Oh, shit."

If it smashed into her car, Tate's plan would be ruined.

But at the last second, the driver somehow managed to come to a stop mere inches from the BMW's bumper.

"What the *mother fuck!*" Jackson shouted as he got out of his car.

The thick cloud of dust from the gravel road that hung in the air was the perfect cover for Tate but, in the end, he didn't need it. As he rushed at the man, Jackson staggered, and Tate realized that he was drunk.

This couldn't be more perfect, he thought.

Jackson never saw him coming.

Tate drove his shoulder into his side in a near-perfect tackle. Jackson, taken completely by surprise made a strange *'ehhrp'* sound as he fell hard onto the ground. His body cushioned Tate and the combined force squeezed every single ounce of air from the younger man's lungs.

Jackson was still conscious when Tate flipped him onto his back, but he was struggling to breathe.

A punch between the eyes didn't help.

The next blow smashed the boy's nose. Somehow this shocked Jackson into breathing again—a horrible, wet gasp. Then he sputtered and spat blood.

Tate squatted over Jackson, bringing his covered face close.

Then he just stared into the barely conscious man's eyes like Jackson had glared at Chase earlier in the day.

This was where it was supposed to end, where he was supposed to make the anonymous call to the Sheriff's Department saying that a driver had had an accident. A *drunk* driver, as it turned out.

But then Tate thought about Marco, the giant Serbian mobster who had knocked the breath out of him with the cinder block fist demanding payment for the loan. Then he thought of the car accident again. The car accident that had put his daughter in a wheelchair and his wife in jail.

He hit Jackson with each memory. Hit him so hard that Tate thought might have actually killed him.

Oh, fuck.

Tate reached down and shook Jackson's shoulders.

Nothing.

Shit, shit, shit, shit.

Tate used the palm of his hand to put pressure on Jackson's chest and then—thank God—the kid sucked in a breath, making a sound like the devil had just possessed his soul. Even his back arched, further adding to the allusion.

He was alive. And he was going to be okay.

Hopefully.

Tate made the call and was about to go back to Chase's car when he just couldn't help himself.

Once more, he squatted over Jackson, only this time, Tate said, "Who fucked who now, Jackson? Who fucked *who*?"

PART IV – Mattress

Chapter 41

"YOU ALMOST READY?" TATE ASKED.

For some reason, Chase had been taking her sweet time today, showering for longer than usual.

"Almost. What's the rush? What did you have in mind?"

"I'm thinking we should speak to Ava again."

"Really?" Chase hollered from the shower. The water shut off and she leaned into the room. Her body was mostly hidden by the door frame, but Tate liked what he saw. The line of her bare collarbone, the outer half of one breast, and the gentle curve of her hip.

"You okay?" she asked with a sly grin.

"Better than okay."

"Well, get that look off your face then—you're in a rush, right? No time for that."

Under pretty much every other circumstance Tate would have just said fuck it and joined Chase in the bathroom. But it had been more than four hours since his encounter in the abandoned subdivision, and if Jackson hadn't rolled into a hospital or to the Sheriff's Department to speak to his daddy by now, then he was probably dead. If that were the case, Tate would hightail it to the Sheriff's Department and turn himself in.

Either way, Tate was destined to end up on Grimes' home turf.

"Any other time, Chase—any other time, but not now. We have to get going. Slip something on and let's get out of here before I change my mind. Because if I do that, we're going to spend the entire day locked in this room together."

***

"I know who did it," Tate said, his eyes locking onto Sheriff Grimes'.

"You just got here. How—"

"It was Daniel Mendoza."

The sheriff made a face as if he'd just gambled with a fart and lost.

"What?"

Tate nodded.

"Yep. Daniel did it."

"What are you talking about? He was here the whole time, locked up."

"So?" Tate asked with a shrug.

The sheriff wasn't dumb, but he couldn't help himself.

"So, how the fuck did Daniel beat up my son when he was behind bars?"

"I guess the same way Daniel managed to beat Brent Dawson when he was miles away at work."

The sheriff growled.

"This is bullshit. You're just—"

Deputy Dean Jardine turned the corner, looking sullen.

"Agent Abernathy, would you like me to administer the blood alcohol test now, or…?"

"Blood alcohol test?" the sheriff snapped. "What are you talking about, Deputy?"

"Jackson drove here, correct?" Tate said, his voice light and airy—deliberately annoying. Hifalutin. "I thought I smelled alcohol in the foyer where Jackson came through. Just in case his injuries were sustained during a car accident, I think it's best if we do our due diligence and test his BAC, don't you?"

"He wasn't in an accident. He was *attacked*."

"*Potayto, potahto*—let's just be sure."

"I don't fucking think so. Deputy Jardine, don't you go near him. Don't even *think* about going near him." The sheriff swiveled his head around. "Where is Jackson now?"

"Holding cell three."

Sheriff Grimes' jaw nearly hit the floor.

"*Holding* cell? You put him in a fucking *holding* cell? He's here to report an assault!" Grimes pointed a stubby finger at Tate's chest. "An assault he says was carried out by *this* man!"

Chase, who had been seeing this confrontation from several feet away as Tate had suggested just in case things went south, suddenly spoke up.

"That's a serious allegation, Sheriff. When did this supposed assault occur?"

"Supposed? This isn't *supposed*. His face is... his face is all beat up."

Chase ignored the comment and spoke as if the man had answered her question.

"Last night, right? Well, Agent Abernathy was with me all night so it couldn't possibly have been him. I mean, not that anybody in their right mind would actually think an FBI Agent, especially one as decorated as Abernathy, would ever do something like that."

"Just like it couldn't have been Daniel who beat up Brent," Tate added, relishing the expression of pure discomfort on Grimes' face.

"You are going to regret this," Sheriff Grimes warned. "You two are going to fucking regret ever coming to Hawkesbury."

"Well, that I don't doubt," Tate admitted. "But, for now, Jackson Grimes is in holding cell three and Agent Adams and I are going to take this opportunity and interview him there."

"You're not—"

"Either you let Daniel Mendoza go," Chase proposed, "and you let us interview your son, or I will get someone to strap him down while I draw blood and perform the BAC test myself. And how do you think that's going to go? Hmm? Local sheriff's son gets into an accident while wasted? Oh, I'll be sure to contact the local paper, too. That'll make it considerably more difficult for you to cover it up, won't it, Sheriff?"

They had him. They finally had him.

Tate hadn't previously believed in spontaneous combustion, but Sheriff Grimes was on the verge of making him reconsider his stance on the subject.

"You don't fucking touch him. And you don't get to talk to him until after I do."

Tate stepped back.

"Fine by me. Need to go ice my knuckles, anyway."

The look that Sheriff Grimes gave him now was so vile that Tate nearly regretted making the comment. But then he stormed off and Tate, who had been holding his breath, exhaled.

"Wow, that was intense," Deputy Dean Jardine said in a huff, suggesting that he, too, had been on edge.

"You're telling me."

Tate looked at Chase, who was the only one seemingly not bothered by the interaction. In fact, she looked delighted.

She was smart and she knew what Tate had done. Tate had half-expected her to condemn his actions, chastise him, tell him that it had been too risky, too volatile.

But she didn't.

Tate's phone pinged, and he looked at it. Then he frowned.

"That was my contact at the FBI," he said. "Got a hit on the DNA from the fetus. The father of Emily Dawson's baby was a first-degree relative to Daniel Mendoza."

"Shit, so Carlos was the father of Emily's baby?" Chase asked.

Tate nodded. He didn't know why, but this information stung. It shouldn't, it didn't change anything, but Tate suddenly felt sick to his stomach.

The three of them just stood there for several seconds before Chase's phone started to ring. She showed Tate the caller ID—STITTS—and then moved out of earshot to answer.

Tate watched her leave and then addressed Deputy Dean Jardine.

"Deputy, when you took Jackson to holding cell three, you didn't happen to pass in front of the room where Ava Morency is being held, did you?"

"I did."

"Do you think she saw?"

The deputy nodded.

"I think everyone in the entire building saw and heard Jackson Grimes being brought in."

Tate smiled.

"Perfect."

Chase got off the phone and hurried over to them. She looked distraught.

"What's wrong?"

She gave Tate a small head shake, then addressed Deputy Jardine.

"Deputy, is Ava's lawyer here? In the building?"

"No, I don't think so. Why?"

"Because I'm pretty sure Ava's going to want him present when I tell her what my colleague back in Quantico just found out."

Chapter 42

AVA'S LAWYER'S DEMEANOR WAS COMPLETELY different today. No longer was he combative. And Chase knew that after she told them what Stitts had uncovered this was about to change again.

Ava looked drawn and worn out, and even if she hadn't seen Jackson being paraded around by Deputy Jardine, Chase thought that one night behind bars was probably enough for the girl to change her mind about pretty much everything.

But the problem was, after what she'd seen—rather, what she'd *heard*—Chase had changed her opinion of Ava, as well.

"Agent Adams, Agent Abernathy, my client has informed me that she has some information about Saturday night that she would be willing to share, for full immunity—"

"Before any talk of a deal, there's something I want to share with you."

Ava swallowed hard but the lawyer kept his cool.

"We've reviewed the footage from the ATM and—"

"No, this isn't about Ava bringing Brent to the hospital. It's about Emily's rape."

Ava whimpered.

"Agent Adams, these scare tactics aren't necessary. My client is under arrest for assaulting Brent Matthews, a bogus charge, but it has nothing to do with Emily Dawson's alleged sexual assault or death."

"Just watch."

Ava shook her head and closed her eyes. She looked like a little kid being forced to watch a horror film by an older sibling.

"Don't want to watch?" Chase asked, pulling out her phone. "That's okay; you can just listen. Whoever sent this video to the school was pretty smart. They hid their tracks well and there's no way to figure out whose phone it was sent from. But they weren't *that* smart. There was audio embedded in the file, it was just muted. My friend at the FBI managed to turn it back on. Here, have a listen."

Chase played the fourteen seconds of Emily's rape this time with the volume turned up.

There was the sound of people drinking, a handful, maybe more, maybe less. At first, the observers sounded raucous, almost giddy. Chase had seen this before, people gathering around two people fighting outside the bar, two people they'd never met before. A sort of crowd-induced blood lust. But then, once blood was shed, they seemed disgusted by it, realized that they were watching something serious.

This happened in the video, too. After a moment, there was pure silence, a silence so deep that the video was indistinguishable from the earlier version that had no audio track. And then, clear as day, a female voice said, "Make it stop."

There was a five count after the video ran out in which nobody made a sound.

And then the lawyer said, "It could be anyone."

Chase cleared her throat.

"It could be anyone, but it isn't. It's you, isn't it, Ava?"

The girl sobbed and buried her face in her hands.

"So, before we talk deals—" Chase's phone rang, startling her. It was Stitts again, and she rejected the call. "Why don't you tell us what happened Saturday night?"

"Agent Adams, if we don't have a deal—"

Her phone rang again—Stitts. Chase rejected it.

"Do you want to get that?"

Chase switched her phone to silent mode and flipped it over.

"Ava, this is your one chance to come clean about what happened Saturday night. Your one chance." She sighed dramatically. "Look, I know you loved Emily, at least at one time you did. And I know that you didn't kill her. But I've told you before, it doesn't matter if you were the one who actually committed the crime if you were there and knew…" More sobs out of the girl and Chase decided to change tactics. "You want to know what I think? I think you're scared. I think Jackson was at The Shack and I think he probably took the video. I understand why you're scared of Jackson—hell, he threatened me, an FBI agent and I'd be lying if I said I wasn't a little scared of him, too. And I know you probably think he's untouchable, with his father being the sheriff and all. But he isn't. He's sitting in the cell next to yours right now just waiting to sing. Despite what he told you, he's not going to keep his mouth shut. Sheriff Grimes is going to coach him and tell him exactly what to say and how to say to make sure he gets to go home at the end of the day. And who do you think he's going to blame for what happened to Emily?"

Ava began to wail. Her lawyer tried to comfort her, but she shrugged him off.

"Her best friend, Ava. That's who is going to be blamed for this—for all of this."

"I didn't—I didn't—" the words were a wet mess coming from Ava's mouth.

"You don't have to say anything, Ava, you're under no obligation—"

Ava glared at Mr. Dawson.

"Yes, I have to." Ava turned her wet eyes to Chase. "I have to tell—Emily deserves at least that much… after what we did to her." She wept freely now. "After what we did to her, Emily deserves for her story to be told."

Chapter 43

"**It was Brent's idea, at** first, anyway. He just couldn't get over Emily. I guess you already know what happened when they broke up: Brent slapped her and that was it. Emily would never go back with him, even if Carlos wasn't in the picture. The thing is, nobody knew that; I mean, until Saturday night, nobody but Em and Brent knew about the slap. I didn't even know it and I was her best friend. That was Em. She wasn't vindictive or malicious. She had a big heart, you know? And she loved Carlos. I… I hate that I had to pick. But I couldn't stay with Em. I just couldn't. Brent was telling everyone who would listen to these nasty rumors about Em and how she cheated on him. Like, I knew it wasn't true, but everyone was saying it. And Carlos… he was different. He was the scholarship kid. I'm not—aw, shit, I'm not proud of it—but I picked Brent. We all did."

Ava took a tissue from the box that Chase had placed in front of her and wiped her nose. She sighed, then continued.

"Brent came to me on Friday. Said he regretted saying that stuff about Em, wanted to give her a second chance. I… I missed her, too. I guess I should have known that it was a prank or a set-up… I dunno. But I was the one who called her, told her to come to The Shack. And the thing that—" she wiped her face again, "—the thing that really hurts is that she sounded… shit, Em sounded *so* excited, you know? So *fucking* excited. I should have known, though. I should have known that something was up the second that Brent said Jackson was coming, too. See, Jackson *hates* Carlos, hates Carlos and his brother with a *passion*. I think it started back when Jackson was at Tenbury, and he said something about Carlos—a stupid joke about how he only got the scholarship because he was Mexican or something. Jackson got suspended but he should have been expelled as Tenbury has zero tolerance for racism. His dad was the one who made sure he got to go back. After that, Jackson was looking for any excuse to get into fights with either of them. And now that Carlos was with Emily—well, he had a built-in excuse."

Ava reached for her glass of water. Her hand was shaking so badly that some of it spilled down her chin. She didn't even bother wiping it away.

"Ava," Chase said, leaning forward ever so slightly. "Tell me what happened Saturday night."

***

"She's not gonna show," Brent muttered under his breath. He took a sip of beer. "She's not showing."

Ava tapped her fingers against the side of a White Claw. On the phone, Emily had sounded ecstatic about the idea of meeting up with the old gang.

"She'll be here."

"I don't know. Maybe—"

"Shut the fuck up and drink your beer," Jackson said out of the corner of his mouth. He lit a cigarette. "She'll show."

"And then what?" Brent asked. "She'll probably want nothing to do with me."

"Let me handle that," Jackson said tossing an empty beer can to the floor.

Ava didn't like the sound of that. In fact, she didn't actually like Jackson at all. She never understood why he wanted to hang out with them all the time. He was three years older, and they had pretty much nothing in common. All six of them, even

Theo, were headed to college next and Jackson had barely made it through high school.

With nervous hands, Ava watched Brent pop two Zoloft.

"You know what? Gimme one of those."

Brent didn't hesitate; he tossed the bottle of pills—*cha, cha, cha*—to Jackson who caught them.

The sour smell of alcohol and urine was becoming noxious. Just like Ava didn't understand why Jackson hung out with them she didn't get the allure of The Shack, either. Sure, there were no parents around to bug them, but there were plenty of places they could go to drink that didn't smell so horrible.

"I'm gonna get some fresh air," she said, looking over at Natalia and Laura, hoping that one of them would offer to come with. They didn't. They remained perched on the windowsill chatting quietly.

It was a cool night and Ava hugged herself as she stepped outside. She turned her gaze skyward, admiring the bright stars. In the absence of light pollution from the city, they seemed to come alive.

Ava moved even further from The Shack, sipping her White Claw as she went.

Jackson was scheming and that made her nervous. His ideas were almost always bad news and unlike him, she didn't have a get-out-of-jail-free card.

Still… *Em*. She missed Em.

Missed their late-night talks, their gossip sessions. Discussing their plans for college.

Carlos… why the hell did it have to be Carlos?

Breaking up with Brent would have made things awkward, but if Emily had just not dated anyone for a month or so, things would've blown over.

But not Carlos.

Ava sighed and finished her drink.

She wanted another but knew that that was a bad idea. She normally only had two or three White Claws but today, nervous about seeing her best friend after so long, Ava had already downed five.

Her head was starting to swim.

How many times did I almost call you, Em? A hundred? A thousand? A million*?*

"Ava?" The voice came out of the darkness, and Ava lowered her gaze from the stars. She couldn't locate the speaker, but it seemed to be coming from the woods.

"Em? That you?"

Emily Dawson stepped out from behind a tree. It was her all right. Pretty Em, who had gotten her period first and developed breasts, that Ava was still waiting to appear. And now, at the ripe age of 18, she doubted would ever come. Em with the cute, petite features, except for her large eyes, Em with the perfect teeth, the hair that looked styled even if it was just pulled up in a bun like it was now. Em who was just wearing jeans and a band T-shirt but somehow made the ensemble look classy.

Emily was nervous; her eyes kept darting to the open door of The Shack from which laughter and shouting could be heard.

"I tried calling you," Emily said softly.

Ava winced.

"I've been so busy," she lied. Emily saw right through this; she always saw through Ava's lies. Suddenly, this didn't feel like a good idea anymore. Jackson had a plan and that meant that someone was going to get hurt. Emily had been hurt enough already. "Listen, Em, I don't think you should be here. I don't—"

"I have no one to talk to, Ava." There was a profound sadness in her friend's voice.

"What about—what about Carlos? Did you guys break up?" Ava couldn't help the optimism from creeping into her voice.

Em kicked at the dirt with the toe of her shoe.

"No, we're together, but I—I can't talk to him about this."

Emily came forward.

"What's wrong? Em, did something happen?"

For a long while, Em said nothing, and they were inundated by boisterous sounds coming from The Shack. Ethan had really tied one off today and he got loud when he got drunk.

"Em?"

Ava saw tears in Emily's eyes. More guilt, this time creeping into her throat like twisted rivers of bile.

"I'm late, Ava."

It took several seconds for Ava's alcohol-fogged brain to register what her friend was saying. When it did, Ava's breathing became shallow.

"Late? How late?"

"Six weeks."

Ava's eyes bulged.

"*Six weeks*? Have you taken a test?"

Em shook her head and then reached into her pocket and pulled out exactly that: a pregnancy test. Even in the near darkness, Ava could recognize the characteristic shape.

"I'm too scared to do it by myself. And I couldn't do it with Carlos. He just got accepted to Penn on a scholarship and he… and he…"

"You have to do the test, Em. It's better to know, no matter what the result is."

"I know." Emily no longer seemed like the confident girl Ava knew, the girl who fell in love with Carlos Mendoza and decided to throw away her entire senior year by dating him instead of Brent Matthews. Now, Emily just seemed scared.

Ava didn't blame her. Nobody got pregnant in Hawkesbury County if you weren't married. And absolutely nobody got pregnant at Tenbury Academy.

At least, if you did, nobody knew about it. Things were… taken care of.

"I just had no one to talk to, and I didn't know what to do. If I am—you know, if it's positive—what do I do? Ava, what do I do?"

Ava went to Emily and wrapped her long arms around the girl in a deep embrace. Emily practically collapsed into her.

This felt good, it felt normal.

"We'll do it together," Ava said. "Em, we're gonna do this together, alright? We're gonna do it together right now."

Chapter 44

BRENT MATTHEWS OPENED HIS EYES. At least, that's what he tried to do but only one of them obeyed his command.

He had no idea where he was or how he got there. All he knew was that he was lying in a very uncomfortable and rather small bed. But a quick look around, with his one slightly blurry and red-tinged eye, told him everything he needed to know.

He was in a hospital, lying in a hospital bed surrounded by medical equipment. A thin, clear tube ran from the back of one hand and there was a blood oxygen meter on his index finger.

A machine pinged and this sent a cascade of memories flooding back. Not of how he got to the hospital, which was still a mystery, but now he recalled *that* night, the night he had sex with Emily Dawson on the filthy mattress in The Shack.

"Brent?"

The voice came from somewhere to his right and Brent tried to turn his head to face the speaker.

No dice.

Pain flared from his neck and shot all the way to his tailbone. Stars shot across his vision.

"Brent?" This time, the speaker stepped in front of his warped line of sight.

"Dad?"

"Oh, Brent." His father reached out and gently caressed his bruised face. Brent couldn't be sure, but he thought the man had been crying. He had never seen his dad cry before. "Everything's gonna be okay, son."

Robert Matthews said this because that was what dads always told their sons. That's what parents tell their children, no matter what.

Tears pooled in Brent's eyes. And when they spilled onto his cheeks, squeezing out of his left eye like juice from a desiccated citrus fruit, he felt a burning sensation as if they were made of acid. And perhaps they were. Perhaps this was his punishment for what he'd done... for doing *that* to her.

To his Emily.

"No," Brent croaked, "things aren't going to be okay." Even speaking hurt.

"Son, do you remember what happened? Do you remember who did this to you?"

Brent closed his eyes, trying to make the stinging stop.

"I—I remember."

"Good, *good*." The relief in Robert Matthews' voice was thick, tangible. He felt his dad lean away from his bed, his hand falling from his cheek. "Deputy Jardine?"

This was it; this would make Brent feel better. The guilt was far more painful to endure than any of his injuries.

The door swung open, and he heard the jangle of a utility belt—Hawkesbury Sheriff's Department standard issue—as someone approached.

"Oh, he's awake. Good."

Brent recognized Deputy Jardine's voice. All the kids joked about the Jardine brothers, calling them Tweedledee and Tweedledum behind their backs. Nobody could ever tell them apart, even after one of them—Dean?—grew a pervy little mustache.

Brent didn't like either of them—they gave him the creeps—but it was better them than Sheriff Grimes.

"My son remembers." Robert slid his hand into Brent's and gave it a little squeeze. "He remembers what happened to him."

"I'm all ears."

Brent opened his eyes and looked first at Deputy Jardine—it was indeed the one with the mustache—before staring at his father.

"No," he began, "I don't remember what happened to me. But I remember what happened to *her*. I remember—"

His father's grip on his hand was suddenly very strong. Almost painfully so.

"Brent, you don't need to say anything. You need your rest. You're not thinking straight." Brent shook his head and almost vomited, the pain was so bad. "Brent, don't say anything." And then, to Deputy Jardine, Robert Matthews said, "he's under the influence of a lot of medication and—"

"No, I'm fine. I'm fine, and I know what I'm saying. Dad, please, I need to do this."

"Brent."

Somehow, Brent managed to pull his hand free from his father's iron grip.

"What is it you want to tell me, son?" Deputy Jardine asked, sliding between Brent and his father just in case the latter tried to intervene again.

"You should arrest me because I did it. I tricked Emily into coming out to The Shack. And then..." Brent's voice caught in his throat. When he spoke again it was tight and he barely recognized it as his own. "And then I raped and murdered Emily Dawson."

Chapter 45

WHY IS SHE TAKING SO damn long? Just hurry up and pee, already!

Emily had been standing behind a tree for a good three minutes and still hadn't managed a single drop for the pregnancy test.

"Come on, come on already, come on," Ava said under her breath, but Emily heard her anyway.

"I'm trying here, geez. I just went before I came out here."

Ava thought she knew the answer, anyway. Em had always been regular and missing your period for six weeks usually only meant one thing. The girl could deny it, need absolute proof, but the writing was on the wall.

And the urine should be on the damn stick.

Questions zipped through Ava's mind as she waited. Was Em sure it was Carlos'? Brent had bragged that he'd slept with Emily after they'd broken up, but Ava had thought this was bullshit. But if it wasn't, could it be his?

Most importantly, would she keep the baby?

"There," Emily said with a surprising amount of satisfaction. "I did it."

She stepped out from behind the tree, holding the stick in one hand. Ava backed away from it, hands up.

"Gross—I'm not touching that."

Emily smiled, and for a second, for that fraction of a second, everything felt normal again, everything felt like it used to.

And then someone leaned out of the shack and the illusion dissolved.

"Hey, there you are! Glad you could make it!" Theo said, his wide face split in a grin. "Come on inside. Come and have a drink." His words were slurred, and while he was hard to understand on a regular day, with his oversized lips that he moistened almost continually, it was nearly impossible to understand what he was saying now.

"Go," Ava said in Emily's ear. "Just go. Don't stay here."

Em gave her a strange look and then she laughed, thinking that Ava was joking. After all, she'd asked her to come here. And they were friends. They were best friends—past tense. And maybe they could be again.

"Come on," Theo urged. Behind him, Ethan appeared. Ava didn't like the way he was staring down his narrow nose at Em. "*Lesss* have a drink. We missed you."

"Sure," Em said. As the girl walked by her, Ava realized the pregnancy test was no longer in her hand.

She glanced back toward the tree. Ava couldn't be sure, it was dark, and forests were nothing if not excellent shadow generators, but she thought she saw the pregnancy test lying face down in the dirt.

Had Emily seen a result?

It took all of Ava's willpower not to run and pick it up and look at it.

***

There was something off about this. There was something terribly off about how no one seemed to be addressing the elephant in the room: they'd ostracized Emily Dawson for the better part of three months and now they were just hanging out as if nothing had ever happened. Even though Brent and Emily hadn't spoken yet, outside of a terse 'hello', even they seemed to be on decent terms.

Everyone was smashed now. Everyone except Emily. She wasn't drinking—*did she know or was this just a precaution?*—and Ava helped her keep this under wraps by preparing virgin mixed drinks for her.

Though Ava was also drunk, she managed to observe everyone from a distance. They all looked so... happy. Even Jackson looked happy, and he was *never* happy.

What the hell is going on? What does he have planned?

Twice, Ava almost told Em to leave. Not like outside but order her to get the fuck out of here before something bad happened.

Brent was even more drunk than Theo. And he had no signs of stopping, either. His eyes followed Em wherever she went, and Ava had the strange notion that even if Em was pregnant, and even if it was Carlos' child, if she wanted him back, he would tuck his tail between his legs and rush to her.

He still loved her. Brent may have told everyone that she was a cheating cunt, his exact words, but he loved Em.

"Look," Jackson said, stepping between Natalia and Em, placing one hand on each of their shoulders. "I'm just going to say it: I know things are fucked up between you and Brent." Upon mention of his name, Brent raised his chin. His eyes also lifted, but more slowly than his head. "But things just weren't the same without you, Em. We gotta patch things up. Get back to normal, you know?"

Ava knew with every fiber of her being that this was absolute, one hundred percent a steaming pile of dog shit. Jackson didn't care about Em, or Brent, for that matter. All he cared about was himself.

But Ava still wanted to believe. Somehow, she could just forget the fact that Em was still with Carlos and might even be pregnant with his child, and think, selfishly, that things could go back to the way they were.

She knew Em, and Em was a nice person. Probably too nice, most of the time. It didn't surprise Ava that her friend was nodding. She looked nervous but her large blue eyes were full of hope.

She must have really been lonely, Ava thought.

"It was his idea, you know," Jackson said, pointing at Brent. "He felt bad about how things ended, and he just wants to be friends. We all do."

Lies—all lies. Em, you can see that these are lies, can't you?

Brent slid off the windowsill and kicked a bottle.

"Yeah."

That's all he said, *'yeah'*.

Brent had come to Ava to ask her to get in contact with Em, but now Ava was thinking that maybe Jackson was behind this all along.

And that smile… she hated the rictus on Jackson's face.

"I'm willing to talk," Em said sheepishly. She sipped her non-alcoholic drink.

No, no, no, this is so wrong.

"I think that's a fantastic idea. Somewhere private?"

There was only one place that was private in The Shack.

Em seemed uncomfortable now, but Jackson was encouraging. He subtly slipped his arm off Natalia and then guided Em over to Brent. He put his hand around Brent's shoulder.

"Talk it out, guys. C'mon, I want things to go back to the way they were."

Jackson brought them to the stairs and then he let them go.

There's still a chance, Ava thought. *Em, say you don't want to go down there. Tell them you want to go home. Hell, I'll take you home, and I'm wasted.*

Em looked over her shoulder at Ava then. It was almost as if she knew. It was as if Emily knew that something bad was going to happen and was silently begging for someone to save her.

But she didn't know.

None of them knew just how bad things were about to get.

Chapter 46

TATE WAS SO INVESTED IN the story that when there was a hard pounding at the door he nearly jumped out of his skin. Chase, who had been leaning forward the entire time, also started, not to the same degree as him.

Ava actually shrieked.

Fucking hell, Tate thought. *What is it now?*

He didn't have to wait long for an answer; before they could even rise to their feet, the door opened. Sheriff Grimes looked in at them, his eyes dark.

"Agents Adams and Abernathy," he said, "there has been a development."

A development? What kind of game is Sheriff Grimes playing here?

The timing was off; it was almost as if the big man wanted to put an end to Ava's story. But why? Who was he protecting?

"Sheriff, we're in the middle of an interview—" Tate was cut off.

"This is critical. Please." Grimes gestured toward the hallway.

"We don't work for—" Chase began, but Tate silenced her by squeezing her shoulder and getting to his feet.

"You stay, I'll go."

Chase wasn't fond of this idea, but it was the only logical choice they had. Grimes wasn't going to leave until at least one of them joined him and Chase was leading the interview.

Tate resisted the urge to bump Grimes as he passed him.

"C'mon," Tate snapped, making sure that Grimes closed the door. Then he glared at the man. "What the fuck are you doing? She was just starting to—"

"Brent Matthews just woke up. I guess the doctors decided he was well enough that they could taper back on his drugs."

About fucking time. But Brent's waking didn't warrant an interruption. Not when Ava was just about to get to what happened to Emily.

"And?"

"And he confessed."

Tate, not following, quickly snapped, "Confessed to what?" Grimes craned his neck forward.

"Confessed to murdering Emily Dawson."

Now, Tate wasn't sure that he'd heard correctly. Grimes, seeing his confused expression repeated, "Brent Matthews confessed to raping and murdering Emily Dawson, just a few minutes ago."

What the actual fuck?

Tate had seen the horrible video, heard the audio, and while he didn't put too much stock into gut feelings or premonitions, something seemed off about it. And despite the evidence pointing to the contrary, he had not believed that Brent Matthews was a murderer.

Hal Grimes didn't want them in Hawkesbury County and probably never wanted them there in the first place. But would he lie about this? Was he so desperate not to upset the small-town hierarchy and keep his job that he would make up some insane lie so that Ava wasn't able to tell them what really happened?

If that was the case, why say that Brent confessed? Why not just say that Carlos admitted to it?

An idea occurred to Tate.

Maybe the sheriff finally had it with Robert Matthews telling him what to do. With his son in jail, the principal would likely lose his job and then he'd have no sway in Hawkesbury.

"Who did Brent confess to?"

"Deputy Jardine."

"Dean or Tim?"

"What does it matter?" Grimes said, sounding annoyed now.

"Dean or Tim?" Tate repeated.

"Dean."

Tate backed away from the sheriff and called the deputy. Thirty seconds later, Grimes' story was confirmed.

"You know, it didn't have to be like this. We could have worked together," the sheriff said.

Tate was beginning to think that Sheriff Grimes was bipolar. None of what he said or did was consistent. One minute, he wanted to collaborate, the next, he was doing everything he could to sabotage the investigation.

"Anyways, if you wrap up quickly with Ava, we can head over to the hospital together. Get Brent to sign an official statement. I don't know if Deputy Jardine Mirandized him so it's best if we act quickly."

"We're gonna finish."

Sheriff Grimes tilted his head.

"Why? She didn't do anything. We both know Ava didn't beat Brent and, besides, I don't think that it matters who did that now. Not after Brent's confession."

"Because she's in the middle of the story and it would be rude not to let her finish."

And then, with Hal Grimes looking at him with loathing in his eyes, Tate returned to the interview room.

Chase gave him a look, but Tate didn't acknowledge it.

"Sorry about that. Despite what the sheriff said, it wasn't an emergency." Tate took his seat beside his partner. "Now, where were we?"

He had to give it to Chase, even with the interruption, she somehow managed to keep the terrified girl willing and ready to tell her story.

And that's exactly what Ava Morency did.

Chapter 47

AVA TRIED TO FOLLOW HER friend downstairs or at least eavesdrop on the conversation that Em and Brent were having, but Jackson wouldn't let her. And Jackson wasn't the type of person you could just force past or reason with.

So, she waited, on edge, keeping mostly to herself. There was tension in The Shack, and it wasn't just Ava feeling it. Natalia and Laura were talking, trying to act normal, but every few seconds their eyes would dart to the stairs. Even Theo, who was sweating now he was so drunk, appeared nervous.

Ava crushed two more White Claws bringing her total for the evening up to seven. Or eight.

Maybe nine?

Jackson was the only one who seemed unfazed by the strangeness of the situation. He sat on the warped counter, smoking a cigarette, staring off into space.

"What're you hoping is gonna happen," Ava heard herself saying.

"What do you mean?" Laura replied. She hiccupped, burped, and then laughed. Natalie joined her.

"Not you. Jackson," Ava managed. Even to herself, the words sounded ill-formed, both in her brain and on her tongue. "Why do you want them to be friends so badly."

Jackson didn't even justify this with an answer. He just smoked and stared.

"You hate Carlos that bad, huh?"

Ava wasn't even sure she said this last part out loud. She stared at the descending stairs so long that her vision began to blur.

She must have drifted off because the next thing she remembered was seeing Emily. She was on the ground floor again and while she didn't look pissed, the good humor that had been on her face when she descended into the basement with Brent, was now gone.

"So? You guys work things out?"

He wrapped his arm around Emily's shoulders. She slipped out from beneath his grasp.

"Hey, what happened?"

"Nothing. I just—I want to go." Even though she hadn't said her name, Ava knew that this was directed at her.

"Aw, you can't go," Jackson argued. "You can't go until you work everything out."

"There's nothing to work out. It's… I just want to go."

Now Jackson was staring at Ava. The look scared her.

Ava knew exactly what Jackson wanted and she was torn. The truth was she wanted her friend back. She wanted things to go back to normal as much as any of them. Maybe even more.

"Ava?"

Was it Jackson who'd called her name? Or was it Emily?

She was too drunk to tell.

Jackson released Emily.

"Here, let me hold that while you two talk."

Jackson took Emily's half-finished drink just as a dejected Brent made his way upstairs.

Emily walked over to her, and Ava leaned in close.

"If you want to go, let's go."

When Emily nodded, Ava took her outside.

"What happened?" she asked when they were alone again.

Emily wandered close to the tree line and started searching for the pregnancy test.

"I can't find it," the girl whined, ignoring Ava's question.

"Did you look at it before?"

"No. I just dropped it."

Ava couldn't find it either. And after a few minutes, they stopped looking. It was just too hard to focus.

"Hey, Em?"

"Yeah?"

"What really happened with you and Brent?"

Emily didn't answer right away. Ava was going to ask again when Em sighed.

"I told him I didn't love him. I tried to be nice, you know? I didn't want to hurt him."

"But that's not everything, right? I know you. I know something must have happened."

Em chewed her bottom lip.

"I didn't cheat on him. I didn't do anything with Carlos until after Brent and I had broken up."

"I know. I know he lied about that. But something must have—"

"He slapped me."

Ava recoiled as if she had just been struck.

"What?"

Em feigned searching for the pregnancy test again.

"Yeah. It was an accident. I mean, it wasn't an *accident*, but he didn't *mean* it."

"That's fucked up, Em!" Ava felt her blood pressure rise. "That's really fucked up. Why didn't you say anything?"

Em made a sound, and Ava knew that she was regretting her decision to tell her what Brent had done.

"I—I knew what it would do to him. If the wrong people found out... he might be expelled."

"So, what! He deserves to be expelled. That asshole. That *fucking* asshole." Ava took one unsteady step toward the front door of The Shack, which hung open.

"Hey, man, you got my pills?" she heard Brent ask Jackson. "My happy pills?"

Em grabbed Ava's arm.

"No. Let me talk to him. Let me try again. Please."

"Em. C'mon."

"Please, just give me one more try. *Please*. I know I can fix this, get things back to normal."

If Ava hadn't been so drunk, she would've fought. She would have told Em that it's not her job to fix something that someone else broke.

That piece of shit Brent didn't deserve her in his life. He didn't deserve anybody.

But, instead, Ava said two simple syllables: "Okay."

Em let go of her arm and offered Ava a sad smile.

"I'll be fine. And… thank you, Ava. Thank you."

***

This time when Ava awoke it was to the sound of a commotion. Yelling, hooting, and hollering.

She groaned. Even though it was still the middle of the night—it had to be—Ava had the beginnings of a hangover: pressure behind her eyes, a thickness to her tongue, and her throat was scratchy.

Someone was shaking her.

"You gotta see this," Laura said. She was giddy and her eyes were glassy. "Come on—come on, Ava, you gotta see this."

"*Nuh-uh.*"

Laura's hands went from her shoulders to her wrists and before Ava could so much as protest again, she was hauled to her feet. She stumbled, but now Natalia was there, offering her support. Both were laughing.

Then who was cheering?

The sounds were coming from downstairs.

Jackson? Yeah, that sounded about right. Who else? Probably Ethan because Theo was way too drunk to do much of anything.

The three of them walked to the stairs.

"What's happening?" Ava slurred. "What's going on?"

"Looks like they worked things out, after all," Laura said. Then she and Natalia exchanged a look and broke out into laughter.

"Who? What?"

By some miracle, they made it to the bottom of the stairs without falling. Ava almost went down, thinking that there was one additional step, but managed to grasp the back of a lawn chair to steady herself.

It was Ethan and Jackson. The latter was holding a cell phone, the harsh white light from the flash aimed toward the alcove.

Jackson was laughing, not that fake thing he did so often but a real, genuine laugh.

Ethan looked at her and snickered.

"Check this shit out. Looks like they did a lot more than kiss and make up."

He was pointing and Ava followed his finger.

It took a few moments for her brain to register what she was seeing and when it did, Ava felt sick to her stomach.

"What the fuck are you doin'? Fuck are you watchin'?"

Brent and Em were both naked. Em was on her back on the mattress of all things. They used to joke about that mattress, talk about how if any part of their body came in contact with it, from the tip of their toe to a finger, they would burn that part off.

But there she was, lying on it *naked*. And Brent was fucking her. Thrusting lazily in and out. Ava didn't even think either of them were making a sound. Or maybe they were, and the jeering just drowned it out.

It was surreal.

It was God awful.

What is happening?

Em had gone from telling her that she was still with Carlos, how she never did anything with him while Brent and she were together to… *this*?

Em?

Emily June Dawson?

Her friend was no prude, but she was no exhibitionist, far from it.

It made no sense.

"Make it stop," Ava moaned. Her stomach suddenly flipped, and she turned her head to one side just in time to avoid vomiting all over Ethan's back.

"Oh, Jesus, get her out of here," Jackson groaned. He stopped recording and Ava was on the move again, this time practically being carried up the stairs.

"Why were you watchin' that? Why?"

"I dunno, it was just a joke, I guess. It's funny," Laura replied defensively. "We're not going to send the video. I mean, Jackson will delete it."

Ava shut her eyes. Her world started to spin.

"Not funny. It's horrible… you know *what* Brent did to her?"

Ava stopped moving.

"What?" Jackson's voice. Ava didn't even know he was upstairs with them. "Fuck her? Yeah, Brent fucked her, so what? It wasn't the first time."

"No, not that. He—"

"Get her outta here." Jackson's voice was gruff. "Take her the fuck home so she can sleep it off. All of you, go home, *now*."

Chapter 48

IT WAS IMPOSSIBLE FOR AVA to continue. She was a mess, her entire face red and wet. Over the course of the story, she'd gone through an entire box of tissues.

Chase was disgusted, of course, but she wasn't sure what to make of what Ava had just told them. Sure, it would have been easy to say, "What you did was reprehensible. What you did is inexcusable. You are a horrible, horrible human being, and your actions, or lack thereof, contributed to your friend's murder."

But things are more complicated than that. Life didn't happen in retrospect. Life happened as a result of a series of small decisions, the total weight of which is often only determined in hindsight.

Yeah, Ava was a shitty friend. Yeah, once Ava found out about Brent assaulting her, she should have done everything in her power to get Emily as far away as possible. But Ava Morency was no Moral Machine, she was just a scared, complicated, and conflicted high school senior trying to find her place in the world.

Chase massaged the back of her right hand.

"Ava, what happened to Emily after you went back upstairs?"

Ava wiped her nose. Long tendrils of snot connected her to the saturated tissue.

"I don't... I don't know."

"Okay, what happened to you then? What happened after you got carried out of the basement?"

"We got into the car and left."

"Who drove?"

"I don't know—I *think* Laura?"

"What about the boys?"

Ava closed her eyes as she tried to remember.

"They left right after us. Jackson's car is so loud... I remember hearing it start up."

"And then what?"

"That's it. I just woke up the next day with a terrible hangover."

"What did you think happened to Emily? Did you know that you guys just left her there?" Chase asked.

Ava looked startled.

"No, of course, not. I don't know if I thought that she was in the car with us or if Jackson had taken her. I was too wasted. We stopped like three times for me to puke. But I didn't think we just left her there! I didn't think that something happened to her, either. You have to believe me on that."

Ava couldn't bring herself to say it, to say that she didn't think someone, one of *them*, was capable of murdering her.

Chase leaned forward, intent on pushing her in that very direction.

"Ava, I want you to think very carefully before you answer my next question, okay?"

Ava nodded.

"Are you sure that the last time you saw Emily she was still alive?"

Despite Chase's suggestion, Ava answered instantly.

"Yes, she was alive! Em was definitely alive. I'm sure of it. Oh, God, I should have done something! I should have called someone…"

Chase was tempted to reach out and touch the distraught girl then. If she was lucky, she might see something to corroborate Ava's story. But then she would have to explain her actions to Tate. Not to mention that this likely wouldn't go over well with the lawyer who was uncharacteristically quiet.

"It's okay—Ava, it's okay. According to your story, you guys left right away and so did Jackson. That means, in all likelihood, Emily was left behind in The Shack, but she was still alive. Did someone go back? Did someone stay with her?"

"I don't know. I *hate* that I don't know. Please... I just—"

"Ava, think."

Ava looked skyward.

"I mean, we only had two cars, Laura's and Jackson's. Em must have taken a cab or something or walked from town because her car wasn't there. I don't know if someone went back later or what, but I don't think anyone stayed at The Shack. Otherwise, Laura or Ethan or someone would have said something, you know? Especially after the news came out about... about what happened to her."

"Something didn't *happen* to her, Ava. Emily was murdered. Someone killed her." Chase was aware that she was being harsh, but that's what she thought the girl needed right now. A little tough love. "She didn't strangle herself. So, who was it? Was it Jackson? Did Jackson kill her?"

Ava held her head in her hands.

"I don't know, I really don't. Jackson's an asshole, but could he kill someone? That's... crazy."

"What about Brent?"

Ava's expression suggested that she thought this suggestion was certifiable.

"No! Brent loved Emily. Yeah, he was pissed at her for leaving him, for going with Carlos, but he wouldn't hurt her."

"He wouldn't slap her?"

Ava started to bawl again.

"I'm so fucking stupid," she chastised herself. Ava repeatedly smashed her palm into her forehead until her lawyer made her stop.

"We already know that Brent hit Em and we also know that he raped her—"

Ava suddenly glared at her. Maybe the blows to the head had shaken something free. An anger that had been buried deep.

"Why do you keep saying that? Why do you keep saying that Brent raped Em?"

Chase was confused by these questions. Sure, Ava had been drunk when she'd seen the display live, but she'd since watched the video. It was clear to everyone that Em was out of it.

"What do you mean?"

"You keep saying Brent raped her, but they were just having sex. It looked consensual. I mean, Em wasn't complaining or begging him to stop. Nothing like that."

"Because," Chase said slowly, "Em had a date rape drug in her system." She kept the discovery that Brent had Rohypnol in him as well to herself. No point in confusing the narrative any further.

"What?"

Tate, who had been incredibly silent for the past half hour, which was unusual, especially for him, gave Chase a break and finally spoke up.

"You said you were making Emily's drinks all night, making virgin drinks because she might have been pregnant, is that right?"

Ava nodded and wiped her face again. The tissue was falling apart it was so used. Chase wanted to ask for another box, but Ava was teetering on the edge of a complete breakdown, and they needed to acquire as much information about Saturday night as possible before she toppled over.

"Then how did the drug get in her system?"

"I don't know. I was the only one—" Ava stopped mid-sentence and stared at Tate. She looked horrified.

"Ava?"

Still nothing.

"Ava?" Tate prodded again.

"When Em came upstairs and I went outside with her, she handed her drink to Jackson."

"To Jackson? You sure?"

"Yes. I'm sure. Do you think—do you think he put something in it?"

I'm almost positive that he put Rohypnol in her drink, Chase thought.

But what she said was, "Maybe. It's possible that someone slipped something into her beverage."

"Let's get back to what *you* think happened to Emily," Tate intervened. Chase thought he was pushing a little hard on this, but he had an agenda. Another *secret* agenda.

She let him roll with it.

"Do you think that if Emily told Brent that night that she wanted to just be friends, that she wouldn't leave Carlos for him, he'd be pissed?"

Ava offered some facsimile of a nod.

"Pissed enough to hit her again?"

"Agent Abernathy, what is the point of this speculation?" Ava's lawyer asked. Chase had sneaked a few looks at the man during Ava's story; Mr. Dawson had been as enthralled as they were. "My client has already told you that when she left The Shack, Emily was still alive. She has no idea what happened to her."

"We're just trying to get a better understanding of the players involved here. I just want to know her opinion."

The lawyer didn't look pleased, but he didn't stop the line of questioning when Tate continued.

"Would Brent be upset if that happened?"

"Yeah, he'd be pissed. But pissed enough to really hurt her? No way."

"So, you don't think that Brent could have wrapped his hands around Emily's throat and choked her until she stopped breathing?"

Even Chase found this in poor taste and reached for her partner's leg beneath the table.

Tate shuffled out of reach.

"Agent Abernathy—"

"No!" Ava shook her head back and forth violently, sending strands of her thin black hair whipping about her head. "No, he wouldn't. Not Brent."

"Because he loved her, right?"

What are you doing, Tate? Push any harder and we're going to lose her.

"Yes!" Ava was out of breath. "Yes, that's why!"

"Well, you know what they say: if I can't have you, nobody can."

Ava broke down again, and, as Chase suspected, her lawyer had reached the end of his patience. He rocketed to his feet, the chair screeching across the hard ground behind him.

"That's it, this is over. I'm shutting this down—it's uncalled for. Pure harassment. Is this what you get off on, Agent Abernathy? Torturing high school girls?"

Tate stood nearly as quickly as the lawyer had.

"*I* don't get off on torturing high school girls," he stated. "But Brent Dawson certainly does."

"Tate?" Chase was trying to get his attention, but her partner's eyes were laser-focused on Ava.

"You want to know how I know that?" He didn't wait for a reply. "Because Brent Matthews just came out of his coma. He just woke up and the first thing he did was admit to raping and killing Emily Dawson."

Chapter 49

THE LAWYER FINALLY OFFICIALLY SHUT the interview down. This was fine to Chase because she was desperate to have a talk with Tate. The problem was that Sheriff Hal Grimes intercepted them in the hallway.

"Sorry about that," Tate said quickly, trying to pull Chase away from the sheriff, but not having much luck. "Apparently, like I said in there, the doc titrated down Brent's meds and he came out of his coma and admitted to everything." Like when Tate had said this moments ago, Chase had a hard time believing it. "Deputy Jardine was there when he said it."

Out of habit, Chase was tempted to ask *which* Jardine, but decided that didn't matter.

What mattered was the confession. What mattered was that it didn't make any sense.

Over the past few days, Chase was aligning the facts of the case in her mind. The break-up, the outcast boyfriend, the sheriff's degenerate son with a vendetta, and the reunion at The Shack.

The Rohypnol.

The rape.

The murder.

Occam's Razor suggested that Brent was Emily's killer. He had motive, means, and opportunity. Maybe he had Jackson's help or maybe he just stayed down in the basement after everyone got sick of being voyeurs. And then, when the rape was over, Brent choked her.

It was a terribly conceived plan, but Ava had told them that they were all drunk. Maybe, like Ava, Brent had just woken up with a hangover and had either forgotten about what happened or passed it off as a drunken nightmare.

To try and cover his tracks he quickly swallowed Rohypnol.

Except, that part, at least on the surface, didn't jive with the crime of passion and opportunity theory. That showed forethought, or at least, post-thought.

Chase scratched the back of her head.

"Why now? Why did Brent admit to killing Em now?"

It was a rhetorical question if there ever had been one, but Sheriff Grimes couldn't help himself.

"Guilt, probably. He knew after the video got out that things were closing in."

A reasonable assumption if the timeline made sense, which it didn't. Brent had been assaulted before the video was sent out.

Tate was used to these long periods of silence as Chase worked things out in her head, but Grimes wasn't. Somewhere far away she heard the sheriff tell Tate that they were going to cut Ava loose. Tate countered by saying that both Mendoza brothers should also be freed, and Grimes almost giddily informed him that Carlos had already been processed and released but Daniel was being held on an outstanding warrant.

It was as if the sheriff was just so happy to get a confession, so happy to have this clusterfuck of a case off his desk, that he was offering nearly everyone in the entire County clemency.

Chase banked this information but would save processing it for later.

She was still hung up on certain facts.

If Brent killed Emily as he claimed, why did he go back to The Shack on Monday? Carlos being there made sense; he was probably worried sick about Em when she didn't answer his calls, he followed Brent, the angry ex-boyfriend.

Think, Chase, think.

Something that Grimes said suddenly popped into her head from when they'd wanted to look at Brent's cell.

...you know teens and their phones.

That was it.

The night that Brent had raped Emily, he'd dropped his phone. That's why he went back. Carlos, who followed him there, must have seen Em's body and lost it. He attacked Brent. But who attacked Brent the second time? Carlos was in jail as was Daniel.

Tate suddenly stepped in front of her, and Chase blinked the thoughts away.

"They're cutting Ava loose." He didn't seem happy about it, but Chase knew that this was inevitable.

Her threat about charging Ava with rape after Brent's confession would never hold up in court.

The interview room door opened. Ava came out first, her red eyes down. The lawyer followed.

"Ava, I just have one more question for you," Chase said, blocking their way.

"My client has said enough."

Chase ignored him.

"Ava, what happened to Brent? Who assaulted him? Who put him in the hospital?"

Ava looked up and said a single word: "Jackson."

"That's enough," Sheriff Grimes said, glaring not at Ava, but at the lawyer who all of a sudden seemed skittish. "Get her out of here."

"I'm sorry," the lawyer apologized, "she's not feeling right."

When they were gone, it was Grimes who had a hard time meeting their gaze.

"We should talk with him," Tate suggested. "Just to clear some things up, you know? Then he'll be set free." It was an order framed as a question and they all knew it. "Just a quick chat with Jackson. Brent already confessed so... you can sit in if you want."

"You bet I want." Sheriff Grimes adjusted his belt. "Five minutes, that's all. Then he's going free."

"Sure."

Chase followed the sheriff and her partner to holding cell three. Then she remembered Stitts calling her during Ava's interview and decided to take out her phone.

She had eighteen missed calls.

What the hell?

"You coming?" Tate asked, seeing the expression on her face.

Chase wanted to interview Jackson, put the screws to the prick, but eighteen calls?

"You go ahead. I have to make a call."

Tate eyed her suspiciously, his mind meeting her at the same junction: the kids.

"Everything alright?"

"Yeah, I think so."

Tate nodded and the two men entered the cell while Chase backed away and made a call.

When Stitts answered he was out of breath, as if he had just gone for a run even though she knew that this was impossible with his bummed leg.

"Chase? Where have you been? I've been trying to reach you for an hour!"

No jokes this time.

"I was in an interview. What's wrong??"

"Chase... are you sitting down? You're going to want to sit down for this."

Chase wasn't a fan of the drama.

"No, I'm not sitting down, just fucking tell me."

But a moment later, Chase wished she'd heeded her ex-partner's advice.

"I found more videos from The Shack, Chase. Not just of Emily. And not just of rape."

Chapter 50

IT WAS HARD FOR TATE not to smile when he saw Jackson's swollen face. And then he thought, *Wow, I might be turning into a pussy.* The man had two black eyes and a broken nose, but Jackson's injuries weren't nearly as bad as he'd originally thought. He definitely hadn't come close to killing the man.

"What the fuck is he doing here?" Jackson demanded. He pushed back from the table and started to stand.

"Sit down," Sheriff Grimes ordered. "Sit down and listen."

Jackson was practically smoking he was so incensed by Tate's presence, but he listened to his daddy.

Everyone in the room knew who had orchestrated Jackson's beating—it was one of the few beatings that wasn't an actual mystery—but nobody could do a thing about it. It was a strange and yet undeniably pleasant experience for Tate, and he thought this must be what perpetrators who got away with serious crimes feel. And he knew that this feeling, this dopamine rush, could be addictive.

"I just have a few questions to ask, then you can be on your way." Tate wasn't sure what the best approach with Jackson would be just yet, but he knew that strong-arming this man would only result in another physical altercation.

And he was too tired to beat the kid's ass again.

Jackson sneered but it didn't have the desired effect; the expression was nearly comical with his swollen lips.

"Mr. Grimes, I believe we've met before, but in case you don't remember, my name is Special Agent Tate Abernathy with the FBI. I'm with the CVU—the Children's Victims Unit. We investigate violent crimes against young people."

"And?" Jackson snapped impatiently.

"And as you are aware, Emily Dawson, a senior at Tenbury Academy was murdered three nights ago." No reply this time. "Prior to her murder, Emily was raped by Brent Matthews."

Tate decided that being upfront and direct was the best approach for Jackson Grimes. Obscure the truth with flowery language and men like him, men who had been in the system or around it their entire lives, were likely to think they were being coerced or confused into admitting something.

"No? Nothing? You have nothing to say?" Tate pressed. Beside him, Sheriff Grimes shifted in his chair.

"Okay, you don't have to say anything. I bet your daddy has reminded you of that fact countless times during your misspent youth. But the thing I don't get is I tell you that one of your friends was raped and murdered by another of your friends. And you just sit there, arms crossed, face all puffy—oops, sorry—with no reaction. None at all."

Tate placed his elbows on the metal table between himself and Jackson.

"Brent put his hands around Emily's thin neck and squeezed. Squeezed until she stopped breathing, until her heart stopped beating."

Was that a flicker of emotion?

Maybe.

"Tate, if you—"

Tate interrupted the sheriff.

"You don't even ask how I know this? It's okay, I'll tell you. Brent confessed. He confessed to killing Emily." Something other than hatred flashed in Jackson's eyes, encouraging Tate to dig deeper. "I just have one question for you: how did you manage to drug both Emily and Brent? Was it as simple as slipping something into their drinks?"

"That's enough!" Grimes protested. He reached for Tate's shoulder, but Tate turned and held up a cautionary finger.

"I didn't drug nobody."

That was a lie.

"Just like you didn't plant the Rohypnol on Daniel Mendoza?"

"I didn't fuckin' do that. What are you talking about?"

"Right, sure—just like Brent didn't kill Emily?"

Jackson sucked in his bottom lip and leaned back in his chair.

"Agent Abernathy, we're done here."

Tate glared at Jackson. Oh, how he'd like another chance to beat some sense into this boy. Clearly, one ass-whooping wasn't enough.

But he'd already gotten what he'd wanted out of him.

"Fine. I'm done here, anyway. Thanks for your help, Jackson."

Tate got up and walked to the door. With his back turned he finally let the grin he'd been holding back loose.

Jackson was a simple kid who was easier to read than a James Patterson novel.

He'd denied two things: drugging Emily and Brent and framing Daniel.

He'd done them both.

He'd remained silent for one: Brent killing Emily.

If nothing else, Jackson did not believe that Brent was capable of murder.

And, for the record, neither did Tate Abernathy.

Chapter 51

CARLOS MENDOZA WAS IN A haze. He'd been in a haze ever since he'd found Brent Matthews in the basement of The Shack and attacked him. He vaguely recalled being arrested, printed, and then thrown in a holding cell.

But all of this, including the interviews with the Hawkesbury Sheriff's Department and the FBI, was covered in a greasy film, a veneer of unreality.

The only thing that had any degree of clarity was what the deputy had told him when he was released.

Brent Matthews had confessed to murdering Emily.

Carlos knew it. He knew it had been Brent all along.

But this wasn't what broke him.

It was the other thing the deputy had told him: that Em had been pregnant with his child.

His *fucking* baby.

Carlos had been looking forward to going to Penn with Emily. He'd been excited about getting out of this shit town, a place that never accepted him, a place that had only made things difficult for him and his brother.

And he'd worked his ass off to get into Penn, which was no easy task for someone with money. But for someone like him? Someone who needed a full-ride scholarship just to afford to go?

Next to impossible. And yet, he'd managed to beat all odds and do it.

But none of that mattered. Not since becoming involved with Emily.

Tenbury Academy wasn't overly large; he'd known who she was for years. It wasn't until they'd spent some time together prepping for the SAT that he really got to know her, however.

There was no spark, no lightning bolt, cupid's arrow, or anything like that. But there was something between them. Something strong, something impossible to ignore.

Twice they'd nearly become physical, but Emily had resisted, telling him that she was still in a relationship with Brent. It was the classic forbidden love story and Carlos expected it to end in heartbreak for him. But they just kept getting closer. It was almost as if not being able to so much as touch made what they had even more powerful.

And then Emily did it. She'd been talking about it for at least a week, but Carlos had thought it was just that: talk. It was right after they'd both found out that they'd gotten into Penn. Then Emily had showed up at his house one night, her eyes wet, her face red.

And that was it.

They were just meant to be together. Penn or not, it didn't matter.

Brent Matthews, that jealous, conniving bitch had taken everything from him.

Then there was the video. If the fact that his unborn child had been killed along with Emily hadn't pushed Carlos over the edge, the video had.

He found it on his phone, an anonymous text message.

And it was horrific.

Brent raping Emily.

Carlos wiped the tears from his cheeks as the Uber arrived at the hospital.

"Right here is good."

"You sure you're okay, buddy?"

"Fine."

Carlos got out.

He knew what he was going to do, he just didn't know how.

Loud voices directed him to Brent's hospital room. He recognized Robert Matthews, Brent's father, and he also recognized the deputy as the man who had arrested him: one of the Jardine brothers.

Carlos made himself as small as possible, hoping not to draw attention to himself. The deputy and the principal were in such a heated argument that he wasn't sure that they'd notice him even if he was doing cartwheels while singing Kumbaya. Principal Matthews was begging the deputy to release his son, claiming his innocence. The deputy wasn't budging.

Carlos was within three feet of Brent's room when he thought he saw the deputy notice him in his periphery.

He froze.

This is it. I squandered my chance.

But then Robert Matthews shouted, "Are you even listening to me? You have to let him go!"

Carlos entered the hospital room and the swinging door closed silently behind him.

Brent Matthews was sleeping. His face was bruised and battered and there were bandages wrapped around his head. But Carlos felt no pity for this man.

There was a single chair in the room and on this chair lay a small, ornamental wool pillow. Carlos walked over and picked it up. It felt rough against his skin and for some reason, he liked that.

Carlos returned to Brent and stared down at his puffy face. Gripping either side of the pillow, he started to lower it.

And then he stopped.

This wasn't right. He *knew* this wasn't right.

Deep down, he knew it was very, very wrong.

Carlos relaxed his hold on the pillow and leaned close to Brent's ear.

"Wake up," he whispered. "Wake up."

Brent's eyelids flickered, and his eyes opened slowly.

Carlos expected Brent to scream when he shed the last vestiges of sleep and realized who was hovering over him.

But Brent did nothing even after he became lucid. When Carlos started to lower the pillow again, there was no panic in Brent.

He did, however, speak. Just two words.

Two simple words: "I'm sorry."

"So am I."

Carlos pressed the rough fabric down on Brent's face. The boy's narrow chest began to heave, and his hands and arms flailed. But at no point was there a conscious effort to get Carlos to stop.

Machines beeped wildly and people came running. They tried to tear Carlos off Brent, but he was a man possessed. The entire fire department could have arrived with the jaws of life, and they wouldn't have been able to separate him from the man who killed his girlfriend and child.

It was only after hearing the long monotone flatline beep and Brent stopped moving did Carlos finally release the pillow.

Someone twisted and wrenched him to the ground and his face was forced into the hard epoxy floor.

Carlos closed his eyes.

"I'm sorry, too. I love you, Em."

Chapter 52

"WHAT THE ACTUAL FUCK?"

At first blush, the video that Stitts had sent to Chase via an encrypted FBI channel was very similar to the one that she'd already seen, the one that everybody in Tenbury Academy had seen.

But there were several glaring differences.

The first was that Brent wasn't in the shot. Emily was still there lying on the filthy mattress, head back, eyes closed, legs spread. It was unclear whether she was alive or dead at this point, but there was no bruising or markings on her throat. Chase moved the phone as close to her face as she could without her eyes blurring.

It did indeed appear as if Emily's chest was slowly rising and falling.

The camera jostled as someone came into the frame. Dressed all in black and wearing a leather balaclava with two holes for the eyes and one for the mouth, it was undeniably a man. He was of average height, perhaps on the slimmer side, but there were no distinguishing features to speak of. He was dressed in generic black clothing.

He moved to the center of the frame and approached Emily's unconscious body.

Chase was horrified when he reached down and brushed the back of one gloved hand, black like his outfit, against her cheek. Emily stirred, confirming that she was indeed alive. And then the man lowered his hand from her face to her bare breast, giving it a squeeze before tweaking the nipple.

Chase felt ill, a feeling that continued to grow in intensity when he moved from her breast to her legs, spreading her wide.

When the man unzipped his pants, Chase closed her eyes.

Approximately two minutes later, he was done, and Emily was dead, strangled to death.

The man left the shot then reappeared moments later. The whole in the mask was just large enough to see a hint of a smile on his face before the camera zoomed in on Emily's face.

The young girl was indistinguishable from how Chase remembered her from the morgue. Eyes open, broken blood vessels on the surrounding skin. Tongue hanging loosely out of her mouth, unnatural and thick. Fresh bruising around her throat.

Chase felt like vomiting.

She knew that she had to watch the video again, all of it this time, and that she had to pay close attention to every single detail. If there was even a hint of an identifiable feature that might help her figure out who this monster was, Chase would find it. But not here, not in the hallway of the Hawkesbury Sheriff's Department.

Her phone rang and she somehow managed to answer.

"Yeah?" she said dryly.

"I'm sorry, Chase. I know it was brutal," Stitts said.

Chase squeezed her eyes closed. The doc had said that Em's body had been flooded with Rohypnol. Chase just hoped it was enough that Emily didn't feel anything or even realize what had been going on.

"Where did you find it?"

"I sent the video out to one of the tech guys who managed to recover the audio and he put it through a bunch of tracing programs, looking for similar videos and images, and he got a hit. It was hidden deep on the dark web. That's what I sent you."

"On the dark web?"

"Yeah. It was uploaded yesterday. Apparently, we have someone undercover, posing as one of these fucking freaks who gets off on snuff films. It was behind a paywall, but he managed to obtain a copy."

Chase still wasn't following.

"Stitts, you gotta spell this out for me, I'm too tired."

"Sorry." There was a dryness to the man's voice, indicating that either he too was tired, or more likely, he was disturbed by what he'd seen. Both she and Stitts had witnessed horrible atrocities committed by humans on other humans but some just hit you differently than others.

Some wore you down, and this was one of those.

"I sent the video in to get the audio recovered. While he was doing that, another tech guy used software that searches out similarities between videos across the web and on our local server. The mattress was identified as appearing in several videos on a prominent dark web ring that sells these things for a hefty price. Apparently, about six months ago, someone forgot to hide their IP address when downloading one of these snuff films. The FBI traced it, found out who he was, arrested him, and now poses online as this guy. Anyway, it looks like whoever took this video is selling it on the dark web."

Chase allowed this information to marinate.

Working with Stu and spending time in Cerberus had taught her more than she ever wanted to know about what was possible using computers and the Internet. But no matter how deranged and twisted that experience had been, no matter how real it felt, it was all fake.

This—Emily Dawson's murder—was real.

"I'm guessing there's no way to trace who posted the video?"

"No, these guys aren't amateurs. The guy that the FBI arrested was a rich accountant. Just a user, not a producer."

"So, we just—wait, Stitts, did you say that there was more than one hit on the mattress? Did I hear that correctly?"

A long pause.

"Yeah, there are more. Two more." Now, Stitts' voice wasn't just dry, it was desiccated.

Chase felt bile rise in her throat.

"What are you saying, Stitts?"

"I'm saying that two other girls were raped and murdered on that same mattress, Chase. I don't think you're looking for a pissed-off high school boyfriend. I think you're looking for a serial rapist and murderer."

PART V – Filthy Secrets

Chapter 53

TATE KNEW SOMETHING WAS VERY wrong the second he stepped out of the interview room. The lack of color in Chase's face, which was nearly as pale as her hair, made his flesh ripple with goosebumps.

"Chase?"

She cocked her head to one side, indicating for him to follow her. Sheriff Grimes was saying something about letting Jackson go.

Jackson Grimes was a piece of work who deserved to be behind bars. Tate was convinced that he'd drugged both Emily and Brent and then coerced them into having sex with one another. He'd filmed the act and then sent it to everyone in the school as a twisted plot to fuck with Carlos Mendoza. In the process, Jackson had broken about a half dozen laws. The problem was proving what Tate knew to be true. Nobody had seen him slip either of them the drugs and now with Brent's confession, would anybody believe that Jackson was involved?

Probably not. Those who might be convinced would be discouraged from doing so by the sheriff.

"Let him go," Tate acquiesced. "Just tell him not to leave the county."

Grimes was already heading back into the cell.

"Hurry," Chase said, grabbing his arm, and pulling him away. They walked briskly until they were well out of earshot at the end of a long hallway.

"I don't think Jackson killed Emily," Tate said, preemptively, still wondering what was bothering Chase so much. "I don't think Jackson killed anyone. I'm pretty sure he's the one who drugged Emily and Brent and put them together to get back at Carlos, but he's no killer."

"I know he didn't do it." Chase's voice was husky. "Watch."

A simple directive encouraged by his partner shoving her cell phone in his face.

Every second of the video that was played made the muscles in Tate's neck tighten. When it was over, everything from his chin to his collarbone ached.

"Fuck." It was more a gasp than a curse.

"Stitts found it on the dark web. Someone was selling it."

"Selling it?"

Chase nodded and took her phone back.

"Yeah, but it gets worse."

Tate couldn't think of how. The video was one of the most disturbing things he'd ever seen.

"Emily Dawson wasn't the first. Two more girls were raped and murdered in The Shack on that very mattress."

And that was how.

"*What?*"

Another nod.

"The first was about a year and a half ago, the most recent, other than Emily, was eleven months. Stitts sent me both videos—like this one, they were also sold on the dark web."

Chase waved her finger over the screen and offered Tate the phone again. He declined. That was enough rape and murder for now.

"Just send it to me." Chase nodded and logged into the secure FBI channel on her phone. "What the fuck, Chase? How did we miss this? How did *I* miss this? One fucking murder in

Hawkesbury in the last eight years. That's all I found. Not three in a year and a half. *Fuck*."

Tate's nails made crescents in his palms.

"That's because they didn't happen in Hawkesbury. I mean, they did, but Stitts believes that they've identified one of the victims. Her name is Marianne Lupul and she's not from here; she's from Centennial Oaks. Her body was never found so, technically, she's a missing person with no link to Hawkesbury."

"Where the fuck is Centennial Oaks?"

"A town about an hour and a half from here."

"And she was killed in The Shack?"

"Same mattress, same dirt floor."

"Then why the fuck didn't the FBI say anything? We're running around here—"

"They didn't know. Until I sent them the video of Brent and Emily, they had no idea where these crimes were being committed. They didn't even know that they were taking place in the United States."

Tate threw his head back and sighed.

"Did this Marianne go to Tenbury?" He was still furious that he'd missed the connection, despite the mitigating factors. They'd wasted all this time interviewing kids who a year and a half ago had barely hit puberty. Was he supposed to believe that Brent at the ripe age of sixteen was a serial rapist and murderer?

"Not as far as I can tell, no."

"Well, what the fuck was she doing at The Shack, then? I thought it was only used by Tenbury Academy seniors, three fucking visits like the goddamn ghosts of Christmas."

"Me, too."

Chase appeared lost in thought. Or maybe the stress of the day and the horror of what they'd watched had knocked her into some sort of stupor. Tate didn't think so, given her resolve, but everyone had their limits. Maybe she was thinking about her sister, thinking about how Georgina had been systematically raped for decades after being indoctrinated by Brian Jalston and his twisted brother.

Maybe this hit too close to home.

Chase was the one who normally continued to push forward no matter what. Now, it was Tate's turn to fill that role.

"Stitts said that whoever made these videos was selling them on the dark web?"

"Yeah, said they were behind a very expensive paywall."

Three rapes and three murders. Tate could buy, however unlikely, that Brent was behind Emily's murder and that the similarities in location and situation with the other two victims were entirely coincidental. But to think that Jackson or Brent or the others had anything to do with these other deaths was ludicrous.

So, who were they looking for, then?

Whoever it was knew about The Shack, which narrowed it down to Tenbury alum or someone familiar with the school and their traditions—most likely, anyway. One of the motivations also had to be money, otherwise, the perpetrator would just keep the videos for their own personal viewing. Attending Tenbury was exorbitantly expensive.

A parent? A parent of a student?

Carlos' mother fit the bill, except she wasn't raping anybody.

Then who?

Sheriff Grimes turned the corner and when he saw them, he indicated that he was coming over.

Bingo.

A light bulb went off in Tate's head.

"Agents?" Sheriff Grimes said, waving his hand in their direction.

Tate ignored him and got close to Chase.

"How much do you think a County Sheriff makes a year?"

Chase looked at him as if he was insane.

"Chase? Sheriff Grimes? How much does he make?"

Grimes was only about thirty feet away now.

Chase shrugged.

"I don't know? Around forty? What are you getting at?"

Tate didn't answer. He didn't need to. His next question made things clear.

"What about a principal at a prestigious private school?"

"Eighty? Ninety at the highest end? But he probably gets a discount to send his son there."

"Yeah, but that's still a lot of money."

"Tate, you really don't think that the two of them could have anything to do with this, do you?"

Oh, yes, I very much do.

But Tate didn't have time to answer.

Sheriff Grimes came right up to them, and he looked extremely distressed.

"Look, I was just asking Jackson questions, all right? I know—"

"This isn't about Jackson," Grimes said in a tone that would have immediately grabbed Tate's attention if his expression hadn't already. "It's about Brent Matthews."

Tate saw the kid in a different light now. He saw Brent being overshadowed by his father dressed in a leather mask.

Had Robert convinced his son to confess to Emily's murder to save his own ass?

No, that was jumping too far.

"What about him?"

The sheriff looked as if he was in physical pain when he said, "Carlos Mendoza left here about thirty minutes ago and went straight to the hospital. Deputy Jardine just gave me a call; Carlos suffocated Brent Matthews with a pillow."

Chapter 54

AN HOUR AGO, CHASE WAS investigating the rape and murder of a high school student. Thirty minutes ago, they were searching for someone who had raped and killed at least three young girls and sold the videos on the dark web. Now, they were headed to the hospital to arrest a high school student who had suffocated one of his classmates. A classmate who, Chase was almost certain at this point, had mistakenly confessed to killing Emily Dawson.

What a fucking first case for the CVU.

"No." Chase wasn't even sure what she was in denial of—some, all, or any of what had happened over the course of just a few days.

This ambiguity didn't stop Sheriff Grimes from answering, however.

"Yeah, I guess Carlos saw the video and overheard that Brent confessed to killing Emily. Lost control."

That wasn't it. That wasn't enough. It was about the baby—it had to be about the baby. But how the fuck did Carlos find out about that?

Did Ava tell him?

No, that didn't make sense.

"What I want to know is how Carlos managed to walk into the hospital, walk right by one of your deputies and Brent's father, into Brent's room, and hold a pillow over his face without anybody saying or doing anything," Tate snapped. "How the *fuck* did this happen?"

For the first time since arriving in Hawkesbury County, Sheriff Grimes was at a loss for words. He didn't look angry or annoyed, he just looked confused.

Could he actually be behind this? Chase wondered. That's what Tate had suggested, albeit not explicitly.

Robert Matthews and Hal Grimes, were one or both of them murderers? The man in front of the camera was definitely not the sheriff, their bodies were completely different, but Robert was about the same size and build as the man in the mask.

Was all of this—all of this murder and rape—just a way for them to make enough money to send their kids to Tenbury Academy?

"Chase, you have your car here?" Tate asked. When she didn't answer, he posed the question again.

"Hmm? Yeah."

"You think you can head out to The Shack, see if there's anything we missed?"

Chase frowned.

What was Tate talking about? The place was an absolute mess. They'd long since concluded that there was no way to distinguish evidence from trash at The Shack.

"Why?" she asked bluntly.

"Because of the... video." Tate was clearly tempering his words, not wanting to give anything away to the sheriff.

Had Tate seen something on the video of Em being killed that she'd missed?

"I'll go with the sheriff to the hospital, speak with Carlos."

He stared at her until she grew uncomfortable.

This wasn't about evidence at The Shack, Chase realized. This was about Tate being nervous about her being around Sheriff Grimes or Principal Matthews because he thought they were killers.

Normally, this would have set Chase off. But she felt a little like she had when interviewing Ava the first time. This case was different. This case had affected her.

Back in the hotel room, Chase had read nearly everything Em had written in her Story Planner. She really had been a decent writer. Maybe, in time, she would develop into a great one.

But now the world would never know.

"Okay," Chase said, surprising even herself. "Just keep me updated. And be safe."

Tate, still holding her gaze, reached out and squeezed her shoulder.

"You, too."

***

The closer Chase made it to The Shack, the more she thought that maybe they had missed something. She was well aware that this might just be a compensatory mechanism, her mind trying to make what she was doing seem useful after acquiescing to Tate's well-meaning chauvinism.

But maybe not.

Stitts called just as Chase turned onto the dirt road leading to The Shack.

"Hey," she said, worried that the man had found even more videos.

"Hey, so I think I might have found something else. Marianne Lupul didn't go to Tenbury, but she applied and was rejected. As for the other victim, facial recognition has it at a 65% probability that she's a missing girl named Tanya Belk from Brookfield Hollow, about an hour from where you are. If it is her, then she also applied but was rejected from Tenbury."

Tate's theory suddenly held more weight. The principal would definitely know who applied and was rejected from the school. It wasn't a smoking gun, but it wasn't exculpatory, either.

"Chase? This help?"

Chase stopped in front of The Shack. Knowing what happened here gave it an even more ominous quality. This wasn't the Blair Witch house, it was Dahmer's apartment.

She shuddered.

"I think it does. Stitts, I need your help with something. In about half an hour, I want you to place a call, and there's something very specific I want you to say. Think you can do that for me?"

"Sure."

Chase explained what she wanted Stitts to say and then hung up.

Recalling Ava's story, she decided to search the exterior of The Shack first. To the right of the building was a series of trees, thin for the first five or so feet until they became much denser. Chase envisioned Ava standing in her exact spot, tapping her foot, urging her friend to hurry up and pee on the pregnancy stick.

What a whirlwind the last few hours of Emily's life must have been. Highly emotional because she was pregnant and optimistic at the prospect of getting her friends back. Did she think she could bring Carlos into the fold?

Probably.

Meeting Ava must have filled her with elation. Just like old times.

How quickly things turned.

Chase walked over to the first few trees and used her foot to gently disturb the dirt.

Nothing.

She scanned right and left and then stopped. There was something, something white, a nub, poking out of the ground.

Chase walked over to it and pulled a tissue out of her pocket. She squatted and picked it up.

It was a white and blue pregnancy test.

She blew dirt from the window, revealing two lines.

Chase was thinking about Emily never knowing for certain that she'd been pregnant, and wondering if this was a good or bad thing, when another car pulled up.

She lowered the test back down to the dirt and flicked the retention snap on her holster. Even when Chase saw that it was a Sheriff's Department vehicle, she kept her hand on the butt of her gun ready to draw.

But it wasn't Sheriff Grimes. Instead, Deputy Dean Jardine, the one with the mustache got out. Chase re-clipped her holster and waved. The deputy looked as surprised to see her as she did him.

"Agent Adams, what are you doing here?"

"I could ask you the same thing," Chase replied. "But instead, I want to ask you something else. I want to ask you about Sheriff Grimes."

Dean had told Tate that there was something rotten in Hawkesbury County. She wanted to know exactly how deep the infection went.

"Yeah, I think I can do that," Deputy Dean Jardine said. "What do you want to know about Hawkesbury's own Hal Grimes?"

Chapter 55

ROBERT MATTHEWS WAS ON HIS knees, wailing.

All in all, it was a pretty natural reaction for someone who had just lost his son.

But was it natural for a man who had killed three women?

Sheriff Grimes wasn't helping. He was so angry that, for a split second, Tate thought that he was going to physically assault Deputy Tim Jardine who looked bewildered and a little confused.

"How the fuck did you let Carlos in here? He murdered Brent while you were standing outside the *fucking* door?"

"We didn't see him," Jardine said as if this was an adequate excuse. "We were talking outside the room and—"

"You fucked up, Jardine. You *fucked* up."

Sheriff Grimes backed away from the deputy and Tate, convinced now that the temperature had simmered, turned his attention to Carlos Mendoza.

Carlos was an adult but with his head and his hands cuffed behind him, he looked like a little kid.

A little kid capable of murder.

Deputy Lane idiotically paraded Carlos right in front of Robert Matthews. Even in his extreme grief, the principal noticed the kid and jumped to his feet.

"You killed my boy!" Once again, Deputy Jardine was slow on the take and Tate got between them first. "You killed my fucking boy!"

"Easy, Robert, easy." Then to Deputy Lane, Tate said, "Get Carlos out of here."

Carlos had no reaction to Robert's anger. He didn't defend himself, although that would have been difficult with his hands cuffed behind his back. But he didn't try to get out of the way, either. Nor did he say anything. He simply accepted it.

"No, you take him. Jardine, you fucking take Carlos to the station," Sheriff Grimes ordered, clearly wanting the deputy out of his sight.

Lane gladly relinquished the prisoner but, knowing that Sheriff Grimes was liable to lash out to anyone close, followed Jardine down the hallway.

Robert collapsed again.

"He *murdered* my boy…"

A nurse tried to console Mr. Matthews and Tate backed away.

This place is fucked up, he thought.

"How did this happen?"

Tate looked at Sheriff Grimes, but the man hadn't been speaking to him, he'd been mumbling to himself.

Was this man really behind those videos?

He was absolutely defeated.

"Why didn't you want us here?" Tate asked, trying to get to the bottom of this.

"What do you mean?"

"I'm just saying," Tate gestured toward the two deputies who were nearing the entrance to the hospital. "Looks like you could use our help."

Sheriff Grimes' brow wrinkled.

"What do you mean?"

Are you being deliberately dense?

Tate decided to lay on his patented charm.

"Look, I overheard you and Deputy Jardine arguing when I first got here. And then my partner told me that her Deputy Jardine said that you were furious that he called in the FBI. I get it, you didn't want someone else mowing your lawn, right?"

You didn't want anyone to find out you were murdering young girls on film?

Sheriff Grimes grimaced.

"Is this a fucking game? A trick? What are you playing at, Tate?"

Tate took a cautious step backward.

"Look, I—"

"No, you fucking look." Grimes got in his face and Tate tensed. "First of all, *I* was the one who called you guys in, not Tweedledee or Tweedledum. *Me.* And we weren't arguing about your involvement. I was yelling at Jardine because he fucked up. The night that Emily was murdered, we got an anonymous call that there were cars out by The Shack making noise. He was dispatched and said he saw nothing. But, obviously, I—"

"Hold on a second. There was a call and Deputy Jardine went out there, but he didn't see anything? Why the fuck didn't you tell us about this earlier?"

Sheriff Grimes backed off.

"Do you know how hard it is to get deputies in Hawkesbury? It's next to impossible. I tell you he fucked up that bad and I have no choice but to fire him. I *have* to. And I just can't do that. Not after—"

"Hal, how long have the Jardine brothers been deputies in Hawkesbury County?" Tate interjected.

"I hired them about two years ago. Why?"

"Are they local?"

A sudden gasp and a sob drew their attention before Hal could answer. Both Tate and the sheriff looked at Robert Matthews. He was holding his cell phone in his hands but as they watched he began to shake so badly that it fell to the ground. He made no effort to pick it up.

"Robert?" the sheriff asked. The nurse was still by his side, and she tried to get him to tell her what was wrong.

Robert said nothing. He just got up and started to walk away. His gait was strange, uncoordinated.

"Robert?" Sheriff Grimes tried to grab him, but Tate got in his way.

"Let him go."

"But—"

"Just let him go. Hal, I need to know if the Jardines are from Hawkesbury. Did they attend Tenbury Academy?"

"Yeah, yeah, they did. What's going on, Agent Abernathy?"

Tate felt his world closing in on him.

They had it wrong. This whole time, they had it *all* wrong.

"Fuck, fuck, fuck, fuck."

He recalled the bizarre expression on Deputy Jardine's face when Tate had said, 'Thank goodness you called me in.' At the time, he'd thought this was because Dean felt uncomfortable about going behind his boss' back. But that wasn't it. It was because he hadn't made that call.

Sheriff Grimes had.

"Hal, tell me something. Did you speak to Mrs. Dawson? Did you tell Mrs. Dawson not to talk to the FBI?"

"Tate, I don't know—"

"Just fucking tell me!"

"No—no, why would I do that?"

Another assumption foiled.

What had Jennifer Dawson said? Something along the lines of, "The Sheriff's Department told us that Carlos murdered Emily."

The *Sheriff's Department*, not the *sheriff*. And why would Deputy Jardine do that?

Tate swallowed hard.

Because they wanted the FBI gone.

And Carlos... how did Carlos find out that Emily was pregnant with his baby, which probably put him over the top?

There was only one way.

Tate had told Chase when Deputy Dean Jardine was standing right fucking next to them.

"Sheriff, who released Carlos this afternoon?"

"Tim."

Of course. And he just happened to let Brent's confession and the pregnancy slip.

With the surfacing of the new video, it was only a matter of time before the legitimacy of Brent's confession was called into question. And what better way to make sure it couldn't be stress tested than if Brent was dead?

And what do you know, Dean Jardine, Tim's brother, just happened to be looking the other way when Carlos showed up with ill intent.

"Goddamn it," Tate cursed.

He pulled out his cell phone and loaded the video that Stitts had sent Chase. It was a risk showing it to Sheriff Grimes, but he was desperate now.

"Just watch this, okay?"

He started the video.

"What the fuck?"

"Just watch!"

Sheriff Grimes cringed and groaned but to his credit, he managed to get through it.

"That's horrible. When—"

"*Listen.* When the man in the mask goes behind the camera and returns, is it the same person?"

"I don't know what you mean. Where did you get this—"

"Focus," Tate shouted in the sheriff's face. "When the man leaves the shot and returns, does it look like the same man?"

Grimes cleared his throat.

"Show it again."

Tate did and the sheriff immediately shook his head.

"It's a different person. Look, you see that? When the guy comes out it looks like he has a thin mustache there, in the mouth hole. He doesn't have that at the beginning."

And that was exactly what Tate had seen but hadn't registered.

Tate pocketed his phone and broke into a run. Like when Robert had strangely wandered off, Hal yelled after him, but he wasn't stopping.

A deputy with his back to him was loading Carlos into a car.

Tate pulled his gun.

"Deputy Jardine?" the man turned. It was Deputy Lane. "What the fuck happened to Deputy Jardine?"

The man made a guppy-like face.

"I—I don't know, he told me to take Carlos in."

Tate clenched his jaw and scanned the parking lot. There was only one other Sheriff's Department vehicle, and he recognized it as the one that Grimes drove.

"Fuck!"

"What's going on?"

Tate whipped around. He'd forgotten that his gun was still out, and Sheriff Grimes ducked.

"Easy!"

Tate put the gun away.

"Where's Deputy Jardine?" he demanded.

The sheriff looked over Tate's shoulder, saw Carlos and Deputy Lane, then glanced back, confused.

"I don't know. You were there, I told him to take Carlos in."

"Not him, the *other* Deputy Jardine. Where is he now?"

"I don't—"

"Don't fucking tell you don't know! Where is the other Jardine?"

"I think—I think he said he was going to The Shack."

Something inside Tate broke.

Chapter 56

"**WHAT DO YOU THINK OF** Sheriff Grimes?"

"Well, Chase, I think that Hal is a fucking pussy. He thinks he owns this town, but he doesn't own shit. Never did. He has no fucking idea what goes on right under his nose."

Chase had asked for honesty, but this was more candid than expected.

"Really?"

Deputy Dean Jardine laughed.

"Oh, really? Did you know that he likes to keep tabs on the girls who apply to Tenbury but don't get in?" Chase's eyes widened, remembering what Stitts had told her about Marianne Lupul and Tanya Belk. "Yep. I wonder what he likes to do with them?"

Chase had a pretty good idea of what Sheriff Grimes liked to do with those girls.

"What about Robert Matthews?"

The deputy laughed again.

"What about him?"

"I mean, are he and the sheriff close? Robert seems to have something that he holds over Grimes."

Deputy Jardine closed his eyes and started to chuckle like he was remembering an old joke.

"Robert, Robert, Robert. He's a piece of shit, too. Stealing money from the school just to give it back in tuition for Brent. Kinda fucked up if you ask me. All seems for naught now, don't it?"

Chase made a face.

"Robert was stealing from the school? Wait—hold on."

Her phone was ringing, and she saw that it was Tate.

"You're not going to believe this," Chase said, putting the phone on speaker. "But Deputy—"

"It's Jardine!" Tate shouted. "Chase, it's not the sheriff, it's the Jardine brothers!"

"Wha—"

Something struck her in the base of her skull and Chase dropped. The phone flew from her hand and landed face up in the dirt not all that far from Emily's Dawson's positive pregnancy test.

***

"Chase?" Tate screamed. "Chase, did you hear me? It's not the sheriff, it's Deputy Jardine! Chase? *Chase?!*"

Take shouted his partner's name into the phone several more times before finally giving up.

Sheriff Grimes grabbed him by the arm. If he was upset that Tate thought he was capable of such heinous crimes, it didn't show. Even more impressive was that even though Hal only had half the information that the FBI was in possession of, he seemed to have come to the same conclusion Tate had.

Tate was pulled toward the sheriff's car and got into the passenger seat. Grimes started it up and flicked on the lights.

Then he gunned it.

But no matter how fast they drove it wouldn't be fast enough. The Shack was on the outskirts of town and Deputy Dean Jardine was there with Chase already.

It had taken the twins less than two minutes to rape and kill Emily Dawson on camera. About the same for Marianne and Tanya.

And as much as Tate could tell himself that the call had cut out because reception was poor, he knew this wasn't the case.

"You have anyone close to The Shack? Someone you trust?"

"Nobody," Sheriff Grimes said. "The only other deputy we got is Barill but he's off today. Lives in the west end."

"Fuck!"

Grimes drove even faster.

"Is there anybody you can call? *Anybody*?" Tate was desperate.

"No. I don't—"

A car slowed unexpectedly in front of them, and the sheriff yanked the wheel to one side so hard that the car hovered on two wheels for a whole second before slamming back to the ground.

"There's nobody. I can't—" Grimes stopped. "Wait, oh fuck, there's someone I can call. You're not going to like it, but he's close and—"

"I don't give a fuck who it is!" Tate yelled. "If you trust them, get them out there, get them out there, and save my partner!"

Save my partner before Deputy Jardine makes another snuff film this time featuring Chase Adams.

Chapter 57

"THE FIRST TIME WE RAPED someone on this very mattress, my brother and I were still in the Academy." Dean Jardine adjusted the phone mounted on the tripod as he spoke. "We were seniors, and it was only our second time coming here—after prom. Everybody was wasted and I mean *everybody*. Most people had already hopped in a cab and left but not me. Remember when I said everyone was wasted? Yeah, count me among that list. I passed the fuck out. Must have had maybe fifteen beers, probably more. Anyway, I was asleep on the floor upstairs when I felt something digging into my side. It was Tim kickin' me in the ribs."

Dean walked around to the back of the phone and adjusted the line of sight. Chase tried to shout something, but the filthy gag across her mouth swallowed all consonants.

"'Come on, get your ass up,' he said. I didn't want to get up. I was happy where I was, drunk as a skunk. I was also kind of pissed. To be honest with you, I thought I was going to fuck my prom date. Maggie Bartok… she had these big fucking tits." He stepped out from behind the phone and held his hands in front of his chest. "I'm talking big ass milkers. But she got drunk and puked all over herself. Had to go home early. Anyway, Tim tells me again to get my ass up, but I decline his gracious offer. So, he pulls me up. 'Where the fuck are we going?' but he doesn't tell me." Dean chuckled. "That's Tim for ya. He takes me downstairs and there's this one guy, I think his name was Brian, I don't know, and he's actually lying face down in the dirt. I shit you not. I laugh, thinking that this is what Tim wanted to show me, but he tells me to shut the fuck up and takes me over here, where you are now. And then, very slowly like a magician with his big reveal," the deputy is miming this now and Chase realizes for the first time that he is no longer wearing his uniform—he's dressed all in black and there's something on his head. Something balled up like a wool hat folded on itself.

Chase knows it's the mask.

"*Yank!* He pulls back the curtain and I see her: Stephanie Millward. Now, let me set the stage for you, Chase."

Again, Chase tried to yell, but the sound was pathetically weak and unintelligible. Her hands were bound in front of her with zip ties and in order to get up, she had to roll. But as soon as she started to move, Dean rushed over and planted a boot on her shoulder, holding her painfully in place.

"You ain't going anywhere. Just fucking listen. None of you bitches ever wanna fucking listen. So, as I was saying, her name was Stephanie Millward. She's not the hottest girl in school, but close, you know? Like, let's say that she hangs out with the hot girls, and she's cute but just a notch or two below the others in terms of hotness. But here's the thing: she had the sweetest body you ever saw in your entire life. Not huge tits like Maggie, but nice firm ones, and a fucking ass—oh baby, you could bounce quarters off that ass. And here she is, lying on the mattress completely passed out. Her hand is above her head and she's wearing this cute skirt—it's prom, right? And this is her second outfit. The top two buttons of her shirt are undone and she's not wearing a bra—never needed one. I can see the outline of one pink nipple and I'm not going to lie to you. Drunk or not, I was rock hard in seconds."

Dean took his foot off Chase's shoulder and started to pace. He also started to not subtly rub his crotch through his black jeans.

"Now, I was happy just cranking one out right there, but I had my brother beside me, which is a bit weird. Tim, he gets this idea, right? He gets down on his knees and he pulls Stephanie's shirt back just a little bit. And then he stands straight up as if he expects her to wake up and say, 'What the hell are you doing.' And I'm half-leaning towards the curtain, ready to bolt. But she doesn't stir. We wait a few seconds and then Tim bends down and pulls her shirt back a little more. And then a little more. Then guess what? Stephanie moans. She's fucking liking it. She's *loving* it. Encouraged, Tim twists her nipple a little and she moans even louder. Next thing I know, he's massaging her pussy through her panties. I don't really know why I take my phone out, but I do, and I start to record. And when Tim is done fucking her, he records my turn. I think it's gonna take me a while 'cause, you know, I'm wasted, but I come so fucking quick. And she *still* doesn't wake. And that's the hottest thing ever, Chase. Really, it's so fucking hot."

Dean was so excited that he was starting to sweat.

Chase, on the other hand, was only half listening to the madman's deranged fantasy.

How could they have been so wrong about everything?

They were so focused on the teenage drama that they missed the bigger picture. Something was rotten in Hawkesbury County, Ava had said as much, and Chase had known deep down that this was true.

No, not some*thing*; two *things*. Tim and Dean Jardine.

"The next day, I swear to God, I'm so scared that I can barely function. I can't even look at my brother. I just keep thinking that the cops are gonna show up at the door and arrest us. But nothing happened that first day or the second. Or the third. And after about a week, I was beginning to think that maybe I just imagined the whole fucking thing. After all, sex couldn't have been that good, could it? But then I looked at my phone and found the video. Oh, it happened all right. It happened, and it *was* that good. At first, it was just mine and Tim's dirty little secret. A filthy secret, one might say. Like that mattress." He laughed as if this was the funniest joke in the world. "I'm going to skip ahead about six months. At some point, Tim got the video off my phone—no idea how, but he did. And he posted it. He promised that it was anonymous—you couldn't see our faces, not really—and that we could never be found out. I was pissed, *really* pissed, but then the strangest thing happened. People were commenting on the video. They loved it. They wanted more. And they wanted to *pay* us."

Dean was so entranced by his own story that he didn't hear the low, resonating rumble coming from outside. It was distinct and faint, and if Chase hadn't heard it before, she wasn't sure she would have recognized it for what it was.

The engine of a classic car.

Chase hated this story and up until this moment, wanted desperately for it to stop. But now she begged Dean to keep speaking. The more he spoke, the more aroused he got, and the less likely he would hear the car.

"Marianne," she said, although because of the gag, it came out *ahihahn*.

But Dean understood her. And he grinned.

"I figured you'd eventually find out about her. But you're jumping way too far ahead, Chase Adams. But okay, I can see you're excited. I'll skip the boring parts. We'd just been hired as deputies and our first case was looking for money that had gone missing from the Tenbury coffers. Fucking small-town shit. Anyways, it was a joke. All we had to do was look at who had access to the money and follow them around. Robert Matthews was the one stealing from the charity fund and then paying it right back for Brent's tuition. And he was so fucking obvious about it.

"All this money business got us thinking… and in the mood to make another video. But we weren't going to be stupid like Robert—don't shit where you eat, right? We didn't want to target Tenbury girls because that would bring all the heat down on us. But Tenbury draws applicants from all around the state. We thought about it and decided that, although Tenbury students were off limits, girls from afar who applied but didn't get accepted might make for good targets. Desperate chicks, you know? We made a deal with Robert; he could keep on stealing chump change from Tenbury as long as he gave us a list of all applicants who fit certain criteria. And, *voila*, a relationship was born."

"*Ihd he owe?*" Chase asked.

"Did he know?" Dean repeated.

The sound of the engine was getting closer. Soon it would be impossible not to hear it.

"That's a good question. You know, I'm on the fence about that. Tim thinks, yeah, he has to know. But I'm not so sure. Robert is a bit of an idiot. That guy is so desperate to remain relevant, to stay principal, that he'll do pretty much anything. So, who knows?

"Back to the story… the first girl we narrowed in on like you said, was Marianne Lupul. It really wasn't that hard to convince her to come out here, we just made up some bullshit about a background check or—I don't even remember exactly what. It was Tim's idea to give her a drink spiked with a little Rohypnol in it. The funny thing is, we actually got it from Daniel Mendoza. Well, technically it was Jackson Grimes' date rape drug, but he planted it on Daniel, and we scooped it from evidence. This time around, with Marianne I get to go first. And it was good. Not as good as Stephanie, but close. Then when Tim was fucking her, she started to wake up."

Chase cringed. She knew this part of the story because she'd seen the video. It was one of the ones that Stitts had sent her.

"I don't know if Tim was trying to kill her or if he was just trying to get her to shut up by putting his hand on her mouth and nose. Then she started kicking and he just kept on squeezing. I thought he was just going to make her pass out, but he squeezed her so hard that the bitch just died. And then Tim finishes sort of at the same time. I guess it was by accident—never did ask him about it, to be honest.

"Makes for a good video, but panic sets in quick. We can't leave her there. The good news is that it was summer, and no seniors were coming to The Shack for a while. We just dug a fucking hole and buried her out back. Simple as that. And then, like with Stephanie, the first day goes by and I'm so fucking anxious. But nothing happens. *Nothing.* We don't get a missing persons alert through the Hawkesbury system, nothing from State, either. We waited three weeks, just to be safe. Then Tim uploads the video and this time, he makes these freaks pay. Ten thousand bucks to watch the video. Fucking absurd, right? But you want to know what happened, Chase?"

Dean paused for a reply, but Chase refused to dignify his question with one.

He shrugged and continued.

"Too many people wanted to see it and too much money came rolling in. *Way* too suspicious. We kept it up for two weeks and that made us both more money than our annual salaries *combined*. Then we took it down and got on with our lives. We even told each other *never again*. But you know how it is. You get an insane hangover one day and promise to never have another drink. Time passes. And, you better believe it, that next beer three days or a week later tastes so fucking good. Besides, it wasn't fair. Tim got to have all the fun. It was my turn. We did the same thing with Tanya Belk. Only I got to kill her, and I have to tell you, it was better than with Stephanie."

Dean definitely heard the car now. Chase could tell by the way he was speeding up his story.

"Tim posts this new video, and the same thing happens. We're rolling in it. Fast forward to Sunday morning and I get this call about a disturbance right here in The Shack. My first thought is that somebody discovered Tanya's or Marianne's body even though that didn't make sense; the call was a noise complaint. But I come here and there's nobody. I'm feeling a little nostalgic, so I head down and… I can't believe it. It's Emily Dawson. Naked. Passed out. It's like a gift from God. I call Tim right away and tell him to get his ass out here. *Heeeee's* not as impressed as I am. And he doesn't want to do it, says it's too close to home. But he can't resist and there's really no way this can come back to us. We didn't lure her anywhere; Emily was already here. Tim does her and we get the video. And then, as we're wrapping up, we hear someone come back. *Oh fuck*, right? Tim manages to get out, but I stay behind, just happy that we parked far enough away—just in case—that it was unlikely that whoever it was saw our car."

Dean looked up and squinted, obviously concentrating on the sound.

Chase shouted nonsense to try to distract him, but he hushed her.

"It's Brent Matthews of all people—Emily's ex-boyfriend. He comes downstairs, looking for something, his phone, and then sees her. I'm like, right over there." Dean points to the corner of the basement. "All he had to do is look in my direction, but he doesn't. Then he freaks out and runs away."

"Wha ihihn you buwah ehihi lie the ohher?"

Why didn't you bury Emily like the others?

"Well, that's the thing, we talked about it, and to be honest, we were going to. But then, Brent and Carlos and that whole mess… still, we were gonna come back, but then things got all fucked up..."

The car was close now, on the dirt driveway, maybe.

"Wha hahhen nehh?"

What happened next?

Dean hushed her again and stared at the ceiling.

"Wha hahhen nehh?" Chase shouted the words this time.

"Shut the fuck up."

But Chase wouldn't shut up. She started screaming and when Dean reached down to adjust her gag, she bit down hard on his finger. He cried out and she tasted blood. But then he reared back and punched her in the forehead.

Chase saw stars but didn't black out.

And then Dean Jardine leaned down and kissed her on the mouth.

"Don't worry, Chase. That's just Tim arriving to join the party. Get ready because this is going to be our best video yet."

Chapter 58

"**PRINCIPAL MATTHEWS? WHAT ARE YOU** doing here?" Mrs. Story asked. "Principal Matthews?"

Robert didn't hear the secretary, much less respond. The only thing he heard was the words the FBI Agent had uttered over the phone.

He heard them over and over and over again.

"We're looking for information about two girls who were murdered: Marianne Lupul and Tanya Belk. I understand that they once applied to Tenbury Academy but never actually attended. We believe that they were murdered by the same person. If you have any information regarding these two individuals…"

Marianne Lupul and Tanya Belk… murdered.

Every quarter for the better part of two years, Robert Matthews supplied a list of rejected applicants to one of the Jardine brothers. In return for this list, they looked the other way when it came time for Robert to 'raise money' to pay Brent's tuition.

All told, the lists included between one hundred and one hundred and fifty applicants. Some applicants were rejected so quickly that Robert never even looked at their names. Others, like Marianne Lupul, were hard to forget.

She'd been a second call back and she would have been accepted had the girl's parents been able to afford it. But they couldn't, and Robert remembered feeling terrible about the situation. Marianne didn't qualify for assistance either because her estranged father made too much money, which Marianne and her mother never saw a dime of.

A month into the school year, the scholarship rules were amended, and the income of a parent who didn't live in the same house as the applicant no longer applied. Robert immediately reached out to Marianne, but he was informed that she'd gone missing.

Robert knew something was very wrong. But it was easy to push these gut feelings aside when you had duties to perform.

Money to steal.

He didn't recognize Tanya's name but as Robert entered his office, locking the door behind him—much to the chagrin of Mrs. Story who wouldn't stop asking him if he was alright—he just knew she was going to be on one of those lists.

Robert opened his computer and signed in using his password. Then he scrolled through the records of applicants from the last two years.

Please don't be there, please don't be there, please don't be there.

But of course, she was.

Tanya Belk. Fourteen years old.

Dead.

Raped and murdered by Tim and Dean Jardine.

And Robert had served her up on a silver platter.

Or a filthy mattress.

Robert thought he was all cried out from weeping for his son.

He wasn't.

His vision blurred with tears as he loaded the notepad app on his computer and wrote a single line of text.

Then he opened the desk drawer and pulled out what looked like a humidor. It was locked and the key was taped beneath his desk.

The humidor did not hold any cigars.

It held a Ruger 9-millimeter pistol.

As if sensing that things were about to take a turn, Mrs. Story knocked even more aggressively on the door.

"Principal Matthews? Principal Matthews, is everything alright in there? Robert?"

He didn't reply.

There was nothing for him left to live for. His son had been murdered, and he'd helped two corrupt deputies rape and kill three women.

For what?

For his son to attend this fucked-up entitled school?

Was it worth it?

Was it *ever* worth it?

"I'm sorry," Principal Robert Matthews whispered as he pressed the barrel of the gun to his chin. "I'm sorry for everything."

And then he pulled the trigger.

Chapter 59

Deputy Jardine might have been convinced that the car arriving was his brother's, but Chase knew definitely.

The sound belonged to an old-school car.

A black Chevelle with thick tires that chewed up dirt and mud.

It was Jackson Grimes' car. The same Jackson Grimes who had roofied Brent and Emily and had coerced them to have sex together.

Without that having happened, Emily would likely still be alive today.

The second Dean ascended the stairs, Chase rolled onto her side, wincing at the pain in her shoulder where the deputy had stepped on her. Then she made it to her knees and finally, onto her feet.

If Dean had made one mistake it was tying her hands in front of her. Behind her, Chase would never have been able to make a call. As she struggled to turn the phone, an incomprehensible thought popped into her head: if the Jardine brothers made so much money selling their snuff films couldn't they have afforded a better camera rig and setup?

The phone wouldn't turn—the tripod held firmly in place. As Chase scrambled around the other side, she heard voices and then someone coming downstairs.

Working frantically now, Chase struggled to get the phone out of camera mode and to the dialing screen.

"Shit! She's got the phone!" someone yelled, someone who wasn't Dean or Tim.

Chase almost made the call—she had two of three numbers before someone was on top of her.

"No!" she screamed, desperately trying to hold on to the phone as she was tackled onto the mattress. The tripod crashed to the floor and Chase focused her efforts on trying to beat off her attacker.

But he was stronger than her.

And younger.

Even if her hands hadn't been zip-tied Chase doubted she would have been able to shake him off.

In mere seconds, the man bested her. He mounted Chase, pinning her hands beneath him as he lowered his weight on her chest.

It was Jackson Grimes, his face hideous and swollen.

She's tried to scream at him, to spit, to bite, but the stupid fucking gag was still in her mouth.

Bucking didn't help either. It only made Jackson's malformed grin grow even wider.

Behind her, Chase caught a glimpse of Dean who had just stepped foot on the basement floor. The mask was still high on his head, and he was holding his service pistol in one hand.

"Look at me!" Jackson suddenly screamed.

Chase refused, turning her face side to side.

Jackson roughly grabbed her chin and forced her head straight. Chase closed her eyes.

"Look at me!" he yelled again. Spit peppered her face. "Open your fucking eyes and look at me! Your partner did this! Your fucking partner did this to my *face!*"

The hand that was gripping her chin slipped lower, the long fingers wrapping around her throat. Then her left eyelid was peeled back.

Her vision was blurred but now she couldn't help but see Jackson.

"He did this!"

The hand on her throat tightened even more.

What the fuck is happening?

But she knew what was happening.

Jackson Grimes was part of this, too.

Jackson removed his hand from her eye and joined the other one. And now, as much as Chase wanted to keep her eyes closed, she couldn't—they were bulging out of her head.

As a last-ditch effort, Chase bucked wildly but Jackson barely budged.

Darkness started to close in.

"Stop! Don't kill her yet!" It was Dean Jardine. She'd forgotten he was even there. "Jackson, stop!"

But Jackson didn't stop.

He squeezed even harder.

"*Stop!*"

The deputy grabbed one of Jackson's shoulders.

"Jackson, you're ruining this! Fucking *stop!*" Deputy Jardine adjusted his grip and pulled Jackson again.

This time something happened.

It was a strong tug but not strong enough to elicit the reaction that followed. Jackson seemed to fly through the air, letting go of Chase's throat and spinning at the same time. The younger man's shoulder struck Dean in the midsection, taking him by surprise. Then Jackson collapsed on top of the deputy much like he'd done with Chase moments ago. This time there was no mattress to cushion their fall and a cloud of dust filled the air.

Chase heard something else hit the ground too, assumed it was the gun, but she couldn't see it—her vision was still littered with black spots.

She coughed, gagged, and spat.

There was no shouting now, just grunts of exertion as the two men writhed on the ground, filling the air with an almost comical amount of dirt and dust. And yet, somehow, Chase found the gun and tried to scramble for it, but her legs, deprived of oxygen, failed.

As she dropped on her stomach, Chase heard a resounding smack, something hard hitting skin, something else breaking, followed by a wet spray.

Three massive gulps of air later, pins and needles attacked her legs.

The gun was still there, no more than six inches from someone's—Jackson's?—hand.

Chase crawled toward it.

She actually arrived first but with her hands bound she fumbled it. And this was the break one of the men needed.

They picked it up and before Chase could even scream, the entire basement was filled with the deafening sound of gunshots.

Chapter 60

When Francie, the Hawkesbury Sheriff's Department secretary and *de facto* dispatcher, wasn't at her desk, all emergency calls were automatically forwarded to Sheriff Hal Grimes' radio.

This call was nearly incomprehensible.

"Slow down. I can't understand you. Who is this?"

The female on the line slowed but not by much.

"It's Tabitha Story, the secretary at Tenbury Academy. I only came back here to pick up some of my things that I left earlier, that I forgot, and then Principal Matthews showed up. He looked like a ghost and locked himself in his office. And then… and then I heard a gunshot!"

Tate's eyes bulged.

"What the fuck?"

Sheriff Grimes clicked something on the in-dash radio.

"And you can't get in there?"

"I can't! I don't have the key. It's supposed to be in my desk but it's not here. And I… he's not answering!"

"Mrs. Story, here's what I want you to do: back away from the office."

"What?" She sounded more desperate now than before.

"Listen to what I'm saying: back away from the office. Do it now."

Mrs. Story was a heavier woman and her breathing got more intense as she moved.

"Now, I want you to keep going. I want you to leave Tenbury Academy. Then I want you to get into your car and drive to the furthest spot in the parking lot where you can still see the front doors. And then I want you to wait. If you see the principal come out, I want you to drive away. Don't talk to him, don't look at him, just drive. Do you understand?"

"But there was a gunshot and—"

"Do you understand?"

"Yes. Yes. I understand."

"Good. If he comes out, you drive a good five miles in any direction. Then, when you're sure he's not around, I want you to call me back and tell me that he left. Got it?"

"Okay."

"Repeat it back to me."

Mrs. Story repeated Sheriff Grimes' instructions. As she spoke, Tate thought back to Robert in the hospital.

He'd gotten a call and then, like a zombie, had just wandered out. And that was with his son's corpse lying in the next room.

Who the fuck called and what did they say?

Sheriff Grimes switched off the radio and turned to Tate.

"I knew he was dirty. I just knew it."

Tate was less sure about anything. He'd thought Sheriff Grimes and Robert Matthews were behind the murders and while one of them not being involved didn't speak to the other's innocence or guilt, the theory that Tate had come up with no longer made sense.

"I don't know," Tate said.

Sheriff Grimes bristled.

"He was busted, and he knew it. So, we went—"

"To be honest, right now, I don't really give a fuck," Tate said. "Just fucking drive."

Chapter 61

CHASE ROLLED ONTO HER BACK and then scooted away from the gunshots. She was nearly deafened by them but could still hear somebody moaning in pain—muted as if underwater.

And then there was the dust.

There was so much dust in the air that it made it impossible to tell who had been shot.

At this point, Chase wasn't even sure it mattered.

All she could do was wait. Trying to find the stairs now would likely result in her either walking into a wall or a gun.

Chase closed her eyes and counted to ten.

When she opened them again some of the dust had settled.

Deputy Dean Jardine lay on his back, his eyes wide, blood spilling from three distinct bullet holes: two in his lower abdomen and one higher, just below the neck. He was staring blankly at the ceiling and small red bubbles formed on his lips in time with intermittent gasps.

Beside him stood Jackson Grimes. The man with the bruised and battered face was sneering and the gun he gripped in his hand was aimed directly at Chase's head.

She closed her eyes again and took a deep breath.

This was it. This is where her life came to an end.

It wasn't the first time that Chase had come face to face with death, but it was one of the few times experiencing this while completely sober.

An eerie calm fell over her.

Nothing happened.

Another three count and when Chase heard nor felt a bullet, she dared open her eyes. Jackson was still there, gun in hand. Only it was pointing the butt at her instead of the barrel.

"Take it," Jackson said, wagging the gun. "Take the gun."

Even though Chase's hands were still bound she didn't want to risk him changing his mind. She reached for the gun just as a shadow moved behind Jackson.

"Look out!" she yelled.

Somehow, Dean Jardine had not only managed to get to his feet, but he was staring at them from halfway up the stairs.

And he was no longer bleeding.

What the fuck?

But it wasn't Dean, it was Tim.

Jackson spun and fired two shots. His aim was wild. The first bullet struck the stairs just below Tim's foot. The second, following the trajectory of the arc from Jackson's turn, hit the wall next to Tim's head. Dirt sprayed the left side of his face and then he was gone.

Jackson made a move as if to go after him, but Chase stopped him cold.

"My wrists! Cut the wrists!" she begged. Jackson was conflicted, his eyes darting from Chase to the stairs and back.

"Fuck."

Jackson pulled a switchblade from his boot and used it to slice through the thick plastic.

Chase moaned when her shoulders were finally able to relax.

Now Jackson was on the move again, sprinting up the stairs.

"The gun! Give me the fucking gun! Jackson! *Jackson!*"

Upstairs the Chevelle's engine growled to life.

Chase started after Jackson when she heard a groan, and something snagged her pant leg.

It was Jardine.

She thought the man was dead.

"Chase." His voice was almost unrecognizable.

Chase yanked her leg free and stared down at the rapist and murderer.

Out of sheer spite, she was inclined to grab the man's phone and tripod where it lay in the dirt and record his death.

She wouldn't sell it, though; she'd give it away for free.

But Dean Jardine did not deserve to be immortalized in film or martyred. He didn't deserve for his words to be entertained, either, but that look on his face...

Chase was forced to crouch low to hear what he was saying.

"The people who watch our videos all say the same thing." Dean coughed and Chase turned her head to one side to avoid the blast of hot air. "They say… they say…"

And then Dean Jardine died.

Chase watched his chest. It didn't move.

Just leave him. Leave this prick to rot.

But she had other ideas.

Chase took the first two fingers of her right hand and stabbed them into the bullet hole near Dean's neck.

He gasped and his back arched. Chase continued to grind her fingers in the wound, feeling thick tissue like a tendon.

"What do they say?"

Dean coughed blood.

"That they want to see… want to see someone younger."

Chase felt such revulsion that she drove her fingers even deeper. She touched something rubbery and Dean Jardine's body seized.

And yet, somehow, before his body went slack and stayed that way until rigor mortis set in, he managed to say something else.

Something that would haunt Chase.

"We know all about you, Chase Adams."

Chase retracted her fingers and wiped them on the man's pants. No longer hearing the Chevelle's engine, she turned her head to the stairs and was surprised that Jackson was standing there.

How much did he see?

"Motherfucker stole my car," the kid said.

And then Jackson finally gave her the gun.

Chapter 62

TATE SAW THE TWO HAWKESBURY Sheriff's Department cars first and his heart skipped a beat.

Sheriff Grimes was driving too quickly, and he couldn't stop in time. He bumped into one of the other cars, but Tate didn't even notice. He was already out, gun in hand.

"Chase! Cha—"

Two people stepped out of The Shack.

The first was Jackson Grimes. He was covered head to toe in dirt and his face was lumpy with swelling.

The second was Chase Adams. She was pale and dirty and there might have been the beginning of a bruise near her hairline but other than that, she seemed no worse for wear.

Tate rushed to Chase and embraced her while the sheriff did the same with his son.

"Dean's dead," Chase said as they separated.

Tate stared down at her.

He didn't give a fuck about Dean or Tim Jardine. He cared about her.

Tate grabbed Chase again, squeezing her so tightly this time that she groaned a little. Then he kissed her, and she kissed him back.

"Motherfucker stole my car," he heard Jackson Grimes say.

Tate didn't know what to make of the kid now.

He'd done some horrible shit. He'd framed Daniel Mendoza, and he'd drugged Emily Dawson and Brent Matthews. And Tate thought that that might only be the tip of the iceberg.

But he'd also saved Chase's life.

Saved her from being featured in another one of the Jardines' snuff films.

Tate didn't say anything, Jackson didn't deserve that, but he did give him a nod.

Jackson returned the gesture.

"I shot Dean in the basement," Chase told Tate and the sheriff. "He admitted to raping and killing Marianne Lupul, Tanya Belk, and Emily Dawson with his brother. He also admitted to raping a girl named Stephanie Millard. Tim came downstairs and I shot at him, too, but missed. He ran and managed to steal Jackson's car."

This account, sparse as it was, sounded odd, but Tate was in no position to challenge his partner. Sheriff Grimes didn't question it; he immediately got on his radio and put out an APB for his son's car. Then he addressed Chase.

"You're sure Dean's dead?"

"He's fucking dead," Chase confirmed. "His phone is down there, too, but I don't know what's on it."

Tate hugged Chase again.

"All I want to do is shower," she whispered.

"We can head back to—oh, shit."

"What?"

Tate huffed.

"Something happened with Principal Matthews."

Tate recounted the call from the secretary. With each word, Chase's eyes grew wider.

"What? What is it?"

Chase bit her lip and lowered her voice.

"When you said you thought Robert was involved, I asked Stitts to do me a favor. I told him to call Robert and mention the girls' names, tell him that he thought they were murdered. I figured if he didn't have anything to do with their deaths, the names would mean nothing to him."

Tate remembered the call and the look of sheer horror on Robert Matthews' face as he staggered out of the hospital.

"Oh, they meant something to him alright."

"Yeah, Dean also said that Robert was feeding them the names of applicants that didn't get into Tenbury."

"Fuck me."

Chase drew in a full breath and stood up tall.

"Tate, you come with me," she said, all business now. "Jackson, you go with your dad. Let's finish this and then get the fuck out of this place."

Chapter 63

"ONE, TWO, THREE!" ON THREE, Tate delivered a kick to Principal Matthews' office door. The wood was thick, and it bowed but didn't break. "Fuck."

Tate kicked the door again and this time there was a splintering sound, but it still held.

"Wait!" Chase reached into her pocket and pulled out a single key.

Tate made a face.

"Don't ask."

She put the key in the lock and turned. Then Chase stepped to one side and opened the door. Grimes and Tate rushed into the room.

A second later, they holstered their guns and Chase entered empty-handed.

Robert Matthews was seated in his chair, his head back and his arms out to his sides, palms skyward. There was a gruesome hole beneath his chin.

The books on the wall behind him were covered in blood and brain matter.

"Jesus," somebody whispered—*Tate*, Chase thought.

She walked past the burly sheriff and around to the other side of the desk to peer at the open laptop.

There were two things prominently displayed on the screen. The first and most obvious was a notepad with a simple line of text that offered no clarity to her conversation with Deputy Dean Jardine.

I didn't know.

Chase was disappointed.

She had hoped for a declaration of guilt.

This—*I didn't know*—meant nothing.

"What do you think?" Tate asked as he came up beside her.

The second thing on the screen was a list of past Tenbury Academy applicants. Tanya Belk's and Marianne Lupul's names were highlighted.

"I think I want to get the fuck out of this place," she said under her breath.

Tate reached over and gave her shoulder a squeeze.

"Fucking small towns, am I right?"

***

It wasn't like either of them to leave without everything being wrapped up with a neat little bow. But sometimes, at least according to Tate, that's just what happened.

Sheriff Grimes had a crew excavate behind The Shack and they discovered two highly decomposed bodies, which they assumed were Marianne and Tanya. Attempts were made to contact Stephanie Millward, a Tenbury alum, but they were unsuccessful.

Chase hoped that this was the result of a name change and not something more sinister.

Somehow, Tim Jardine had managed to slip by multiple statewide barricades and roadblocks while driving that obnoxious Chevelle, but eventually, they'd catch him.

After everything that had happened, Sheriff Grimes's opinion of Carlos Mendoza had changed. With his recommendation, the DA had struck a deal—a sweetheart deal: ten years for second-degree manslaughter. Your girlfriend being raped and murdered while pregnant with your son sometimes drove people to empathy.

Daniel Mendoza was less fortunate. He got a full two years for failure to appear for some bogus warrant.

Sheriff Grimes was surprisingly forthcoming with all this information, but the one thing he neglected to mention was what happened to his son. If Chase had to bet, she'd put her money on Jackson Grimes' name not appearing in any documents. When asked why Grimes had told his son to follow them, he'd been obtuse. Something about wanting to make sure he had a line on everyone coming and going in his town.

Chase wasn't so sure if Jackson hadn't just done that on his own accord and his father was, once again, covering for him.

As much as Chase wanted to get the hell out of this town, they both did, there was still one thing she had to do.

"Mrs. Dawson—wait. Before you close the door, I wanted to give this back." Chase slipped Emily's Story Planner through the crack in the door. "Mrs. Dawson, your daughter really was an excellent writer. I'm so sorry about what happened to her."

Jennifer Dawson took the book without a word and shut the door.

Back in her car, Chase sighed.

"And we thought that Director Hampton was going to make our first case at the CVU an easy one," Tate said.

Chase wasn't listening.

Something was nagging her, and it was more than just the fact that Tim Jardine had yet to be apprehended.

"You have that look on your face, Chase. What're you thinking?"

Chase debated not telling him, but they'd agreed to be honest with one another.

"Before he died, Dean said something. He said, 'Everyone who commented on the video said they wanted to see someone younger.'"

"Fucking savages."

"Yeah, but then he said, 'We know all about you, Chase Adams'." Tate went silent. "You think it means anything?"

"I think it means you should give Stitts a call and see if he can check on the girls."

Chase was already getting her phone out.

"I'm sure they're fine, but just in case."

"Yeah, me, too."

So much for honesty.

Epilogue

"Do you think this counts as our first case?" Floyd asked.

Stitts leaned on his cane with one hand and knocked on the door with his other.

"You wish. This wasn't our case—it was Chase's and Tate's. You're not getting your cherry popped that easily."

Floyd laughed.

"Okay, old man. Remember, this will be *our* first Cold Case. Not just mine." He leaned back and glanced up at the bedroom window over the front door. "What exactly are we doing here, anyway?"

"No idea. The thing about Chase is, the more questions you ask the less answers you get."

"What the hell is that supposed to mean? You asked a lot of—"

The door opened and they were greeted by a pretty middle-aged woman with caramel skin.

"Hello?" she had a hint of an accent.

Columbian or Cuban, Floyd thought.

Stitts held up his FBI badge.

"My name's Jeremy Stitts and I'm a friend of Chase Adams. This is my partner, Floyd Montgomery."

Floyd showed his badge, and the woman took her time reviewing both of them.

"What can I do for you, Agents?"

"Chase asked us to come by and see if everything was alright, to see if—"

A flurry of movement came barreling toward Stitts.

"Uncle Stitts!" Georgina screeched. "I haven't seen you in *sooo* long!"

If Stitts hadn't been leaning on his cane, he would have been toppled.

"Way too long," he said, hugging the girl as best he could with one hand.

She let go of him and then hugged Floyd.

"I miss you too, Floyd."

"Come on inside now, Georgina, leave the good men alone," the woman said.

Georgina gave Stitts another hug before ducking back inside.

"When's Chase coming home?" Georgina asked.

"Today. Not sure when, exactly," Stitts replied, unable to wipe the smile off his face. Behind Georgina, he saw a young girl in a wheelchair. Rachel, presumably. He said hello and she waved before wheeling off. Georgina, the ball of energy that she was, bounded after her.

Stitts tipped an imaginary hat at the woman who had answered the door.

"Sorry for bothering you. Have a nice day."

"It was nice to see you, Georgina!" Floyd shouted into the house.

Georgina's face magically reappeared.

"Come back soon!" she said with a huge grin. "You have to! Chase misses you!"

On the way back to the car, the smile still etched on his face, Stitts called Chase.

"Yeah, no need to worry, they're fine. They're absolutely fine."

***

"Thanks, Stitts. I owe you one."

Chase hung up the phone and then stared at the blank screen.

"Why do you not look relieved?" Tate asked.

They were about an hour outside of Virginia, but the closer they got, the worse the twisting in Chase's guts became.

We know all about you, Chase Adams. Everyone wants someone younger.

"Chase? I can't help you if you don't talk to me."

Chase wished that Tate would just shut the fuck up so she could concentrate. But she knew he wouldn't leave her alone until she said what was on her mind.

"Something's wrong."

"Is it Tim? Because they'll find him."

It was Tim but not in the way that Tate was thinking.

"Let me ask you something. If you looked me up, if you learned 'all about me' what would you find?"

"Oh, that's easy. I'd discover that you were pretty but complicated and—"

"I'm serious, Tate. What would you find?"

There was no better person to ask because Chase knew that Tate had done just that: look her up.

"Well, most of the shit after your faked 'death' at the hands of Dr. Mark Kruk has been completely erased. I mean, if I'm being honest, stuff from before that time is well-hidden, too."

"Yeah, but Tony Metcalfe found out everything and threw it in the metaverse."

"Tony Metcalfe was a deranged psycho with PTSD who just happened to also be an expert in computers. I am neither."

"Okay, but you would find something about my past, though? My marriage to Brad and—oh, fuck."

Chase scrambled for her phone.

"What?" Tate sounded concerned. "What is it? Chase?"

Chase ignored him and scrolled through her contacts.

"Chase? I was just about to call you," Brad said.

"Where's Felix?"

The pause that ensued couldn't have lasted more than a second, but it was, without a doubt, the longest moment of Chase Adams' life.

"I thought he was with you."

"What are you talking about?" she gasped.

"Well, the camp just called and said someone from the Sheriff's Department picked Felix up this afternoon. Said he was a friend of yours."

"What was his name?"

"Chase, is everything okay?"

"Brad, what the fuck was the name of the man who picked our son up from camp?"

"Tim," Brad said slowly. "The camp told me the man's name was Tim Jardine."

END

Author's Note

Filthy Secrets marks Chase's return to her roots, so to speak. I've always envisioned her coming back to the FBI but, until now, I was never sure how it would work. Chase has burned so many bridges over the years that it seemed inevitable that she was destined to exist on an island. Alone. Unless, of course, she has her own unit to run and the only person to report to is, effectively, herself. And maybe Tate. He seems to be the only person capable of standing up to her and is unwilling to bend to her will. But we're talking about Chase Adams here, so you never know.

I think we all have someone in our lives like Chase—okay, not *really* like Chase, but someone who shares certain traits with her. Someone who hurts you, hurts themselves, hurts others, but is generally well meaning. And no matter how often you try to put distance between them, they keep sucking you back in.

For better or for worse.

That's Chase. Deep down, she's (mostly) a good person. The reality is (or should I say, *her* reality is) that the tragedy she's experienced has left an indelible imprint on her soul.

I hope you'll continue experiencing her adventures through her eyes. And it's *soooo* easy! No heroin or electroshock treatment required. All you have to do is pre-order TAINTED BLOOD, the next Chase Adams adventure.

Before I go, I just wanted to take a quick moment to say that I appreciate all of you and I genuinely thank you for your support over the years.

I love writing books. I love creating characters and worlds and fucked-up scenarios that sometimes pale in comparison to the real world. *Sometimes*. Because the world can be a fucked-up place and we all need an occasional escape.

Enter books.

Exit author notes.

You keep reading, I'll keep writing.

Pat

Montreal, 2023

Printed in Great Britain
by Amazon